Dos Equis

Also by the author

Amuse Bouche
Flight of Aquavit
Tapas on the Ramblas
Stain of the Berry
Sundowner Ubuntu
Aloha, Candy Hearts
Date with a Sheesha

Dos Equis

A Russell Quant Mystery

Anthony Bidulka

INSOMNIAC PRESS

Library and Archives Canada Cataloguing in Publication

Bidulka, Anthony, 1962-
Dos Equis / Anthony Bidulka.

(A Russell Quant mystery)
ISBN 978-1-55483-067-1
Ebook ISBN 978-1-55483-080-0

I. Title. II. Series: Bidulka, Anthony, 1962- . Russell Quant mystery..

PS8553.I319D68 2012 C813'.6 C2012-900759-5

The publisher gratefully acknowledges the support of the Canada Council, the Ontario Arts Council and the Department of Canadian Heritage through the Book Publishing Industry Development Program.

Printed and bound in Canada

Insomniac Press
520 Princess Avenue,
London, Ontario, Canada, N6B 2B8
www.insomniacpress.com

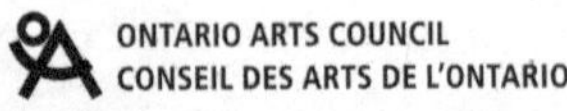

Recent praise for the books of Anthony Bidulka:

"Bidulka mixes fun and seriousness in his fiction, and this sixth episode in Quant's life and times is no exception."
– ***The Globe & Mail (Toronto)***

"Bidulka serves it all up with warmth, wit, and savvy, making for a delicious read that will leave you hungry for more..."
– ***OutFront Colorado (Denver)***

"Some writers get all, or most of, the technical components in order...but miss the feeling behind good story telling...Bidulka has that gift and uses it with more finesse with each succeeding novel."
– ***The Hamilton Spectator (Hamilton)***

"...beautifully written and deeply wise."
– ***Lambda Book Report (Los Angeles)***

"It's an endearing series, and Russell Quant is just the kind of guy you'd want for a big brother."
– ***NOW Magazine (Toronto)***

"Bidulka's books, once started, are hard to put down."
– ***The Star Phoenix (Saskatoon)***

"His characters [have] the happy side effect of making Saskatoon an intriguingly lively spot on the map."
– ***The London Free Press (London)***

"...what lifts Bidulka's books a level above other well-crafted mysteries is the human element he has created in the character of Russell Quant."
– ***Wayves (Halifax)***

"Bidulka pulls out all the stops to give the reader an exciting ride."
– ***Lavender Magazine (Minneapolis)***

"Bidulka seasons his novels with rich ingredients..."
– ***Xtra (Toronto)***

"...you will be swept away..." – ***Out in Print, www.outinprint.net***

From where I live, I see rolling hills, vast fields of prairie,
oceans and rivers, cities and towns.

From where I live, I see people I love, places I've visited,
and the many more I've yet to.

From where I live, I hear laughter, I feel healing, comfort,
and caring.

From where I live, support and safety and salvation
rise up around me.

All this comes to me easily
From where I live
Atop a mountain
Put there
By you

For Herb.

Acknowledgements

Dos Equis (meaning two X's) was created in 1897 by a German beer maker to celebrate the start of the twentieth century. For me, it is a celebration of this eighth Russell Quant book. As many of my readers will know by now, the titles for the books in this series have always included two things: an ingestible, and a hint (sometimes more subtle than others) about where in the world Russell Quant will travel in the story. This title, quite obviously, fits the bill nicely. I also chose it for three other reasons. One: X's over a person's eyes are often used in drawings to indicate they are dead, which, as a mystery writer, is a symbol I cannot resist. Two: in the course of this story, two of Russell's exes make a brief but meaningful appearance. Three: Dos Equis is a drink most people equate with Mexico, a country I've greatly enjoyed, especially during the cold winter months of my own home country. In particular, I, along with Herb, and a number of our friends to whom we've introduced the place, have had a long love affair with a lovely place called Zihuatanejo. So I'm very happy to immortalize in this book just a small part of what we enjoy about that place, and to say a warm *gracias* to our little Zihua.

As the time since the last Russell Quant book grew a little longer than usual, an interesting thing began to happen. Instead of fewer emails and messages, I began receiving more. Most of them asking: When is the next book coming? So I'm thrilled to be able to say: Ta Da! Here it is! And thank you to all the dedicated Russell Quant readers for your unflagging interest and support.

In the meantime, we have been busy releasing new editions of the early Quant books, and I'm pleased to welcome all of our new readers to the series.

As always, I am indebted to the fine people of the media—reporters, interviewers, reviewers, bloggers—local, provincial, national, international—who pay such kind attention to my books, and indeed books of any kind. Some say you are a dying breed. I say you are pioneers, in an as yet not fully formed, new literary landscape. Stay with us. Keep up the good work.

I would like to thank all the organizers and volunteers of literary festivals, reading series, conferences, and special events which I was fortunate enough to take part in across Canada and the U.S., including Blue Metropolis Literary Festival in Montreal, Vertigo Reading Series in Regina, Bloody Words Mystery Conference in Victoria, Festival of Words in Moose Jaw, University of Saskatchewan bookstore's Reading in a Secret Garden, Bouchercon in San Francisco, Saskatoon Writers Coop Up Front and Personal, the Professional Writers Association Workshop in Saskatoon, the Arthur Ellis Awards, and a very special thank you for the kind recognition of the University of Saskatchewan's College of Education by including me on their Wall of Honour. XOXO to all of you who made a point to be there to celebrate with me and sent notes and cards.

And to my fellow writers with whom I've spent time on panels, at readings and signings, on boards or committees, at special events…or in the bar…including Barbara Fradkin, Louise Penny, Nat Grant, Garry Ryan, Geoffrey Ursell, David Carpenter, Judy Fong-Bates, Yann Martel, Lorna Crozier, Denise Chong, Stephen Galloway, Lorna Goodison, Greg Herren, Ellen Hart, Susan Calder, Joan Donaldson-Yarmey, Sharon Wildwind, MJ Maffini, Don Hauka, Phyllis Smallman, Hilary MacLeod, Sharon Rowse, Gail Bowen, Neil Plakcy, Cathy Astolfo, Deryn Collier, and many more, thank you for the fellowship, support, many good laughs, and fine companionship on this mighty ride. Much appreciation to those fearless mystery writers who braved the rigours of my "10 Silly Things You Didn't Know About Canadian Mystery Writers" blog series: Joan Boswell, Madelle Morgan, R.J. Harlick, Lou Allin, Vicki Cameron, Nicola Furlong, Gail Bowen, P.A. Brown, Suzanne F. Kingsmill, Maureen Jennings, Catherine Astolfo, Jeffrey Round, Garry Ryan, Louise Penny, Vicki Delany, and Cheryl Kaye Tardif. Not only are you fantastic writers, but I thank you for your grand senses of humour, matchless pluck, and endless grace.

In my writing life, and life in general, I am supported by and grateful to so many. I cannot begin to name everyone. I do want to say thank you to the many readers who write to me, not only to say nice things about the Russell Quant books, but to share parts of their lives, their stories. I am honoured to be entrusted with them. Dori, my *Date With a Sheesha* toques have kept my ears *and heart* warm. Shelley N., thanks for keeping my posters up long after anyone else. Jill C. and Jessica, I think you give more Russell Quant novels away as gifts than anyone I can think of. Paul, my biggest fan who's never read one of my books, and Jan for keeping him informed about the funny bits—not to mention your incomparable dinner parties with Bugger, Taylor, John, and Marie. Shelley B. for a fantastic pre-launch party, and Rhonda for organizing things as only you can. Carl and Tony for hosting me in Palm Springs. The Russell Quant Wannabe buttons from Edmonton — love 'em! Laura and Alison for bringing Russell along on your Friendship trips. For spending time with us in Zihua—Pat, Lynne, Dori, Shelley N., (Eldeen and Moo for one afternoon too), Jill M. and Rami, thanks for the memories. To all the members of all the book clubs I was invited to join for a visit, thanks for including Russell Quant on your reading lists. In the year it was released, *Date With a Sheesha* was #1 on McNally Robinson's Fiction list of Saskatchewan Bestsellers—thank you Saskatchewan! Thanks to my agent, Robert Lecker, and my editor at Insomniac Press, Gillian Rodgerson, for your continued support and the hard work I know you put in on my behalf. I love a good bookstore, and the booksellers who go with them. Thank you to those special places and people for keeping Russell on your shelves. To all of you who come to my readings/signings, I was reviewing pictures the other day, and remembering your kindness in taking the time to join me at these special events—you make a writer's day by doing so. I am a man who considers himself exceedingly rich in family and friends, sisters, and mothers, and in-laws. We share good times at dinner parties, pool parties, Christmas parties, just-because parties, family get-togethers, during travel, sometimes with nothing more than a quick email or phone call or shot of tequila or limoncello, drinks at the end of the day, or visit at a special event…every moment of laughter, love, a quick hug or hello, is cherished and remembered.

And Herb.

Part One

Chapter 1

"Quant, *you* are the only one who can help me."

Those were the ten simple words that brought me back to life.

I didn't know it at the time, but this is where it all began. This was the moment I began to understand it was time for me to go back. Back to living my life. The life I'd worked so hard to discover, build, mould, into something I truly loved. The life I abandoned just over a year ago.

Why?

I abandoned my life, because I felt it had abandoned me.

I know it didn't look like that from the outside. I had family. Friends. I had my health. I had a great house. Great job. Great dogs. And a man whom I adored with all my heart, who came with two more dogs, and a daughter I loved as my own.

Unfortunately, what appeared too good to be true, was. Every aspect of my life actually was as wonderful as I perceived it to be. The parts, however, simply did not...would not...fit together.

A year ago, after a great deal of heart-wrenching indecision, I had decided to give up the home I loved. It was worth it to be with the man I loved. His name was Ethan Ash.

Then disaster struck.

I am a private detective. Therein lay the problem.

During the course of a particularly harrowing case, a young woman died. I blamed myself.

The events of that horrible winter day occurred on a prairie slough, just a stone's throw away from Ethan's house. That young woman could easily have been his daughter. The thought of it haunted him. And me.*

In my line of work, a certain amount of danger is expected. As a former police constable and a private detective, I *voluntarily* accept risk. My loved ones don't have that luxury. They are left to accept the chance of danger by virtue of their relationship with me.

Ethan could accept it no longer.

He ended our relationship.

I was left feeling empty. I'd lost my partner. My adopted daughter. My career seemed nothing but a cancer, eating up the love in my life. I was miserable. Pathetic. A mess.

So I left.

I closed up my office. I arranged for my mother to move into my house and look after my dogs, Barbra and Brutus. Then, one cold day in February, I caught a one-way plane to somewhere hot with plenty of alcohol.

I admit it. I ran.

For the next twelve months I lived like a gypsy. Some might call it being a mooch.

I am lucky; I have friends in hot places. I started with my neighbour Sereena, who was cavorting in Marrakech and Agadir. After that I spent a while in the south of France with my mentor and oldest friend, Anthony, and his husband Jared. Then it was back with Sereena in Greece and Italy, once again with Anthony and Jared, then some time alone in the South Pacific and Hawaii,

---

**Date with a Sheesha*

and now I was staying with my lawyer landlady, Errall, in her condo in Zihuatanejo, Mexico.

In all that time, I returned home only for a few days here and there, but as soon as I could, before real life could tap me on the shoulder and say, "*Uh, what the hell do you think you're doing?*" I was gone again. It was hedonistic. Greedy. Self-indulgent. But most of all, my god it was healing.

On occasion, I'd take on a small job wherever I was. Mostly these were compliments of Sereena's endless cast of friends and acquaintances, with their endless lists of petty woes and worries. Usually the work entailed nothing more than following a wayward husband or wife, or investigating who was being invited to what party and, more importantly, who was not. I did this for three reasons: to keep my detecting skills limber; for a good laugh; and to earn a few extra Euros, dirhams, or Fijian dollars.

When I think about it now, although I started out believing life had done me wrong, the *opposite* was actually true. Life was in the process of saving me. And these people—Sereena, Anthony, Jared, even Errall—my friends, were there for me every step of the way. All I'd really done was change the venue. And added some sun, sand, rum, and rebound romances to my daily routine.

In my real life, Sereena is my neighbour. Jared is a trusted friend, and Anthony is my mentor. Errall, however, is something else altogether. Our relationship defies easy explanation. We only know one another because she was the prickly, irritating, opinionated, pushy lover of my dear friend Kelly. Eventually she ended up being my landlord, owning the building that houses my PI office, just off the edge of downtown Saskatoon. Then she became my lawyer. Sometime confidante. Sometime dog-sitter. Sometime travel companion. And before we knew it, we were in each other's lives, long after Kelly no longer was. Funny how that goes sometimes.

In every way that counts—on the surface, and below—Errall is all dark and sharp. Dark hair. Dark sense of humour. Dark heart (I don't say that in front of her), with sharp edges, sharp wit, and a very sharp tongue.

Dos Equis

Several years ago, Errall began the annual habit of escaping Saskatchewan winters for a week or two. She'd hop a plane to whatever Mexican resort had a seat sale that month. She'd been to Acapulco, Cancun, Puerto Vallarta, but it wasn't until she was spending a week in Ixtapa, having taken a short cab ride over the hill to a neighbouring fishing village, that she began to fall a little in love. On the Mexican Pacific Coast, known as *Costa Grande*, just two-hundred-and-thirty kilometres northwest of Acapulco, she found Zihuatanejo. It was a Mexican diamond in the rough.

Zihua—as locals call it (pronounced Zee-wah)—manages to maintain a traditional, fishing town feel, by resisting the glitzy nightclubs, pricey shops, glass high-rises, and Señor Frog nightclubs that proliferate in every other coastal Mexican resort. Yet amongst the rocky hills, steep cliffs, and private, craggy bays are hidden a surprising number of fine restaurants, beautiful hotels, and large residences and guest houses. In fact, Errall was so impressed during her first visit, she immediately packed her bags and left Ixtapa for a place on Playa la Ropa. She had found her "spot." Once there, before the margarita salt had time to encrust her lips, she'd purchased a fractional ownership with stunning beach views, at the Canadian-owned Club Intrawest condos.

I was on Errall's expansive balcony when I heard those ten words that brought me back to life. We'd just returned from a late dinner at Bandidos, next to the church on *Calle Cinco de Mayo*, where they make to-die-for fresh salsa right at your table. Although everyone raves about Bandidos's fish *molcajetes*, my all-time favourite dish is an appetizer called "Shrimp in Love." It's bacon wrapped shrimp, soaked in some kind of sweet sauce that makes love to the tongue.

The night was achingly beautiful, as most were in Zihuatanejo. The sun had long ago found another place to smile, the temperature hovered near perfect, and somewhere, in the distance, someone was murdering the lyrics to the ubiquitous "Guantanamera." While Errall was getting us a couple of Dos Equis beers to round out the night, I decided to make my bi-weekly call to my home machine to check on messages. I didn't expect much. As my exile had progressed, I noticed the quantity of messages decreasing in direct proportion with my increasing weeks away. So when I heard the voice, with its potent message, "Quant, you are the only one who can help me," I was unprepared.

"What's up?" Errall asked when she set down the beer on a table next to the lounger where I sat. A juicy sliver of lime was perfectly balanced on the bottle's lip. "You look like you just saw a ghost."

"That's original," I shot back. Errall doesn't suffer fools easily. So I always seize any opportunity to return the favour.

"Give me a break," she answered back, uncharacteristically calm as she plopped down on the chaise next to mine. "You're the one who insisted on tequila shots after we'd already had coffee."

"It's a Saturday night." I defended my decision.

"Every night in Zihua is a Saturday night," she cooed with pleasure.

Now, you must understand. Errall Strane is not a cooer. *That* is the magic of Zihuatanejo.

"Actually, I didn't see a ghost, but I think I just heard one."

"Oh yeah?"

"I checked my messages. Guess who called me?"

"I don't play that game. Tell me who, or I'm going to bed." Now there's the Errall I know and put up with.

"Jane Cross," I told her.

That got her attention. She nearly spit up a bit of beer. "Jane? Wow. Talk about a blast from the past."

Errall and Jane had a past. A romantic one. Well, probably more like a let's-have-sex-a-couple-times-to-piss-off-Russell one. Jane was a private eye, like me. Thankfully, she ran her shoddy, unprofessional, low-rent practice (not quite how she saw it, I'm sure) out of Regina, a city about two-and-a-half hours south of Saskatoon. Even so, that didn't stop her from becoming a royal pain in my ass every now and again as our paths inevitably crossed in the pursuit of bad guys and gals.

"Do you still keep in touch with her?" I wondered, as I tried to remember the last time I'd set eyes on the plaid-loving gnome. I was ungracious about her, I know, but she'd once shot me! (In the spirit of full disclosure, I must add that it was with a can of Herbal Essences hairspray...but she got me right in the eyes.) She did make me laugh though. Especially when she got all heated up about something. She looked like a cartoon bug whose head was about to explode.

Errall thought about this for a moment, contemplatively sipping her drink. "I think the last time I talked to her was over three years ago. Probably haven't seen her in five."

"Same."

"So what does she want with you after all this time? If I remember correctly, you two aren't exactly kissing cousins."

"Hardly. Actually, it was kind of a strange message. She's on a case, something serious, she said. And listen to this, her words, not mine...she said I was the only one who could help her."

Errall threw back her head and laughed.

I screwed up my face. Somehow I wasn't sensing anything good from her hilarity. "Okay, I know that laugh. What are you thinking?"

"Good old Jane. Knows how to play you like a board game."

"What are you talking about? You think she's playing some kind of game? Some kind of joke on me?"

"Oh no, I have no doubt she needs your help with something. But she's probably heard how you're on this extended *Eat Pray Love* voyage, so she's using your ego against you to get what she wants."

"My ego? I don't..."

"Russell, don't tell me you're not a little bit flattered by her..." And here she went into her best girly-girl voice impression: "Oh Russell! My big hero! Only you can save me. Please help me, help me, help me!"

"First off, that is as far from how Jane Cross talks as you can get. Secondly..." Hmmm. I suppose she had a point. I *was* feeling rather good about being needed, wanted, for something that only *I* could do, particularly for a former nemesis.

"Ah hah!" Errall caught me. "There! You see? I'm right, aren't I?"

I decided to answer without words. Instead I gazed out at the endless black veil surrounding our balcony. Somewhere out there was a beach, an ocean, blenders taking a well-deserved rest until the next day when they'd be put back to work combining tequila with a dizzying array of fruit juices, and the promise of another sun-drenched day. Was I *really* ready to leave all of this behind? Sensible, smart adults don't just run away and never go back home. That was kid's stuff. And I was far from being a kid. You see, there'd been one other big-ticket item I'd had to deal with during my time away. One that reminded me of this fact in no uncertain terms. It was the headlong, unstoppable, fateful, full-speed gallop towards a major milestone event, one which likely had contributed to my general malaise.

My fortieth birthday.

As the occasion marched into my life, unwanted but inevitable, my apprehension and depression grew. And then, magic happened.

On the day—late last July—I was in Santorini, with Sereena. She was the only one around who knew it was my birthday. I'd accepted an invitation to join her and her friend, Spiros, for a sail around the island. I spent my time sipping a cheap but immensely satisfying white wine, eating delicious breads with cheese and fresh tomatoes, and flirting shamelessly with the cabin boy. (I suppose he might actually have had a more auspicious title—Captain, I think I heard someone call him—but I still prefer to think of him as the cabin boy.)

Under the gentle ministrations of the Mediterranean sun, my skin had turned a colour somewhere between gold and bronze. My hair was long, and bleached near white. Shoes were a thing of distant memory. I felt carefree, and next to naked in lighter-than-air, white cotton yacht-clothes. By the next morning, I too felt lighter. That day, my fortieth birthday, I now believe, was the first, small step, on a long bumpy road taking me back home.

I remember turning to Sereena at some point that morning after. All I said was, "I think I'm feeling better." She seemed to know exactly what I was talking about.

I am not a dawdler. Once I make a decision, I act on it. By the next morning I had left several messages for Jane, my flights were booked, and my bags were packed. I was going back. Suddenly I couldn't wait, even though I knew the forecast for Saskatoon was minus thirty, while Zihua languidly entered its hundredth day in a row of plus thirty. I missed my home. I missed my people. I missed my dogs, my office, my own bed, my backyard, my favourite restaurants, my BluRay collection, my books, curling up on my caramel coloured couch on a stormy day, my kitchen, my…I could go on and on.

It was time to go home and take back my life. I was grateful beyond words for the precious gift of the past year. But of any gift I have ever been given, this one was totally, completely, entirely used up. It's been said that gay people experience a retarded adolescence. We're too busy fighting doubt, fearing revelation, hiding who we are, to deal with all the other "regular" stuff adolescence throws our way. We have to do that later. Maybe this past year had been my time. My adolescence. My turn to get my hormones in check, and figure out exactly who I was meant to be. Well, mission accomplished. Russell Quant, PI, was back, and better than ever.

Although Saskatoon is the larger city, Regina is the capital of Saskatchewan. There is a good-natured (usually) rivalry between the two centres, but for the most part I see them as two quite different cities. Whereas Saskatoon is a university town with strong ties to potash, pulse crops, and biotechnology, Regina is a government town. It's home to legislature, football, and oil. With the South Saskatchewan River flowing right through the city, Saskatoon is known as the City of Bridges. Regina has Wascana Lake, outstanding museums, and is home to the training facility for the Royal Canadian Mounted Police (the RCMP).

The vibe of each city is also quite distinct. But I saw none of that as my plane landed in the Queen City well past sunset. My calls to Jane's numbers had gone unreturned. I was becoming a bit nervous about my decision to make a layover in Regina to find out what was up with her. Suppose it was a joke? Suppose she no longer needed my help? Suppose she'd decided to take off for a week's holiday on the island of Lesbos?

It wasn't such a big deal, I decided as I caught a cab outside the airport terminal. If I couldn't find her tonight, I'd have a good meal, drop by the casino, catch my twenty-minute flight first thing in the morning, and be home before lunch.

I'd gotten Jane's home address from Errall before leaving Zihua. After dropping my luggage off at the hotel, I directed the cab there, telling him to wait while I knocked on the door. The woman who answered said she'd been living in the apartment for over a year and had no idea who Jane was. Great. She'd moved.

On the off chance she was still at work this time of night, I asked the taxi driver to take me to Jane's office.

Jane worked out of a petite, clapboard house she rented on a quiet street near the warehouse district. I could see the low wattage shimmer of a light somewhere inside as we pulled up. I walked up the narrow, shovelled walkway to a covered porch, and pulled out my cellphone. I tried her office number once more. Mounting the steps I could hear a phone ringing inside. I had the right number. But no one was answering. Hope dwindled.

I stepped into the porch and knocked on the interior door.

No answer.

Again.

Nothing.

I was about to head back to my waiting ride, when I heard a noise from inside. It sounded like someone stumbling on hardwood floors. I stepped over to the nearest window and peered through the slats of a blind. I thought I caught a glimpse of a dark mass moving from one side of the room to the other. What the hell?

I rapped on the window.

"Jane? Jane, are you in there? It's Russell Quant."

No response.

Back at the door I tried the knob. It turned all the way. Unlocked. Not very smart of Jane, if she truly wasn't here.

Slowly I pushed open the door. It actually creaked. This was all beginning to feel a little like a bad horror movie. I glanced back toward the street, hoping for the comfort of a kindly cabbie watching over me. Instead I saw exhaust puffing from the rear end of his car as he sped off. I should never have paid him for the fare to get here.

I was getting cold. The temperature was hovering in the minus twenties. The jacket I'd brought with me was meant for airports and cabs, not for actual protection from winter elements.

"Yoo hoo, Jane!" I called out. "Ready or not, here I come!" I stepped inside, closing the door, leaving the frozen air behind it.

At this point in a typical Jane Cross-Russell Quant repartee, she'd be shaking her little fists, cheeks all red and rosy, calling me bub, or Priscilla, Queen of the Prairie Desert, and yelling at me to get the hell out of her office, unless I had an appointment. Since none of that was happening, I was guessing Jane Cross, Birkenstock PI, was not in.

Another noise.

I was back on high alert.

I was definitely not alone.

The light I'd seen earlier must have been in another room, because the one I was in was pitch black. I could barely see a thing.

Something moved on my right.

Shit, what the hell was that?

"Who's there?"

I reached out, looking for a light switch or lamp. I stumbled over something on the floor. Typical lesbian; a lousy housekeeper.

More hurried movements.

"I know you're there," I announced, trying to keep the quiver out of my voice.

Seeing what I hoped was the silhouette of a lamp, I headed toward it.

Next thing I knew I was flat on my face.

I swore a little.

What the hell? Did she have the place booby trapped against intruders? My ankle tingled where it had caught underneath the bulky item I'd tripped over.

If I'd thought it was dark standing up, it was even darker down here on the floor. I reached out for something to hold on to, to help pull me up to my feet. My hand landed on something soft.

The pain that coursed through me in the next milliseconds was enough to elicit a discordant choir of screeching. From me.

I immediately felt drops of blood dribbling down my face. My cheek was throbbing. My eyes watered.

From beneath what I was guessing was a bureau, I heard a low, warning yowl. It was coming from the cat whose tail I'd just grabbed in the dark.

I called the cat some not very nice names. To be fair, I did not know her actual name. And, I was hurt. To be equally fair to the cat, I had just broken into her home, and yanked her pride and joy. I supposed we were even. By the time I found a Kleenex in my pocket and dabbed up most of the blood from the scratches, I was ready to forgive and forget.

With the yowling and shrieking having subsided, and the wound tended to as best I could given the circumstances, I decided it was time to make a move. I reached into my jacket pocket and pulled out my cellphone. The display screen lit up with its silvery glow. I directed the meagre light around me, looking for the nearest public-utility-provided light source. What I found instead, was one of the greatest horrors of my career.

Chapter 2

You'd think, in my line of work, that I'd have seen a long line of dead bodies. But there really haven't been that many. Being a detective in a small prairie city, where murders per year average under a dozen, I rarely come face to face with death, never mind grisly death caused by the violence of one human against another. They say that murder is often committed by someone known to the victim. I disagree. To do the unthinkable, to look someone in the eye and intentionally rob them of the thing most precious to them, to...end...them, well, I don't think that victim ever really knew that person at all. No one can truly know a monster.

A monster had been to Jane Cross's office.

Displayed in the glow of my cellphone was the most dreadful sight. Not only was I looking at death. Not only was I looking at death caused by something other than accident or natural causes. I was looking at unnatural death in the unseeing eyes of someone I knew.

Jane Cross was dead.

Shot. Many times.

For a full minute, it seemed, I did not breathe. The world was a still life painting, a rendering of hell on earth.

Although Jane Cross hadn't been someone I loved, cherished, or even liked very much, she had been part of my life. She was a colleague. She was someone who'd made me laugh, who'd once saved me from a pack of hooligans intent on beating me up, who'd romanced a friend, who'd attended a birthday party for me. She was someone I had a history with. Someone who had thought to call on me when she needed help.

But I was too late.

"Oh Jane..."

A mournful feline wail sounded from beneath the bureau.

I pulled the phone close and made to dial 9-1-1.

The cat's lamenting wail suddenly morphed into a growl.

I should have taken it as a warning.

An arm wrapped itself around my throat and yanked back with such force, I thought my head might actually pop off.

I hadn't had time to consider whether the murderer might still be in the house. I guess I knew now.

It was too dark to tell much about my attacker, other than that he was about my size, maybe a little smaller, but strong and wiry.

Being taken by surprise immediately puts the surprisee in a bad position when it comes to hand-to-hand combat. This guy was choking me from behind, seemingly intent on cutting off my air supply. Not a bad strategy. But, being fond of breathing, this made me rather intent on breaking his hold. Adrenaline is a fine adversary of surprise.

I began pushing into the other guy, forcing him to move backward if he wanted to maintain the chokehold. This also allowed me to gain my footing on the floor. For a few seconds we did this crazy dance around the room. Except for the sound of us crashing into things, the room was oddly silent. I could hear him breathing hard, as was I. But neither of us grunted or moaned or screamed out. We were conserving our energy purely for the goal of doing in the other guy.

Once my knees had recovered from the fluttering weakness you get when someone is attempting to kill you, I enacted my hastily devised plan. Waiting for just the right moment, I firmly planted my feet in front of me, then dropped to my knees like a sack of potatoes, curving my back into his torso. The unexpected change in our propulsion sent him swinging over my head, releasing his grip on my neck and landing him ass down in front of me. It would have been a perfect move if the jarring motion hadn't wrenched my neck, causing me to spasm as a bolt of pain tore up my spine to the base of my brain.

The guy scrambled to get up. I grabbed his trousers and tripped him. This gave me enough time to recover—slightly—and throw myself over his body. This time I was going for the death grip around *his* neck. Instead, his elbow caught me in the side. I bellowed, and he flipped us over so that now I was on the bottom and he was struggling on top of me. We must have looked like two drunks at a wedding reception, doing The Worm on top of each other.

In a dirty move, the jerk arched his back up, and then came down on me hard, with his butt meeting my groin. Fortunately, I guessed what he was about to do, and skittered to the side just before he made full contact. Mercifully, the effect was somewhat muted. I decided if he was going to go all Jerry Springer on me, I could do the same. With my right hand I grabbed a shaft of hair and yanked as hard as I could.

"Yoooooowwwwwwwwwwwwwwwww!"

No sweeter sound, I thought.

We went on like this for a while longer, perfectly matched for strength and low down, dirty moves. It was becoming obvious neither of us was going to win this. But I had to find a way. This maniac had just killed Jane Cross. It was when I reminded myself of that, that I remembered how Jane had died. Oh geez. This guy had a gun. I did not.

And that's all it took. That one fraction of a second distraction was all he needed to land a sucker punch in my gut. I went down. As I rolled on the floor, holding onto my throbbing abs, I waited for the pummelling that was sure to follow. Instead, I heard the rumble of retreating footsteps, then the slamming of a door.

I jumped up, pain screaming out from every pore, and ran for the door. I threw it open and searched the scene. All that greeted me were the quiet, peaceful sounds of a late night street asleep. My hand landed on an elusive light switch. I flipped it up and looked at the room behind me. It was a nightmarish scene. At its centre, the body of Jane Cross. I couldn't leave her like this. I had to let the killer go.

For now.

I knew I had only a few scarce minutes to myself before the cops responded to my 9-1-1 call. I worked quickly. I found that Jane's filing system was arranged much like my own, so I was quickly able to locate her current case files.

My typical rule when dealing with police on a case I'm involved in, is to neither intentionally impede nor facilitate their progress. But this was different. This was murder. This was Jane Cross. So, instead of simply swiping her files, I hurriedly ran the pages through Jane's copying machine. I only hoped that no smart guy cop noticed that the copier was warm when they got here.

While the pages were duplicating, I performed a quick scour of the rest of the place. The only thing of note was the sofa near the desk. I imagined Jane taking afternoon naps on the sagging thing when business was slow, or spending the night on it when a particularly tough case kept her late at the office. I lowered myself to my knees and studied the undercarriage. It looked as if someone had ripped away the bottom lining. The sorry looking sofa had Garage Sale written all over it, so I couldn't be certain if this was actually important or not. Had Jane been hiding something in the couch? Something her murderer was looking for? Did they hold her at gunpoint until she turned it over? And then shoot her anyway? Or did they find it themselves after they killed her? Or was it simply nothing more than a torn couch lining?

I maneuvered myself in order to get a better look. There certainly was room enough in the sofa's body to conceal something, like a small box or a file of papers. I studied the wood frame from which the lining had been pulled. In the corner from which the fabric had let go, there were tacks. The rest of the lining was held in place with industrial-size staples. Someone had either tried for a home repair, or had purposely created a hiding spot for...something.

Hearing the telltale wail of approaching sirens, I hopped up. I returned the case file to its original location, and stuffed the copies into my waistband. Thank goodness the weather necessitated a bulky sweater under which the sheaf of papers would not readily be visible. When the cops came crashing in, I was crouching near Jane Cross's body, saying my last goodbyes to a real pip.

The next hours were gruelling. Given the disarray of the place, the fact that I was covered in bloody scratches, thanks to the damn cat, and contusions, thanks to the damn killer-who-got-away, and that I was found standing over the body, I was not surprised to be suspect numero uno. It wasn't until the coroner inspected Jane's body and determined she'd been dead for at least twenty-four hours that I was cleared. Fortunately I still had a copy of my boarding pass proving that when the murder was committed, I was still living *la vida loca* in Zihuatanejo. My, how a few hours change everything. Even so, none of this kept the constables from questioning me endlessly. They asked me the same questions, over and over again, only in slightly different formats. They were hoping for a slip up or discrepancy they could exploit. Luckily, I used to be one of them. I know all the tricks.

Of course, the best defence against getting caught up in the spider's web of police questioning, is to tell the complete truth. Which I did. To a point. I didn't lie...exactly. I simply withheld the bit of information about why I was in Jane's office in the first place. I didn't tell them about the phone message from Jane saying she needed my help. I simply said I was a friend who decided to stop in for a visit on my way home from holiday in Mexico. Once I was ruled out as a suspect, they were too focussed on detecting the identity of my attacker and likely killer, to go into it any further.

Figuring out the identity of the man I'd caught red-handed in Jane's office was not going to be an easy task. I'd asked myself all the same questions the cops did. What did I know about this guy that could help identify him? Sadly, it was bloody little. It had been dark. I'd been consumed more with saving my own life than studying facial features. As night smudged away into the early hours of a new day, the only thing I could come up with was his smell. The guy wore nice cologne. I thought it might be Tom Ford. The cop questioning me at the time quite obviously had no idea who or what Tom Ford was. I elaborated. He rolled his eyes and walked away. Soon after, I was allowed to go back to my hotel.

I was beyond exhausted by the time I locked the door of my hotel room. But I knew I wouldn't sleep a wink without taking at least a cursory glance at the papers that had been adding an extra inch to my waist size for the past several hours. I ordered a stiff drink from room service, stripped down, took a quick hot shower, donned the hotel's cozy white bathrobe, and, with feet up on the bed, dove in.

Although Jane was up to date in her notes, she was not what I would consider overly verbose in her written reports. I guess she just assumed most of it would be safer stored in her noggin. She was wrong about that. But there was enough in the papers to get a sense of what she'd been up to.

Jane had been hired by Millie Zacharias. Millie asked Jane to look into the death of her neighbour, a woman named Hilda Kraus. According to police and hospital reports, Hilda had died, quite suddenly and unexpectedly, from botulism. I was surprised to see the cause of death. I'd have to do some research on it, but I was quite certain death from botulism was virtually wiped out years ago. Not only was inadvertent creation of the poison easily preventable, but also treatment was foolproof...assuming the victim received help in time. Obviously that had not been the case with poor Mrs. Kraus. Apparently there was something about the passing that did not seem quite right to Mrs. Zacharias.

A knock at the door told me my Manhattan had arrived. I retrieved it and had taken a deep swallow before I was back on the bed. It was strong and sweet and cold going in but hot going down. Perfect. I yawned and placed the drink on a bedside table. I needed sleep. But I needed information more. I continued to scan the remaining pages I'd...appropriated...from Jane's office.

From her notes, it looked as if she'd begun by doing a background check on Hilda Kraus. She made the typical inquiries and computer checks and intended to talk to friends and family. But either she hadn't gotten to it yet, or she simply hadn't had the time to record the results of her work. I was confident she must have found something out. Something important. Or else she wouldn't have deigned to call and ask for my help. And, she probably wouldn't be lying in a Regina morgue. There wasn't a lot to go on in the files. But there was enough. Enough to get me started. I knew the police would do a good job investigating Jane's death. But I couldn't leave it at that. Jane Cross, in one of the last acts of her too short life, had reached out and asked for my help. I had no intention of denying her request.

The next thing I knew, the rude buzzing of an alarm clock was burrowing into my brain like some kind of crazed drill. I slapped at the unfamiliar bedside device several times in an effort to locate the shut-the-hell-up button. Opening one eye to the new day, I reached for the watered down remains of my Manhattan and downed it. Not so bad really.

Abruptly, like a jack-in-the-box, I bolted up and out of bed.

Something was very wrong.

I darted to the windows and yanked open the blackout curtains to throw some light on the situation. Remembering that I was naked and that my room faced an office tower, I quickly pulled back the filmy drapes to obscure and discourage any early morning would-be peeping Toms.

Scanning the room, I tried to focus my brain on revealing

why I was so sure something wasn't right. Everything looked to be just where I left it. Tired set of luggage full of shoes and laundry. My favourite airplane slip-ons on the floor. Watch, cellphone, and laptop on the bureau. Toiletries—the only thing I'd bothered to unpack—set out in the bathroom.

My eyes widened as an unwelcome thought hit me.

I'd had the good sense, as I grew more and more tired the previous night, to stuff Jane's papers between the mattress and box spring of the bed. I almost tripped over myself in a rush to check if they were still there.

They were.

So what was it? What were my senses warning me of?

And then I had it.

The air.

It smelled of Tom Ford cologne.

Chapter 3

Never one to shy away from bloody inconvenience in the quest for good looks, I'd once again purchased a car that was wholly unsuitable for my daily needs. Annabelle is a British racing green Solstice convertible, with imperceptible trunk space and non-existent back seats. This makes it almost impossible to buy more than a sack or two of groceries, haul any piece of luggage larger than a knapsack, or ferry about my two Schnauzers, Barbra and Brutus, without discomfort. But my god, it is a sexy looking automobile.

And so, it was up to my mother to pick me up at the airport with her circus-sized van. It all worked out fine anyway, as Mom had been looking after my house and dogs while I was away. Generally, I am not a fan of being met at the airport, especially if it's been a long day of flying. I'm usually bagged, and not up to sparkling conversation, and would rather just get in and out of the airport without much fanfare. This, however, is not my mother's style.

"Oh *sonsyou*!" she wailed before I'd even completely crossed the threshold into the arrivals area. "Vhere haf you been all dis time! You must be so hungry, *tahk*? Come, I take you home for some goot food. I brought sandweech for now."

I accepted the salami, red onion, and Velveeta on homemade white bread thrust into my hands. "Mom, we have to wait for my luggage."

Mom wasn't used to the idea of air travel, or really any sort of travel at all. She'd never been out of the province of Saskatchewan, never mind on a plane. God help the first stewardess who tried to pass off airplane food as a proper meal.

"Vhere haf you been?" she asked again as she followed me toward the luggage carousel.

"Mom, I was in Zihuatanejo. With Errall. I told you that when I talked to you on the phone last week."

"I don't know about such place. Mebbe I didn't hear so goot. Vhere is Carol, den?" Mom either couldn't say, or didn't approve of, the name Errall. Who ever heard of such a name? So, in such cases, she came up with another name that suited her better. Thus, Errall became Carol. "I haf extra sandweech in da car for her den."

"Errall's still in Mexico. She has a few more days of holiday left."

"Okay, den. But you stay here, *tahk*? You come home for goot now, uh huh?"

"Yes. I'm back now, Mom. I bet you'll be happy to get back to the farm. I really am sorry I was away for so long." We'd covered all this before, but it never hurt to repeat apologies.

"Yah, vell, eets cold now. Not so much to do on da farm. But still, it vill be goot to be back home again."

Mom still lived on the family farm where I grew up, about forty minutes north of the city. At one point, after Dad passed away, I—no doubt suffering some kind of hallucinatory haze—invited Mom to come live with me permanently.

But, at the spry age of seventy, she still preferred her independence and the peacefulness of the farm, compared to the "vild, crazy vays" of the big city. Mom had given up a lot to look after my home and dogs. During the summer months, she'd simply closed up my house and took the dogs with her to live on the farm. In the winter, they'd stayed in Saskatoon. I was exceedingly grateful. But she seemed to take it all in stride. A mother's job is never done.

"I go home tomorrow, den," she told me. "Tonight I feex you goot meal."

I smiled and hugged her. "I can't think of a better welcome home."

Stepping up to my front door, bags and mother in tow, I was surprised at how nervous I was. Everything looked and smelled and felt wondrously familiar. Nothing had changed. Except me. Was I a stranger in my own world? I was excited to see my Barbra and Brutus again. We were a tight trio. It had been difficult to be away from them for so long. I missed their smell, their quirky ways, their undying, unqualified love.

Taking the key from my mother, I unlocked the front door. Before it was fully open, I could hear the clomping of multiple feet rushing toward me. I dropped to my knees just in time to get an armful of Brutus. Normally my dogs are graciously restrained, keeping excessive shows of affection for our private moments. But not now. Brutus was all over me, like skin on bones . As he covered me with kisses, he whimpered with nearly uncontainable joy. If only he could talk, I knew he'd be saying something like: "I love you I love you I love you did you bring me treats?"

Momentarily sated, Brutus went to see if perhaps Mom had been smart enough to bring him something tasty. I glanced around expectantly, awaiting the next furry onslaught by Brutus's sister. Instead, Barbra was sitting on her haunches, in the distant entranceway to the kitchen. She was watching my welcome home with a calm, detached gaze.

I felt a sudden sharp stab of pain in my heart.

For a time, long before Brutus came to live with us, it had just been Barbra and me. We had a special bond. A bond which, I suddenly realized, I'd damaged by being away for too long. A bond which would not immediately be repaired, just because I'd decided to suddenly reappear.

Barbra's eyes narrowed as they moved to regard her exuberant, love-starved sibling. If I were to guess what she would say, it would go something like: "What a slut." She slowly rose and, leaving me with one last withering look, slunk away.

Promising to be home no later than seven for my welcome home supper, I found Annabelle in the garage and dusted her off. After warming her up for about five minutes, I was off. I hadn't seen Anthony and Jared since spending several weeks with them at their rented place on the Amalfi coast in early fall. So when I called to say hello and tell them I was back in town, they insisted I drop by for a bite of lunch at their downtown penthouse, atop the Radisson building.

Anthony and Jared, although already having been together for several years, were legally married in the middle of a prairie plough wind a couple of years ago. That the ceremony barely skipped a beat is testimony to a relationship that has heartily withstood the test of time, trials and tribulations. Anthony Gatt is the owner of a string of high end menswear shops nattily called gatt. Once upon a time, Jared Lowe was the male equivalent of Gisele Bündchen. At sixty, Anthony continues to be a successful entrepreneur. At twenty years younger, Jared's modelling career is long over. Now he runs Ash House, a care home for the swinging senior set, along with my ex, Ethan Ash. Anthony speaks with an English accent; Jared speaks the low, throaty language of sexiness. Anthony is Robert Redford. Jared is a copper-headed, olive-skinned, sweet-natured, man-boy wonder. Anthony was my mentor when I was coming out, and the man whose opinion I probably most respect. Jared was the object of my unrequited man-crush for a number of years. Given our history, they were the perfect sounding boards to help me figure out if I was doing the right thing in pursuing Jane's final case.

"I can see how you'd remember a Tom Ford scent. They're

very distinctive," Jared said. He was serving us moderate helpings of hot rotini pasta mixed with shrimp, slivers of brandied salmon, caramelized onion, broccoli florets, baby tomatoes, and just enough basil-cream dressing.

Anthony tasted the wine and asked, "But aren't there at least a couple of dozen Tom Ford colognes—he really went to town at the scent factory. How can you be sure the one you smelled in your hotel room was the same one worn by the fellow at Jane's office?"

"I guess I can't be one hundred percent certain," I admitted. "Or I suppose it could have been some sort of olfactory dream I was having."

"No such thing as coincidence," Jared decided, taking his seat. Living with it every day, he was oblivious to the stunning view of the South Saskatchewan River valley many stories below and behind him, a winter wonderland landscape of whites, greys, silvers, and muted browns. "And you say nothing was missing from your room?"

"No. But the door was unlocked. And I'm positive I locked it as soon as I stepped inside. I always do. It's a habit. But maybe I forgot to re-lock it after room service left."

Jared let out a low whistle. "So he broke into your room while you're sleeping and you don't hear a thing. This guy—whoever he is—he's good, right?"

I had to agree.

"Let's assume you're right," Anthony said, tasting the pasta. "Oh sweetheart, this is delicious."

Jared winked and tipped his wine glass toward his husband. "Bon appétit."

We repeated the toast to each other, and Anthony continued. "If you're right, it means the killer didn't run away after you beat him off from Jane's office…"

"Well," I acknowledged, "I didn't so much beat him off as we simply wore each other out. It was a stalemate. He got in a good shot, and by the time I recovered, he was gone."

"So he runs out of Jane's office," Anthony said, not giving up on his line of thinking. "Then waits for hours outside, in the freezing cold, until the police are done with you. He follows you to the hotel. Waits for you to fall asleep. Then he breaks into your room, and...what? Takes nothing? You are a lovely looking man, Puppy, but do you really think he went through all that just to watch you sleep?"

"I know, I know. It makes no sense."

"If he thought you saw his face and could identify him as Jane's murderer, you'd think he'd have finished you off when he had the chance," Jared added.

Suddenly, the pasta wasn't tasting quite so good. But the guys had a point. Why would the killer break into my hotel room and do nothing? He took quite a chance for no apparent payoff.

"Unless..." I began, a new idea buzzing around my head. "...unless he was after something he thought I had...but didn't."

"You mean like some kind of evidence that tied him to the murder?"

"Or to whatever it was Jane was doing that brought him there in the first place. Maybe he ripped the lining of the couch but didn't find what he was looking for."

"So he killed Jane for nothing?"

I shrugged. Stupider things have happened.

"So maybe this thing he was looking for had something to do with the case Jane was on."

I nodded. "I'm quite sure the death of Hilda Kraus was the case Jane was working on when she called asking for my help."

"So of course you're planning to look into the case yourself?" Anthony pointed out, waiting for the expected answer before taking another sip of wine.

I sucked in my cheeks and nodded.

"Of course."

"Russell," Jared began, sounding tentative. "You're not doing this out of some false sense of responsibility, are you...because Jane called for your help, and you weren't here to give it?"

"Not until now I wasn't."

Jared's face froze.

I laughed. "Just kidding."

Jared was speechless. Anthony, as usual, was not.

"Puppy, you've just put poor Jared off his food for a week. Shame on you."

I reached over and gave Jared a quick friendly forgive-me hug. "I know what you mean, Jared. And maybe a year ago I would have felt exactly that. But I know there was nothing I could do from Zihuatanejo. I rushed back here—even though no one asked me to—as soon as I could. The way I look at it, if I hadn't come home when I did, who knows how long it would have been before someone found Jane? And, if I hadn't been in her office when I was, I wouldn't have seen the killer. That's got to count for something.

"To tell the truth, partly I am looking into this because Jane asked for my help. She wanted me to do something for her. I don't know yet what that was, but I'd like to do it for her if I can. I'm also doing this because she was a colleague, someone in my life, and Errall's life. It doesn't feel right just to let this go and see what the police dig up. Like it or not, I'm involved. She was a bit of a pain, that Jane. But underneath all the bravura and snarky name-calling, she was okay. I liked her. She deserves some extra effort from me."

"Not to mention poor Hilda Kraus," Jared added.

"Ah, yes, poor Mrs. Kraus, dead of botulism," Anthony commented dryly as he forked in another helping of lunch. "I do hope you cooked the shrimp long enough, darling."

When I called Millie Zacharias after lunch, she told me to come right over. This was a little easier said than done. Millie lived on a farm just outside a village with the rather unusual name of Muenster. It was an hour and a half drive directly east of Saskatoon.

Although February in Saskatchewan can be nasty, with the possibility of surprise storms, the day was sunny and bright with nothing sinister on the horizon. I checked my watch, and saw that I'd have just enough time to get there and back in time for Mom's supper. So I gassed up Annabelle and away we went. I left the city via Highway 5, past the Sundown, Saskatoon's only remaining operating drive-in theatre, and headed due east.

With plenty of time to kill, I used my Bluetooth to make a phone call. It was time to check in with my Saskatoon Police Service contact, the über macho and mustachioed, Darren Kirsch.

"So why are you telling me all this, Quant?" Kirsch asked after I gave him a brief rundown of all that had transpired over the past twenty-four hours. "As much as I appreciate your story-telling prowess, I don't really have time for it until beddy-bye."

"Prowess? My, someone has been reading his dictionary again. Finally at the 'P's, huh?"

"How *pernicious* of you to say so."

"Oh, wait, I feel a *paroxysm* of laughter coming on."

"Quant, you're such a putz."

"Perhaps."

That bit of wordplay dispensed with, Kirsch got right to business. "So what's the real story here? I know you can't be stupid enough to ask me to stick my nose into a case being handled by Regina ?"

I hesitated, then: "I can't?"

The cop made a kind of steam-blowing-out-of-ears sound.

"Listen, I just want to know what's going on. Or if they've made any progress. Besides, they know I'm involved. They had me in their clutches for most of last night."

"Did you at least get any phone numbers?"

"That's a homophobic comment. I could file a complaint with the Saskatoon Police Advisory Committee on Diversity."

"Quant, I'm asking you one more time: What is really going on? What are you up to?"

I try never to ask Kirsch for a favour. There is nothing worse than being beholden to a guy like him. He takes advantage of it, making my life miserable. Even worse, he always expects something in return. What a jerk. But he's my jerk. And like it or not, I needed a someone in the Saskatoon Police Service. Fate gave me Constable Darren Kirsch. I've often wondered what horrible thing I did to deserve him.

"Okay. I'll tell you. But you have to promise to keep it between you and me for now. Deal?"

"No deal."

There was dead silence on the phone. He had me by the short hairs.

"It's nothing illegal. It's nothing that would impede their case...very much."

"Quant, I'm counting to three. If you haven't said something worthwhile by then, I'm hanging up."

I wisely decided it was not the best time to share my long-held opinion that I did not believe Darren Kirsch could count that high. Instead, I spilled a few of my beans. "Jane was a colleague. I have a vested interest in seeing that her murderer is brought to justice. You have to understand that, Darren. It's the same with cops." I knew I had him with this. If a cop went down—anywhere—every cop in the country stood up en masse in an awe-inspiring show of solidarity to take responsibility, provide support, and most of all, seek justice. "I know she was working on a case when she was killed. It would really help if I could find out if it had anything to do with what happened to her." I'd chosen my words carefully, only divulging what I wanted to, and making little noise about getting involved in the case. But words are just words, right? I did feel a little bad about not revealing the phone message from Jane that led me down this path in the first place. But a private detective isn't called private for nothing.

I could hear Kirsch breathing as he considered what I'd said. "I've got a few buddies down there." I smiled to myself. Got ya. "I'll ask how things are going. But that's it, Quant. Don't call me, I'll call you."

And he hung up.

That went very well.

Millie gave good directions. They took me right to the long, fir-lined driveway, which led to a large, brown, one-storey, ranch-style house. The snow had recently been cleared, including a shovelled path from the pad in front of the garage, where I parked. When I knocked on the side door, a chorus of barks greeted me. After a full minute, a woman and three dogs of questionable parentage appeared.

"Don't you worry about them," the woman squawked as she threw open the door and motioned me to come in. "They're all bark and no bite, usually."

Usually?

"You must be that Russell Quant fellow who called a couple hours ago then, is that right?"

"Yes, that's right," I said. I slipped off my boots and followed the woman and her mutts up three steps into a cavernous kitchen.

"Why don't you sit yourself down right there," she said, nodding at a kitchen table already set with placemats, coffee cups, cream and sugar, and napkins. "I'll pour the coffee."

I did as I was told, allowing two of the three dogs to have their way with my crotch. The third plopped down near an unlit wood fireplace, probably too old or too jaded to care. You've smelled one crotch, you've smelled them all. I know a couple of guys who see life in pretty much the same way.

"And you must be Millie?"

The woman was in her seventies. She was tall and thin, with wiry, silver-white hair, chopped short to frame a sharp, angular face. When she smiled, her features softened somewhat, revealing perfectly white dentures made a touch too big for her mouth.

"Oh yeah, that I am. All my life." She laughed at that.

Right about then, the dogs abandoned me like day-old roadkill. They trotted off to greet a newcomer, coming in through the back door at the far end of the room. It was another woman. Ignoring the dogs, she dropped an armload of freshly chopped wood by the fireplace. I was hoping she'd use it to set a fire. Even with my winter jacket still on, there was a persistent chill in the room, nipping at my nose and fingertips.

"This is that Russell fellow who called," Millie told her.

"Oh yeah," was her thrilled response.

She turned and took off her outer cloths, then joined me at the table. "I'll have one of those coffees too," she said, giving me a studied once over.

I'd describe the second woman exactly the same as Millie,

with the exception of her hair, which was much darker. And she was probably about seven to ten years younger.

"I'm Russell Quant," I said by way of introduction.

"Yeah, I heard. I'm Barb."

"We've been friends for over forty years," Millie explained as she deposited three cups of weak-looking coffee in front of us. She took a seat opposite mine. "Lived here ever since my parents died when I was just a young gal."

"Rent's cheap," Barb added. The two women laughed at what must have been a well-worn joke between the two of them. It was the only bit of softness I'd see between the two "friends."

"I'm surprised you came all the way out here," Millie said. "The other guy sure didn't want to."

"Other guy?"

"The Regina cop who called this morning."

So they'd read the file too. Good for them. Sort of. Obviously no one wanted to make the three-hour trip all the way from Regina. Not unless they were sure it would be important to their case. And maybe it wasn't. Maybe I was the one barking up the wrong tree. We'd just have to see.

"You're not a cop, are you?"

"No. I used to be. In Saskatoon. But now I'm a private investigator. Like Jane."

Millie sighed. "I still can't get over it. Her being killed and all. It seems so unreal, you know?"

I nodded. "I'm curious," I began. "I know you hired Jane to look into the death of one of your neighbours. But why did you hire a detective all the way from Regina instead of someone closer." Not that Saskatchewan is crazy with people in the PI business, but er, uhm, what about me?

"She was a friend of ours, that's why. We've known Jane since...when was it, Barb?"

Barb made an noncommittal movement with her shoulders and remained mute, as she'd done for the entire conversation thus far.

"Anyways, we met at the Spring Valley Guest Ranch in Cypress Hills. Gosh, gotta be a dozen years ago now. We don't see her all that much, with us living way out here and her in

Regina. But we keep in touch on the phone and email. So when all this business with Hilda came up, we decided to ring her up."

"You decided," Barb stated, keeping the lip of her coffee mug near tightly pursed lips.

I regarded the younger of the two as I sipped on my own coffee. It needed a little something...like maybe a scoop of coffee grounds. "You didn't think it was a good idea to call Jane?"

Barb looked at me, as if surprised that I'd heard her, or maybe surprised that I'd say something in response to it.

She put down her coffee cup and held up her wrinkled, work-worn hands as if in defence. "This is her story, not mine." She gave Millie a look. "Thanks for the coffee. I'm going to get back to that woodpile. Never know when another storm is going to hit."

We watched in silence as Barb put on her coat and boots and left through the same door she'd entered.

"She's not really very social," Millie said by way of explanation. "She didn't know Hilda very well. Didn't think we should get involved."

Millie rose and ambled into the kitchen area. I thought she was getting the coffeepot to offer refills. Instead, she dug out a bottle of Kahlua from one of the cupboards.

"I think this coffee needs a little something, don't you?" She held the lip of the bottle over my cup, waiting for my answer.

I smiled. "Oh thanks, that would be nice, except I have to drive back to the city right away. My mother is expecting me for dinner."

"Okay for you then. Don't say I didn't offer." She poured herself a double portion, mine and hers. Millie had obviously found a better way to keep warm. Why keep a fire going when there's alcohol around?

"So you and Hilda were good friends?"

"Oh, I don't know if I'd say that," she answered when she'd returned the bottle to its hiding place and sat back down. "But she was our nearest neighbour. Has been all my life. Her place is just over the hill to the north. Big place. She pretty much owns most of the land around here. Something like seventy quarters or more.

"We weren't best friends or nothing like that. But we were friendly. Like neighbours are friendly. At least in the country. We look after one another out here. She'd buy eggs from us every now and then. Our hens have always been better layers than hers. Don't know why. They just are. So if she needed extra, for baking or company at Christmas or something like that, she'd call and ask if she could buy an extra dozen or so. I'd take them over there and we'd have coffee and talk sometimes."

"What was it about her death that made you think you needed to hire a detective, Millie?"

"It's what that doctor said. And the police. That she'd died from that food poisoning thing."

"Botulism."

"Another thing that country folk know about is that botulism. Used to be that people were afraid—city people, that is—they were afraid to eat home-canned food, because they thought they'd die from it if the canning wasn't done right. But that was years and years and years ago. All you have to do is boil everything long enough and hot enough. It's not hard. And let me tell you, if anyone knew how to preserve safely, it was Hilda Kraus. She would never make that kind of mistake. I'd stake my life on it. And besides, they say it was a jar of canned asparagus that did her in. There's no way."

"Why's that?"

"Can't grow asparagus around here. Comes up all reedy and woody. Must be the soil, I don't know. But in all my days, I've never known Hilda to grow asparagus. Never mind can it."

"I suppose she might have bought it somewhere else. Like maybe at a Farmer's Market or something like that."

Millie swigged her coffee / cocktail. "I suppose, but I doubt it. Besides all that, I had another reason for calling in Jane."

Excellent. "What was that?"

"I know who killed Hilda."

Chapter 4

"I saw the car."

"You saw the murderer's car?" I asked, a little gobsmacked.

"You see, I have to pass right by Hilda's yard on my way to town. I go into town at least once a day. It was strange, the first time I saw her car..."

"Her?"

"Lynette. Hilda's daughter."

Okay, wow. Millie was accusing Hilda's own daughter of killing her. Matricide. Tsk tsk tsk. It was shocking. Unbelievable. So much so, that I wasn't sure I believed it. And I certainly couldn't begin to connect how a daughter killing her mother in Muenster could lead to Jane Cross being shot to death in Regina.

"The first time I saw her car, it wasn't even in the yard. She'd left it on the side of the road, just short of the driveway into the yard."

"Like maybe it had broken down or had a flat tire?"

"Well, I suppose so. The next day, when I passed by, the car had been moved. It was in the yard, next to the house. Probably plugged in on account of how cold it was. The day after that it was gone. So I pretty much forgot about it. Until we heard about Hilda being found dead over there."

"What did you do then?"

"Well, I told the police what I thought. But they couldn't care less. They probably thought I was just another crazy old farm woman scared about her own imminent death from poisonous asparagus." She chuffed at that and took a healthy swallow of coffee-flavoured Kahlúa.

"What exactly did you tell the police, Millie?"

"I told them everything I just told you. And I told them about Lynette, and how she and her mother never got along much. I know Lynette Kraus. Known her all her life. She was as spoiled as spoiled comes. They gave that child everything under the sun. Especially Bill, Hilda's husband. And guess what happened? When you give a child everything they want, the only thing they want is MORE.

"Lynette grew up thinking everything should be handed to her on a silver platter. But then she moved to Saskatoon, and found out pretty quickly how the real world works. Then Bill died. Poor Lynette. That was the end of easy street for her. Hilda loved her child, but she knew they'd made a mistake with her. She decided the best way to teach Lynette the value of things was to make her work for them. Do you know they were still paying that full-grown woman an allowance? Shameful. Well, Hilda cut that out pretty darn quick. Lynette finally had to get and keep a job if she wanted clothes on her back and food on her table. The only way Hilda would give Lynette any money was if she provided some sort of service for her. Like drive her into Humboldt or Saskatoon for a doctor's appointment, or to pick up groceries. You can imagine Lynette wasn't very keen about any of this."

"So their relationship was not a good one?"

Millie barked a laugh. The three dogs, none of which had cared to go outside with Barb, looked up from their various resting spots around the room. "Not good is an understatement. You see, even at that, Hilda didn't really have all that much cash to hand out to the daughter. Like a lot of us out here, our fortune—such as it is—our savings, everything we have, is tied up in land, buildings, and machinery. The only way Lynette was going to get her hands on any real money was if Hilda sold some of it. And she swore to me, she had no intentions of selling so much as a hayseed until her last will and testament was read over her dead body."

Hilda Kraus had been a headstrong and willful woman. In my experience—and from watching episodes of *Murder, She Wrote*—people like that seldom bulldozed their way to a natural death. Was that the case here?

"Did the police or RCMP investigate Lynette Kraus?" I asked.

"They didn't seem very interested in my 'theories.' As far as they were concerned, they had an open and shut case. The murderer was botulism."

"But Hilda did die from the poisoning?"

"Yes. But how she got it into her system is another matter."

Without knowing the details of the official investigation, I'd have to say that although Millie had some interesting points, I could see where the police would have had doubts.

"So I did the only thing left for me to do. I called on Jane. She was like a daughter to us, so I knew she'd help if she could. Sweet thing drove all the way down here from Regina one Sunday, just to talk to us about it."

Sweet? Jane? "And what did Jane say after you told her your story?"

"She didn't say much, now that you ask. But she did tell us she would do some snooping around and let us know if she found out anything. I was happy with that. It was the only hope I had left to find out how Hilda really died. Like I says, we were neighbours, and neighbours look after one another. Dead or alive."

Minutes later, as I was leaving, I saw Barb watching me from around the corner of the house. I waved a goodbye. She didn't wave back, only stared, unsmiling.

Dead or alive, the one neighbour I knew I could rely on was Sereena Orion Smith. I'd spent a good part of my sojourn away with Sereena, at some of the various ports of call around the globe which she treats like home. She knew I was going through a tough time. So she'd made herself, and wherever she happened to be at the time, fully available to me. It was her unobtrusive, yet strong, quiet support, not to mention her willingness to dive into a pitcher of anything at any time of the day or night, that got me through the worst of it.

That night, however, it was Sereena herself who was having her own resolve tested.

Having somehow sensed that I was finally home, and wanting to share gossip, a few bons mots, and some laughs, Sereena had unwittingly found herself in my kitchen with her nemesis: my mother.

There can be no two women more different than Sereena Orion Smith and Kay Quant. My mother is as Ukrainian as Easter eggs and borscht, with a thick accent to match. Just shy of five feet tall and leaning toward stocky, she has generally kept the same dress size since giving birth to her last child, which was me. She sports a tightly permed head of greying hair, horn-rimmed spectacles, and a face that can be sweet as cream or sour as...well, as sour cream. Mom goes to church. She gardens, and cooks to excess. Her family is her life. And, according to her, the last true movie star of any note was Doris Day.

As for Sereena: if you could think of the last person in the world you'd imagine finding living on a quiet street in Saskatoon, Saskatchewan, Canada—or watching a Doris Day movie—well, that's Sereena. Her past is elusive and fantastical, filled with tales of madcap adventures across every continent. She's bedded kings and dined with emirs. She's danced at midnight under the stars of foreign lands and lived in palaces and Bedouin tents. She's enjoyed great loves and suffered deep tragedies. Her greatest feat is to have survived it all. Just barely. Now, somewhere north of middle age, Sereena still continues to trek into the worldly wilds of the rich and famous every now and again. But in between, this ravaged, damaged beauty is content to live a quiet life in Saskatoon. Well, quiet in an indisputably Sereena fashion.

Returning home from Muenster, I left Annabelle in the garage and trudged up my back walk (which was badly in need of a good shovelling). It was when I'd just reached the back door, which opens into my big, brightly lit kitchen, that I'd caught sight of the unlikely scene. It was a picture worth a million words not all of them nice. Sereena had obviously mistaken the lights in the kitchen for a sign that I was home and open for company. Instead, she'd walked in on my mother preparing "just a leetle someting for *sonsyou.*" Although Sereena is not above rude behaviour if it suits her, bless her heart (it was in there somewhere), she wanted to see me and decided to wait until I arrived.

With both Mom and Sereena unaware of my presence, I caught the best sight of all. The look on Sereena's face was particularly priceless. She was watching, utterly horrified, as my mother poured cream, thick as molasses, into a stovetop pot, while, at the same time, squirting half a bottle of Heinz ketchup into the same pot.

I knew that Mom was preparing one of my favourite dishes: meatballs in red sauce (aka cream and ketchup). But to Sereena's eyes, it was some kind of Hallowe'en prank in a saucepan. Her body recoiled, her eyes grew wide, incomprehension turned to disgust. Her dark red lips curled into a near snarl. Her hand tensed around her champagne glass as she threw back all that remained in the flute. It was as her eyes darted about the room, no doubt looking for something stronger to drink, that she noticed me peering through the window.

I smiled and waved. My only hope was that the cat scratches on my face would curry me some sympathy and forgiveness. Sereena gave me one of her famed *I-curse-you-and-all-your-pets* looks, and motioned me inside with the crook of her middle finger. I knew that, if nothing else, it would be both an amusing and delicious evening.

By nine-thirty I was done in. It had been a long day. And the night before I'd had very little sleep, what with all the murder, attacks on my person, and police interrogation. So I sent Sereena home and Mom to her room, with instructions on how to use the Blu-ray player. I thought she'd like to watch *Send Me No Flowers* (the last movie in which Doris Day, Rock Hudson, and Tony Randall all appeared together).

My bedroom is a large room, with ensuite bathroom and walk-in closet, that takes up the whole north end of the house. French doors open onto a small, bricked pad surrounded, in summer, by flowerbeds. The latest re-do, supervised by Sereena, had turned the space into a cozy, colourful room with a faintly Middle Eastern feel to it. It is my private kingdom, particularly when I have houseguests, as I did now. I can close the door and have everything I want.

Except, in this instance, for one thing.

Every night, when it's time to turn in, the usual routine is that Barbra and Brutus follow me (and the doggie treat they know is in my pocket) down the hallway into the bedroom. Once the treat is hurriedly chomped up, they curl up amongst the piles of fringed pillows artfully arranged throughout the room. Sometime during the night—only if I'm alone—one or both will inevitably find their way onto the bed. I wake up the next morning with a furry tail or ear in my mouth. I like to complain about it, but really I love it.

But tonight our routine was out the window.

I must admit, the fact that Barbra had chosen to follow Mom into her room, to watch Doris bewilder Rock yet again, stung a little. Throughout the evening, I had made a special point of giving her a lot of attention and hugs and ear scratches to remind her of how much I loved her. She'd accepted the affection with good grace. But she was obviously intent on sending me a message, loud and clear.

Message received. I was repentant. She, not yet mollified. So, tonight, it would be just me and stalwart Brutus.

I ran a bath with essences of mint and eucalyptus thrown in. As the flavoured steam spread its pleasant scent throughout the room, I decided to check my phone messages. I'd been pretty good about keeping up with them while I'd been away. But I hadn't checked since hearing from Jane and deciding to come home. First, I collected my bath necessities—a book (this time it was Gail Bowen's latest mystery), reading glasses (no comment), and a glass of wine (a 2006 Acacia Lone Tree Vineyard, Napa Valley Carneros Pinot Noir). Then I stripped down, and pushed the button on the machine just before lowering myself into the tub.

The first two messages were from friends checking in to see if I was still alive, and ever intending to return home. The third was a solicitor, the fourth and fifth were hang-ups, and then came the climactic final two calls. It was as if the first messages were intentionally orchestrated to lull me into a false sense of ease, then BAM! right between the eyes.

The callers were Alex Cross and Ethan Ash.

My very own Dos Equis...Two Exes.

Two men with whom I'd recently had serious relationships.

Calling me on the same night.

WTF?

Alex: "Russell, it's Alex. I...I was thinking about you." Hesitation. "I know we haven't talked since...anyway, I was thinking of you, and thought I'd call to see how you are. I'm doing great. I'm in Bahrain right now." Alex was a personal security specialist. And a very nice guy. "Hot as hell." *So are you,* I thought.

Ethan: "Russell, hi. Jared tells me you've finally come home. Must be nice to sleep in your own bed again." He sounded nervous. "Ah, Simon is doing terrific." His daughter. "She misses seeing you. So, if you're, ah, you know, ever in the neighbourhood, I hope you feel you can still drop by and say hello or something. I just...well, I just wanted to say hi and welcome home. Soooooo welcome home! I hope you're okay." Sweet guy. Also hot.

The real kicker was, they both ended their calls with the exact same words: "No need to call back. Goodbye, Russell."

No need to call back?

Probably not a bad idea.

Despite how it might sound, the past year hadn't just been

about sun, sand, and sangria. There was a fair bit of another "s" word going on: *soul-searching*. I'd done a lot of thinking. About these two men. About me. About love. About me and men and love all at once. Now, I can't pretend I reached some great eureka, some great zenith of personal wisdom. But I can say, most definitely, that I know a lot more about myself, my ways of doing (or not doing) things, than I ever did before. I don't know exactly what it is I'm looking for in life. But I do know that if and when I find it, I will be prepared to recognize it, fight for it until it is mine, then nurture it until I am a grey-haired old geezer, chasing down bad guys on replacement hips. I am Quant. Hear me roar.

With a warm smile at the memories of Ethan and Alex, I sipped my wine and slid deeper into the fragrant suds.

PWC is the converted character house where Russell Quant, Private Investigator, lives. Errall Strane is the wicked stepmother...er, landlady. I share the top floor with psychic Alberta Lougheed, while Errall and psychiatrist Beverly Chaney split the main floor.

PWC looked cold and forlorn that wintry February day when I pulled into the nearly empty parking lot at its rear. Inside was not much better. Now it wasn't that I was expecting streamers and balloons and a *Welcome Back* sign. But was a celebratory cake too much to ask for? Instead, the place had the same empty, echoing feeling that a house has for the first few days after taking down the Christmas decorations. I'd been to my office a handful of times over the past year—checking my mail, making sure that someone was watering the cacti in my office, that sort of thing—so I wasn't completely out of touch with my building mates, but it had been a while since my last visit.

I marched up to the reception desk that dominates the large central foyer. The space doubles as a waiting room for our various clients, guests, patients, and people in need of psychic stuff. Instead of our bubbly, bright-as-a-newborn chick, receptionist Lilly, I found grey-complexioned, dour-as-a-Sour-Patch-kid, Rebecca.

"Can I help you, sir?"

Uh, what? Where was I? I twirled around and took in the emptiness. Not another soul in sight. The doors to Errall's and Beverly's offices were closed up tight.

"Who are you?" I asked.

Her naturally crabby face frowned a little more. "Who are *you*, sir?"

"I'm Russell Quant."

"Do you have an appointment with someone?"

"Where's Lilly?"

"Lilly? I don't know any…ohhhhhhhh, you mean the regular girl."

"Uh huh, yup."

"Lilly is on maternity leave. She had her baby last month."

I knew that.

I think I knew that.

I should have known that.

No, of course I did. I'd just forgotten, with everything else that was going on. I had chipped in for the gift.

"I'm Rebecca. How can I help you, sir?"

"I work here. My office is right up those stairs."

The girl looked a little taken aback. "Really?"

Understandable. I suppose. My name should have tweaked a little something. "Mmm hmm. I've been away for most of the past year. That's why you haven't seen me around much."

"Well, no one told me about this. Are you sure you're expected back? I was told all I had to do was answer phones and take messages. And they said I could go at three. And that I should just lock up at lunch and that the only…"

"Wait, wait, wait a sec. Where exactly is everyone?" I knew Errall was still in Zihua for a couple more days. But what about everyone else?

"As I told you, Lilly is on maternity. And they said all the other offices would be empty."

Empty! "Empty? Who told you that?" What was going on here?

"The temp agency."

"Who exactly hired you, Rebecca?"

"The temp agency." Her voice was getting pouty. As if she was beginning to doubt she'd be employed much longer.

"And who hired the temp agency?"

She shrugged. "I just get told where to go and what to do."

She gave me the information about which temp agency she worked for, then I left her to her myriad of very important duties. I wandered into the kitchen, looking for coffee. Nothing. Only a cold, empty pot. Lilly always kept a fresh pot brewing. Beverly brought in samples of her extraordinary baking on a daily basis. Alberta kept bowls of the candy she was addicted to in here, because she knew if they were in her office she'd finish every last piece in very short order. Today—nothing.

I stomped upstairs and unlocked my office door. The first thing I did after booting up the long-asleep computer, was to start a pot of coffee. I had everything I needed to brew my own, but somehow the stuff that Lilly made downstairs always tasted immeasurably better. For now, this would have to do. I knew I should have stopped at Starbucks. But I was feeling cheap these days.

I plopped my butt into my office chair and wondered what I had missed. I'd just spent the better part of a couple of weeks with Errall. She'd said nothing about anyone closing up their offices. Then again, sharing important information with me was not Errall's forte. She'd been known to take pleasure from surprising people unfairly by springing previously undisclosed information on them. She was, after all, a lawyer.

I grabbed the phone and dialled Beverly's home number. No answer. Then Alberta. Same thing. Had the world gone crazy? Step away from your life for a few months and see what happens. Anarchy.

The phone rang and I hurriedly picked up.

"Welcome back, Mr. Quant!" a singsong voice warbled out of the receiver. Lilly! And that is why she is the best receptionist in the world.

"Lilly! Thank you. How are you? How's the new kid?"

"He's growing like a snowball rolling down a hill. He looks

just like Brad."

"Oh, I'm sorry."

Her sweet laugh tinkled over the phone line. "So are you back for good now? We really missed you!"

"And I'm really missing you, Lilly. It was a rude surprise to show up today and find you weren't here."

"It worked out perfect though, don't you think? You were gone, Errall and Beverly are both on vacation, and Alberta's car won't start." She tittered. "She decided it was a sign; the spirits telling her to work from her home until the weather warms up."

In only a couple of sentences, Lilly had made my world right again. Did I mention that she is the best receptionist in the world? "More like the spirit of the guy at the garage telling her to buy a car worth more than sixty bucks."

"Oh, Mr. Quant. Well, I just wanted to call and say welcome back. Is there anything I can do for you from home?"

"Just hurry up and raise that baby fast, so you can come back to us very soon."

"That's sweet. It won't be too long, I promise."

"Thanks, Lilly. Bye."

"Bye."

Phew.

I stared at the phone. Then the blank computer screen. The barren inbox on my desk. The Day-Timer opened on my desk to some long-forgotten week from the previous year. The dusty filing cabinet across the room. Ta Da! I was open for business. Day one.

Nothing happened.

I drummed my fingers on the desktop.

Still nothing.

I needed work. Over the past year, I'd been careful with funds, not to mention the grateful beneficiary of the generosity of friends. As such, my long-term retirement savings were safe and sound. The same could not be said for short-term cash. Soon though, I knew, upon attempting withdrawal from my chequing account, I'd hear the telltale sound of scraping at the bottom of the barrel.

I hadn't had a rainy day. I'd had a monsoon.

I needed to be patient. In a way, I was starting over. Now that my shingle was officially hung once again, business would surely begin to trickle in. It always had before. There'd been lean times, there'd been feast times. This was just an extra-lean time. I would survive. In the meantime, I knew I should keep busy. So I put my fingers to work and began doing what detectives do best: snooping.

By lunchtime, I had a pretty decent picture of the life lived by Hilda Kraus's daughter. Lynette Kraus was thirty-eight years old, never married, no children. She left home at eighteen and, jiving with what Millie Zacharias had told me, moved into a nice apartment in the trendy Broadway area. After that, she seemed to spend her time flunking out of Secretarial College, Hairdressing school, and several University level classes taken one at a time. It didn't appear she did much of anything else. She was twenty-seven when her father—aka the golden goose—died, leaving her at the financial mercy of her mother. Suddenly, Lynette began to add actual work experience to her paltry resume. Eventually she went back to school to earn a diploma in bookkeeping. She landed a job doing the books for a small local company that specialized in made-to-order cardboard boxes.

I couldn't find anything to indicate that Lynette was involved in any community volunteering, sports groups, or social organizations. The only group I could find which listed her as a member was called The Arm Chair Travellers. They met once a month, and seemed to spend entire evenings ooohing and ahhhing over pictures of other people's trips. Oh dear.

There had to be more to Lynette than this.

Throwing on my jacket, I locked up and jogged down the stairs to the main floor. I tossed Rebecca a *see-ya-later* as I passed by.

"Wait! Mr. Grant! I have to go to lunch!" Her face was the colour of storm clouds.

She didn't really expect me to man her desk, did she?

"Try Colourful Mary's. Have the Blob soup, it's delicious," I threw back, quickening my steps.

"So I'll just lock up then? I'm leaving at three! They said I could leave at three!"

I was out the door.

Boxes Made to Order—catchy name—was located in the Hudson Bay Industrial area, just off Miners Avenue. The building was tired. The signage was tired. The man who stood behind the counter, looking dispiritedly at a computer screen, looked really tired.

"Hi," I said when the noise of the glass entrance door slamming shut behind me didn't seem to attract his attention.

"Yeah, hold on. I'm just in the middle of something here. Be right with you."

I sidled up to the counter. In the reflection of a glass cupboard behind the man, I could see his screen: he was busy spending time in FarmVille, a real-time simulation game on Facebook.

After a minute, without even bothering to look up, the fellow said: "There's a brochure on the counter. You can pick out what kinda box you need outta there. When you're ready, I'll take your order down."

"I'm ready now," I informed him. I resisted the temptation to tell the Boxes Made to Order employee that I'd like some bags made to order. Just to screw with him.

He looked up, but didn't move away from the computer.

"I'm looking for Lynette Kraus. I was a friend of her mother's. I wanted to drop by and tell her how sorry I am for her loss."

"Well, good luck with that," the guy said with a bit of a snort. "If you find her, let me know."

"She didn't come into work today?"

"Hasn't been in all week. Don't know where she is. Didn't call or nothing."

I could have found this out over the phone. But I always find it preferable, when talking to a suspect for the first time, to do it face to face. Especially when they're not expecting you. This plan, however, was not working out too well for me today.

"Did you call her? Maybe she's sick at home or something?"

He shrugged. "I guess the boss'll call her when he really needs her...or to fire her. Either way, can't help you, buddy." His dead eyes lit up. Something quite wonderful must have happened in FarmVille.

Fortunately I didn't need this bozo to tell me where Lynette Kraus lived. Her address was in the phone book.

Catching light traffic on Circle Drive, I was parked outside of Lynette's modest Confederation Park bungalow in under fifteen minutes. The street was quiet. It was the middle of the day and most residents were likely at work or school. I ran through my mind the best approach to take with the woman. Honesty or clever lie? Clever lies are much more fun.

I adjusted my earmuffs against the coming cold. Little did I know I was about to have more to worry about than the temperature.

I didn't see it coming.

As I stepped from my vehicle into the street, I was hit from behind by a force so brutal, I was plowed to the ground.

I never stood a chance.

Chapter 5

I'd never imagined what being run over by a vehicle would be like. Now I didn't have to imagine. That's what it felt like as I lay there, face smashed against pavement, blood running down my cheek, a heavy weight pushing down on me, a nauseating feeling bloating my stomach.

"What the fuck do you think you're doing?" The words were spoken so close to my ear, I could feel them rumble around in my ear drum like bingo balls.

Wait. I recognized that voice.

I hadn't been the victim of a hit-and-run after all. I'd been taken down by yet another big hunk of steel—Constable Darren Kirsch. I realized two more things. First, the blood wasn't coming from some near fatal contusion. Rather, the cat scratch on my cheek, which had reopened when I hit the ground, was simply expressing its distress.

Second, the heavy weight pushing down on me was Kirsch, who'd fallen on top of me. Now, I must admit, this was not a scene (sans the blood part) I hadn't fantasized about once or twice over the years. Although he's a big lug who may have been raised in a barn, Kirsch is still a bit of a hot number—if you're into the Burt Reynolds from *Smokey and the Bandit* type. But there's a time and place for everything. This was neither.

Cursing under his breath, Darren hoisted himself up, and with his ham hock hand helped me up too. I was expecting more swearing. Instead he threw an arm around me and dragged me away from the scene, like a freed hostage at a bank robbery.

When we finally came to a stop around the nearest corner of the block, I spun away from his grasp and asked as politely as I could: "What the hell is going on here?"

In an uncharacteristically gentle move, the first thing the human dumbbell did was raise a hand to touch my cheek. I nearly recoiled, thinking the guy was gonna bitch slap me or something.

"I'm sorry about this," he whispered, inspecting the cuts on my face. "You should have that looked at. I'll call someone."

Call someone?

My eyes moved away from the cop. I slowly took in my surroundings. The street had been cordoned off at both ends. Within the perimeter were at least three police cars, an ambulance, a fire truck, and several other vehicles. There were cops milling about everywhere. What...?

I turned back to Darren. I debated not telling him that the blood was actually from a cat scratch, and not from his unprovoked attack on an unsuspecting citizen of the city he'd taken an oath to protect. But that didn't seem very nice, so I told him the truth.

"Have somebody look at it anyway. You may have gotten some dirt in the wound. You don't want it getting infected. It might ruin your online dating prospects."

And evil Darren was back.

"But for now, let me repeat," his eyes grew smoldering. "What the fuck are you doing here?" When an answer wasn't immediately forthcoming, he blabbed on: "Here we are, not quite finished cordoning off the streets, when who do we see driving into the restricted area, but our happy-go-lucky local private dick, Russell Quant. Now tell me what's wrong with that picture? Quant, why are you here?"

"Why are *you* here?" Not great, but it was the best retort I could come up with.

He'd had enough. "I am two seconds away from slapping cuffs on you for obstruction of justice."

"Ohhhhhh, how *Law & Order* of you." I wasn't too happy about things either.

We glared at each other.

Although it smarted a little, I gave in first. "Obviously, we're here for the same reason. Lynette Kraus lives here. We both think she had something to do with Jane Cross's murder."

"Have you been asked to look into her death? By who?"

"Yeah," I shouted back. "By Jane! Right before she died."

He glared some more.

"Your turn," I said in a quieter voice.

"After we talked on the phone, things happened pretty quickly."

"Yeah, thanks for keeping me in the loop on that." I knew he had no responsibility to do so. It was probably even a little against the rules. But it would have been nice if for once he gave me something I needed without my having to sell a kidney to get it. Yes. I was grouchy. And my cat scratch really burned.

He began to talk. "The investigation moved from Regina to Saskatoon once we got wind of Lynette Kraus, and Jane's involvement with her. We talked to people who said Lynette often joked about needing her mother to kick the bucket so she could inherit the land, sell it, and go see the world. Lucky for us, but unlucky for her, Kraus's fingerprints were in the system. She'd been arrested for shoplifting in her early twenties. She left them all over Jane's office. And, it gets better. Lynette Kraus was one of the few people in Canada who registered their gun, then shot someone with it. So here we are, Quant. Ready to make an arrest. That enough information for you?"

I surmised this wasn't the best time to bring it up, but I couldn't help wonder if Kirsch and his police buddies were making a big mistake. There was a major piece of this puzzle that did not fit. How could Lynette Kraus be the killer when the killer I'd rumbled with in Jane's office was most definitely a man?

I kept my mouth shut, backed off, and tried to blend into the background. By making myself inconspicuous, my hope was that they'd forget about me, and I'd get a front row seat to the arrest of Jane's possible killer.

It was a tense environment. A real live murder suspect on a Saskatoon suburban street was a big deal. I had to give kudos to the law enforcement agencies involved. Other than allowing a rogue PI to slip through the cracks, they seemed well prepared, with plenty of backup firepower should they need it. I suppose it might have seemed like overkill to the casual bystander. This was, after all, a heretofore law-abiding woman in her thirties we were talking about. But I knew, as did the cops, of far less perilous situations that had gone horribly wrong.

What followed was a lot of waiting and many whispered consultations (none of which included me). Finally the move was made. A team of three plainclothes, one being Darren Kirsch, was sent to the front door. I had my great view, albeit from a great distance.

They knocked.

The door opened.

A woman whom I guessed to be Lynette Kraus stood there. She had a short chat with the officers. Everything seemed very polite. Had she been expecting this? Or had they not yet revealed their true intent? Or did she know the jig was up, and decided to peacefully give herself up? She must have invited them in, for we watched as the three men went inside. The door closed after them.

And then all hell broke loose.

We heard one loud pop. That was it. After two microseconds of profound silence, the yelling and screaming and running and drawing of weaponry commenced. It seemed like every cop in Saskatchewan was rushing through Lynette Kraus's door. Whoever had done the shooting didn't stand a chance. My only hope was that the victim did.

My late workout at the gym was punishing. I needed it. For many reasons, not the least of which was to help me exorcise the sound of the senseless death of Lynette Kraus. One "pop" and it was all over for her. The cops didn't even have a chance to talk to her. She must have known they would come for her. She'd invited them in. The moment the door was closed, she looked Darren in the eye, placed a gun to her head, and fired.

I hung around and kept my eyes and ears open. It sounded as if the evidence they'd collected against her, even in the short time they'd had, was damning enough to convict her for Jane's murder. They suspected the gun she used to kill herself would end up being the same one she used to kill Jane. Motive? Jane must have discovered that Lynette killed her own mother. A mother killer. No one on the street that day was sad that Lynette Kraus was dead too.

It all should have felt right. Millie suspected Hilda's death was murder. She'd hired Jane to look into her prime suspect, Lynette Kraus. Jane did what she was asked. She found out the truth. She was killed for it. The murderer met with the ultimate justice: her own death. Case closed.

But Jane hadn't closed the case. Instead, she'd called me, asking for help. That wasn't the action of an investigator who'd wrapped things up. And there was the little matter of my Tom Ford man. I knew the cops were beginning to think that either I was wrong, or by some bizarre coincidence, I just happened to interrupt a break-in in progress which had nothing to do with the dead body lying on the floor. Possible? Of course. Probable? Oh come on!

So I pounded away at the elliptical and pressed hateful iron until the sweat soaked through my clothing and began to obscure my vision.

It was over. So why didn't it feel over?

Saskatoon has more than three hundred restaurants. This is quite a few for a city with a population under a quarter million. Despite the riches of restaurants, Sereena maintains that the only time to try different restaurants is when you're out of town. When at home, you should stick to three or four that you really like. Visit them often. Get to know the staff and management. Tip outrageously. This practice ensures you great service, great food, and a great experience every time. Plus, every now and then, you got a free aperitif or dessert thrown in. I have found her advice to be sound.

Colourful Mary's was one of my "three or four" places. At first, I supported it because it was the only eating establishment in town owned and operated by an openly gay couple. I did this despite my experience that—surprisingly—"gay-owned" does not necessarily equate with three-star, Michelin Guide quality. Either the food isn't very good, the prices are too high, or the ambiance is too raunchy, too trendy, or both. Not to say there's anything wrong with raunchy or trendy, but you've gotta have the culinary goods to back it up. Colourful Mary's blends the cultural gastronomy of the Ukrainian/First Nations backgrounds of the two owners, Marushka and Mary. It has turned out to be an unlikely but unbeatable combination.

Adding to the unique mixture of restaurant and bookstore, and the varied and distinctive menu, Colourful Mary's is also famed for the owners' predilection for redecoration and reinvention. Every change in season or Mary's mood, brings a decor rebirth to the restaurant. Over the years, the place has been a rustic Alpine chateau, an African sanctuary, a medieval castle, and Aunty Em's kitchen from *Wizard of Oz*. Yet, no matter what the place looks like, stepping inside is like visiting the home of your favourite (eccentric) aunt: you feel welcome and wanted, and you know you won't leave until you've been well fed.

This time, I walked into the perfect antidote for the chilly weather. Wandering through the front door was as if I was entering a tent belonging to a Maharajah. The colours were dark and rich, with plenty of gold and silver highlights. The floor was littered with cushions and metal urns. There were fantastic armoured pieces, and fanciful *chauris* (whisks), *ankushas* (sticks used to goad elephants), and swords. The walls were draped with thick fabrics that seemed to embrace you with promised warmth as soon as you entered into this foreign land. It was the splendour of a princely Indian court. As always, the staff was dressed to fit the theme. The most splendid costumes were the vintage saris worn by Collie Flower and Dandy Ruff, two of my favourite servers.

The joint was hopping. Mary, who often acts as hostess, was too busy for a sit down visit, but came over for a quick hi and hug.

"Is it true? Does this mean we can take down the 'Missing Gay PI' poster for good now?" she asked, standing close so I could hear her over the buzzing cacophony of the diners.

"It does."

"Wonderful. You've just made my day. And that's something, because it's been a little more hectic than usual around here."

"I thought the restaurant business was supposed to slow down in February."

"I know. Tell it to these people. But I'm not complaining. Just a little weary on my feet. Been here since six this morning."

"You two work harder than anyone I know."

"Listen, your order is not quite ready. Marushka wanted to throw in an extra treat. I'm sorry I can't offer you a table. They're all full up at the moment. But there should be a free stool in the bookstore."

"Perfect. I'll wait there. You go back to work. I'll come by in a few days and we can catch up."

As I meandered through the convivial restaurant toward the bookstore, I was immediately sorry I was only there to pick up take out. But I had dogs at home, waiting to be mollified. I also had a refrigerator full of Mom's cooking. She'd apportioned the bounty into single meal servings. However, to my mother's way of thinking, "single meal" means enough food for you and five friends who haven't eaten for a week. And, instead of Tupperware, Mom uses decades-old, plastic ice-cream and margarine containers, which she has dutifully recycled since World War II. Don't get me wrong, I adore my mother's cooking. But after the extravaganza of the previous night, I was looking for something a little more...uncreamy. To be fair to my mother, many of Marushka's recipes include their own tonnage of cream and butter, but the place also serves the best homemade hamburgers this side of a Texas BBQ, and I had a hankering for one.

Waving at a few acquaintances as I passed through the mishmash of bustling tables, I suddenly stopped dead in my tracks. Lingering above the many wonderful smells wafting from Marushka's kitchen, was something else. Another scent.

Tom Ford cologne.

Now on high alert, I scouted the crowd more closely. A couple of people took notice and gave me strange looks. Understandably. I was standing in the middle of a crowded restaurant, sniffing at the air and scowling at the diners. I'm sure I looked like some crazy person who'd just been denied a seat and thought he could frown somebody into giving up theirs.

"Russell, are you okay?" It was Dandy Ruff, passing by with a platter of calamari.

"Do you know the smell of a Tom Ford cologne?"

"Does Ivana Trump need a makeover? Of course I do. Why, hon?"

"Is someone in here wearing it?"

Dandy made a show of taking a good whiff of the crowd. "The guy at table ten is close, but it's not Ford. I know my scents. He's wearing Creed. Anything else I can do for you? Maybe a drink while you're waiting for your order?"

"Thanks, no."

Was my brain leading my nose astray? Fooling it into smelling the cologne because of my doubts about Jane's death and who caused it? Or, was there still a killer out there, wearing Tom Ford...and looking for me?

There is a part of me that could totally be one of those hermit guys. The kind who never leaves his house, surrounding himself with all the things he loves—pictures, books, music, movie collection, good food, bad-for-you food, sweet dogs. I created my home as a place conducive to hibernating. My home is my castle.

And every now and again, I like to fill the moat, pull up the drawbridge, and settle in. Tonight I wanted just that.

My mother had gone back to her home on the farm. I had a feast, compliments of Colourful Mary's, a few special treats for my special Schnauzers, and a half bottle of Pinot Noir left in the fridge, which needed drinking. The salesperson at Cava Secreta had promised scents of black cherries, pine tree, and tar, with hints of herbs, vanilla, and oak char. It had delivered on the first go round. I looked forward to more of the same.

Barbra and Brutus were definitely up for some major cuddle time. So we collected our goodies and settled into the front living room. While the large picture window displayed arctic conditions outdoors, miraculously kept at bay by a few thin, plates of glass, we lounged in cozy comfort in front of a roaring fireplace. Along with my splendiferous burger, Marushka had added a basket of sweet potato fries, an order of clam chowder (so much for a creamless meal), and, best of all, two chunks of her toasted cornmeal bread, meant to be dipped in warmed honey and eaten with the soup. Bless that woman. Along with my food and wine, I was in the mood for a little Mozart and more of my book. Barbra and Brutus were happy to work at freeing a couple of Kongs of the goodies I'd buried within their rubber bellies.

Done with dinner, we retreated to the bedroom. Barbra too. The treat-filled Kong, along with some slavish attention, had finally done the trick. Given my line of work, and the amount of time I spend travelling, the dogs are used to my being away from home from time to time. A year, understandably, was too long. Which was okay with me. I wasn't planning a repeat performance.

Cuddled up on the bed, we—well, mostly me—chuckled away as we began re-watching the first season of *Sex in the City*, until sleep gently took us into its arms.

Some time later, in the magical world of dreamland, I somehow landed a starring role in my very own episode of *Sex in the City*. I was in my bed. Stark naked. And spread eagled. My hands and feet were fastened to the posts of the bed frame; my own neckties and bathrobe belt used as ropes. Straddled on top of me was a handsome blond man. I smiled at him in a dreamy haze. He smiled back. He was really something. Wavy hair that shone like strands of gold in the summer sun, the perfect five o'clock shadow on a square jaw, a Brad Pitt grin, and, from what I could see from my compromising position, a finely shaped chest heaving with…what?...lust for me? I was ready for the next scene.

The man held something above me, positioning it within my line of sight so I could clearly see it. I tried to focus my eyes. It was grey, round…

The man began to say something. "Just so you know, if you decide to scream, I'll have to use this. But I'd really rather not." He spoke with a barely-there French accent. Just by his tone I could tell he was sweet and kindhearted.

…but wait a second…

Inside my head, another voice shouted: "Do something you big dummy! This is no dream!"

Chapter 6

The mystery did not last long. A distinct scent in the air told me everything I needed to know.

Tom Ford was in the room.

A killer was straddling me.

Of course. After all, it had been at least a few hours since I'd been attacked, cat-scratched, or knocked to the ground. I was getting bored.

But how had he done it? How had he gotten me into this position without waking me up?

My next thought was one of concern. Barbra and Brutus. God, where are my dogs? What has he done to them? They would never allow a madman to come into the house and do this to me without plenty of fuss. I raised my head—as far as I could, considering the rest of me was fastened to the bedposts—and searched the room.

Next to the Jacuzzi tub, I found my answer. Laid out before the two—obviously undiscriminating—Schnauzers, was a veritable horn of plenty, doggie style. I eyed pigs' ears, antler horns, a bowl of bacon bits, and a selection of my mother's Ukrainian delicacies displaced from my refrigerator. Evidently they'd been at it for a while. Both dogs were sitting while they ate, tasting a bit of this, then a bit of that, all at a leisurely pace. And they say food is the way to a *man's* heart? Apparently it did the trick for canines as well.

I stared up at my captor with hate-filled eyes. He was still waggling the roll of electrical tape in my face.

"Soooooooo?" he queried, the French Canadian accent not quite so charming anymore. "Will I be needing this, or…?"

"I reserve the right to scream later, but for now you can put it away."

"Deal," he said with a sweet smile, setting aside the tape.

"How did you do this?"

He glanced at the dogs. "Them? Oh, they were the easy part. I used to have dogs all the time at home on the farm."

A farm boy. Like me. Maybe I could use that to my advantage. Later. "Not them. Me. How did you get me tied up without waking me up? I know I'm not exactly a light sleeper, but this? Uh uh. No way. How did you do it?" I'd get to the "why" in a minute.

"What?" he asked in mock shock, as if greatly insulted. "And give away trade secrets?"

Trade secrets? So he was a professional captor and killer? What had I gotten myself into? I knew that the longer I dragged out the talking part of this, and distracted him with questions, the better. "If you're going to kill me, what does it matter if you tell me your secrets?"

He seemed genuinely taken aback by what I'd said. Now he was truly insulted. "Kill you? Why would you think I would do such a horrible thing? You actually think I could kill someone?"

"Ah, excuse me. You're the one who broke into my house, bribed my dogs, and tied me up. And now you're sitting on top of me. I'd say that's pretty threatening. Not to mention that I know you were involved in the death of Jane Cross."

He laughed. Yeah, that's all veeeeerrrrrrrry funny. What a

jerk.

"I guess I see your point," he said, "But, Russell, you've got it all wrong. I was the one who thought *you* were Jane's killer."

"Oh right. That's why you jumped me and tried to kill me too, I suppose? Oh, by the way, I'd lay off the Tom Ford cologne."

He was momentarily speechless after that bit of info. He sniffed at his arm. Looked at me with wide, innocent eyes. "You don't like it?"

"Well, I prefer…hold on! Are we really talking about cologne right now? Really?"

"You're right. We'll talk about that later. I'm sorry about all this. Maybe I got a little carried away. But I thought this might be the only way I could get you to listen to me."

"Listen to you? About what? You want me to tell the cops you didn't attack me in Regina, after you killed Jane Cross? Well you're in luck. In case you didn't hear, they arrested someone else for her murder."

He nodded. "Lynette Kraus. I heard."

As we chatted away cosily, I was trying my best to loosen one of the four bindings that kept me from knocking this creep on his ass. It looks so easy in the movies. So far, nothing.

"My name is Jean-Paul Taine. My friends and family…and captives…call me JP."

Oh, a funny criminal.

"I *was* the one who attacked you in Jane's office. But only because I thought you might be the murderer, returning to the scene for some reason. I was pissed off. And scared."

"But if you weren't there to kill Jane, why were you there? Are you a thief or something?"

He chuckled again. "You don't think much of me, do you, Mr. Quant?"

"I have to admit," I responded dryly, "my first impressions haven't been exactly stellar."

"I'll give you that. But I can promise you, by the end of this, you will have changed your mind. Totally." That Brad Pitt smile again. I wished he would stop that.

"I doubt it," I said dryly. "Unless you feel like letting me go? These restraints are really starting to hurt, JP." Playing the familiarity, just-buddies, game.

He studied me, eyes narrowed, lips scrunched to one side. "I think I'm going to wait on that just a bit longer."

Shit.

"Until my charm has a chance to work its magic on you."

"I don't think either of us has that long to live." Good one, Quant!

He smiled. "We'll see." Sensing I was getting a little sore, he shifted his weight a little to the right. "There's a good reason I was in that office, Russell."

"I'd like to hear it."

"I was Jane's assistant. I'm a part-time PI."

Now this I didn't expect.

"I'd just found Jane's body myself, only minutes before you broke in."

"I didn't break in. The door was open."

"Whatever. You can see how I'd think you were the bad guy."

"I suppose," I allowed grudgingly.

"So I tried to take you down. You know how that turned out."

"Yeah. Thanks for the sucker punch in the gut by the way. I'll send you a bill for the hernia operation."

"Sorry about that. But I realized if I didn't do something, we'd have to fight to the death. One death that night was enough. I wanted to get out of there and call the cops. But then you did. I couldn't believe it. It was then I began to figure out you weren't who I thought you were either. We were both wrong."

"Yeah, yeah, okay, we were both wrong. Let me go."

He ignored my suggestion. "I stuck around to see what was going to happen. When you left for your hotel, I followed you."

"Then broke into my hotel room."

"Yup. I needed to find out who you were and why you were in Jane's office. When I went through your stuff… sorry… again… I found out you were Russell Quant. Jane had told me all about you. So I came to Saskatoon to...well, to break into your house, bribe your dogs, and tie you up."

"Some people just make an appointment, but this is okay too." Even tied up and at this guy's mercy, I could still manage a good dose of smarmy sarcasm.

"Apologies."

"You still haven't told me why we find ourselves in this...awkward position."

"I need your help, Russell. There's been another murder."

JP's words were haunting. And a bit familiar. Turns out that JP believed the same thing Millie Zacharias did. That Lynette Kraus had murdered her mother Hilda. He'd also convinced me he wasn't the bad guy. In turn, I convinced him to let me loose.

While I was covering my nakedness with a pair of Rock & Republic jeans and a v-neck T, JP's sparkling green eyes roved freely. This, and a couple of telltale signs while he was on top of me, told me in no uncertain terms that Jane had recruited from the community of Friends of Dorothy.

"I don't see what I can do for you," I said, shooting Barbra and Brutus a wordless *shame-on-you* look. To their consternation, I picked up the bowls of canine junk food, and placed them on top of a shelf out of their reach. Brutus had the good sense to look a little sheepish. Barbra went for a smug *see-what-happens-when-you-leave-for-a-year* sneer. "This is a police matter. I never get involved in police matters," I lied.

"Russell, I can believe Lynette killed Jane," JP said from where he'd settled on the armchair near my bed. "What I'm afraid of is that the police will never find out the real reason why. Once they discover Jane was a lesbian, they'll probably write it off as a lover's quarrel gone bad. Russell, Jane was killed because of what she knew. She would be horrified if what really caused her death never comes to light. And, as a final legacy for her wife and kid, that really blows."

I was hit with a little blow myself. Wife? Kid? Things had really changed in Jane's life since we'd last been in contact. JP could tell by the look on my face that I was more than a little surprised.

"You didn't know about Marie-Genevieve and Joshua?"

"No." I needed to sit down for this. I crawled onto the bed and sat cross-legged, watching JP carefully.

"They were married two years ago. Joshua is one. That's how I know Jane, how I got the job. Because of Marie-Genevieve. She's my sister." After a beat, he added, "And now she's a widow and single mother."

I couldn't help but soften toward JP. This was personal for me, but for him it was much deeper than that. "JP, I know all about Millie Zacharias and Barb Harper. They hired Jane because they suspected Lynette of murdering her mother. The police know about it too. Even if it's true, what does it matter now? Lynette is dead. They know she killed Jane. Is there someone who would gain from Lynette's being posthumously charged and found guilty of her mother's death too? Are you saying that's what Jane would want? Or her wife?"

JP shook his head in frustration. "Russell, you don't get it. Jane suspected Millie was wrong. In fact, she knew she was. She told me so. Lynette *did* want her mother dead. But she's not the one who actually did the deed. She hired someone else to do it. Russell, there's another murderer out there."

I felt the cold hand of fear-tinged exhilaration run its icy fingers over the skin of my back and neck. I wasn't excited that there was a murderer out there, running around scot-free. But, as a detective, I was keyed up by the thought that there was evil on the run, and I the one fated to catch it.

"Jane knew who the real murderer was. Or at least she was close to finding out."

There was something in his voice that gave me pause. "Well, did she or didn't she? This isn't horseshoes or hand grenades; close doesn't count."

He looked down. "I'm not exactly sure. We never got a chance to talk about it after..."

"After...?"

"After I gave her the file."

I just knew this was going to be good. "File?"

JP looked me straight in the eye and said, "Listen, there's something you should know about me."

"No thanks. Just tell me about the file, please."

"No, wait, you need to know…you need to know that I don't have a lot of experience at this…"

"Seriously, Sherlock?"

"What? How can you say that?" he spouted, suddenly indignant. "You've only just met me. How can you possibly have any idea how much detecting experience I have or haven't?"

"First off, break-and-enter and unlawful detainment of a fellow detective are against the rules in the PI handbook."

"There's a handbook?"

Oh good grief!

"Anyway, I just thought you should know this is…." The balance of the sentence was hidden in mumbling.

"What was that? I didn't hear you."

"This is my first case."

"As a part-time detective?"

"As a part-time detective."

"What's your other job?"

"Shoe salesman."

"I can see why you need my help." Inwardly, I had to admit, the guy was doing pretty good for a newbie. Except for the tying me up part.

"Jane was looking into this for Millie for free. As she got deeper and deeper into it, it was taking up more and more of her time. She already had a heavy caseload. I'd been bugging her for a job forever. I just needed her to try me out. I knew I'd be great at it. I have a lot of skills. I just had to prove it to her."

"Oh gawd. What did you do?"

"I didn't do anything until she hired me. When she did, I sort of broke into Lynette Kraus's home to see what I could find out."

"Ah jeez."

"Don't 'ah jeez' me. You can personally vouch for how good I am at breaking into places."

I shot him a dirty look. "Did Jane think so too?"

He hesitated before answering. "No. Actually, she was epically pissed. Tried to fire me on the spot."

"Tried?"

"Did I mention how charming I am?"

I decided to let that one slip by. Curiosity was getting the best of me. "Did you find anything?"

"I did. I found the murderer."

Chapter 7

"Did you truss him up naked on a bed and sit on him too?" I asked JP Taine, when he told me he'd found Hilda Kraus's murderer in her daughter's house.

JP seemed resistant to sarcasm and mockery in general. I'd have to try harder. "I didn't find the *actual* murderer," he told me. "I found a file called MOM."

"You've got to be kidding?"

I've long believed that all murderers are stupid. But some really take the cake. Some, particularly the more pedestrian, one-off murderers, tend to commit their crime before they've had a chance to really develop a sophisticated criminal mind. They tend to truly believe that what they've done was necessary, a one-time thing that won't hurt anybody else. They also believe that they will never be caught. So they do supremely stupid things, like keep a file called MOM. The same MOM who is now dead.

"Nope. She had the sense to keep it in a hiding place. But I found it pretty easily. Obviously I didn't want to hang around there too long, so I only managed a quick look at what was inside. Just enough to make sure it was important to our case." He whistled like a cowboy seeing a pretty filly. "And it was golden. The first thing I found in the file really told me all I needed to know. Gawd, Russell, it was so...horrible."

I might have started panting at that point, desperate to know what he'd seen.

"It was a picture of Hilda Krause."

"What's so horrible about that?"

"Over the eyes...someone...I guess Lynette...scrawled two exes."

I blanched. Lynette Kraus was one sick woman.

"What did you do?"

"I took it and left."

I winced. I couldn't help think about what I'd recently done in Regina. But the difference between me and Sticky Fingers Taine was that (a) I did not break into Jane's office; it was open, and (b) I did not steal the file I wanted; I duplicated it and put the original back where I'd found it. Ah yes, the wisdom that comes with experience.

Suddenly I was feeling like Cary Grant giving acting tips to Shia LaBeouf. I eyed up JP. I decided he was in his early thirties at least. That felt a little better. Now I was more like George Clooney giving acting tips to Shia LaBeouf. As such, it was JP—and not I—who should feel bad. What was a thirty year old doing pretending to be a PI and selling shoes part time?

"I'm not going to comment on your thieving ways," I noted with generous spirit. "Instead, I'd like you to tell me what happened next."

"I took it straight to Jane. She yelled and screamed when I told her how I got it. Blah blah blah, whatever. Then she read it. That's when she got really mad."

"What got her so riled up?" I knew Jane. She was like a little block of dynamite, just looking for reasons to blow up. Her getting "really mad" might not necessarily be particularly newsworthy.

"She didn't tell me exactly. Not right away, anyway. We were just starting to work together. She hadn't figured out how awesome I am yet. But over the next while she did start telling me bits and pieces. She told me she was on to who Lynette used to kill her mother. And Russell…she was scared shitless about it."

I watched as JP tried unsuccessfully to stifle a major yawn. I thought about what the guy must have been through over the past couple of days. His first case as a PI ends up involving a mysterious, sinister killer of old women. He finds his boss, mentor, sister-in-law, shot to death on the floor of her own office. He has to fight off a tall, handsome stranger, whom he believes to be the murderer (that was me). He realizes he has illegally obtained information about the killer, *and* that he's in *way* over his head. He tracks me down, and somehow manages to tie me up until I promise to help him. And, I hadn't even told him the worst of it yet.

The crazy, suspicious, little weebles who live in my brain, were suggesting a slightly different possibility. It was true that Lynette Kraus had killed herself. But what if this unknown killer, who'd Jane found out about, had somehow found out about Jane. Could he have used Lynette's gun to kill Jane and frame Lynette for it? This same unknown killer was still out there. Was he watching? Would he get the same murderous idea if he thought JP and I were getting too close to finding out the same truth?

I looked at the clock next to my bed. It was nearing three a.m. There was nothing more we could do tonight. JP looked spent. I was tired. The dogs were burping up bacon bits. It was time to call it a night.

"Do you have someplace to stay?" I asked.

He nodded. "Yes. I've made a reservation with the couch in your den."

We stared at one another. He tried for a smile. I headed off to get blankets and a pillow. I didn't bother to tell him I had a guest room.

I made up the couch in the den and told JP that Barbra and Brutus would be guarding the door. When I returned a minute later with a requested glass of water, he was already under the covers. All his clothes, including DKNY briefs, were neatly arranged on a chair. I set the water on the coffee table next to the couch and started for the door.

"When we fall in love," he said dreamily, "I'd really like it if there was a fire in the fireplace when we sleep in here."

I stopped cold in my tracks. Took a second. Turned around. The couch faced a dark, cool, unlit fireplace. When the fire was roaring, it was one of my favourite places to hang out on a cold day, with a good book, the dogs, and someone special.

Instead of reacting to what he'd said, I asked once again: "How did you get me tied up like that?" It was killing me not to know.

All he did was slowly shake his head. Then he turned on his side and fell asleep.

It was a pleasant arousal. The aromas sailing down the hall into my bedroom were sweet and solicitous. Had my mother snuck back in the house while I slept?

Then I remembered.

JP Taine.

I jumped out of bed. The dogs had already deserted me. I threw on my navy-with-white-piping housecoat, intent on finding out what was going on. I was about to stomp out of the bedroom toward the kitchen when I caught my reflection in a mirror. It was ridiculous, I know, but I realized I didn't want JP seeing me looking quite so dishevelled. Really, what did it matter? I was about to kick his ass out of the house anyway. Still, I quickly brushed my teeth, rearranged my hair with the help of a dab of gel, and spritzed on just a little CK One. Not exactly perfect, but good enough. It was perfectly feasible that I'd woken up looking and smelling this way.

When I entered the kitchen, it was apparent JP had not gone to quite as much trouble with his own appearance. His golden locks were pointing in too many directions to count, his jaw scruff was noticeably longer and darker, and all he was wearing were his DKNYs and a bright red scarf tossed casually around his neck. He looked delicious enough to eat.

He had, however, gone to quite a bit of trouble to prepare

breakfast. On the table was a stack of steaming French toast, crispy bacon, hash browns—where did he get hash browns from?—and he was just finishing up a skillet of scrambled eggs.

"Great," he said, showing off a row of pearly whites. "You're up. I was about to send B and B to get you."

Barbra and Brutus were sprawled nearby, obviously suffering from a bacon bits hangover.

"Take a seat. I'll get you a coffee."

I did as I was told. I stared down at the lovely food. He brought me coffee. I added a dash of milk and sipped. Sigh.

"You didn't have to do this," I said, as I helped myself to the bounty.

"I didn't do much. I just rearranged your groceries into a more pleasing format." He sat across from me and filled his own plate. "I wanted to repay you for letting me stay here last night. Especially after...well, you know."

"Especially after you tied me up?"

"Uh huh. I love Barbra and Brutus by the way," he enthused, obviously wanting to move on to another topic. Who could blame him? "They're so well-behaved."

I didn't know if I quite agreed with him. As far as I was concerned, they could learn a thing or two about protecting their master from golden-haired boys with rope. Then again...

"So what's our next step?" JP asked. Eager beaver.

"Finish breakfast?"

"Then what? What do you want me to do?"

I am a lone wolf when it comes to my career. I don't play well with others. And that's the way I like it. But, I had to admit that JP and I had similar goals in this case, and there were things he knew that I needed to get out of him. When I did, I'd cut him loose.

"You know what you can do? You can tell me exactly where I can find the MOM file you found in Lynette's house." I needed to see what Jane saw.

JP bit his lip. "It's gone. I think that's what Lynette came to Jane's office to find. It had all the information we had on her, and whoever it was she hired to kill her mother. She knew it was evidence that would put her away forever, so she needed it back. She must have forced Jane to hand it over."

I remembered the torn couch lining.

JP kept on. "And when Jane did hand it over, she killed her anyway. God, Russell, this is my fault, isn't it? If I hadn't stolen that file in the first place, Jane would still be alive today."

I saw the anguish in the man's face. This was why he'd been so intent, so over enthusiastic, so foolhardy in his attempt to get to me. He thought he was the cause of Jane's death. He wanted to make things right. To do that, he needed help.

"JP, don't do that to yourself. Jane Cross was a fine detective. She eventually would have found out everything that was in that file one way or another. And as soon as she did, she was painting a target on her back. What happened was going to happen, no matter what you did."

"Do you really think so?" For the first time, he sounded a bit like a little boy.

I nodded. Some lies are also kindnesses.

"Okay, so we don't have the file," I said. "I assume Lynette destroyed it as soon as she retrieved it from Jane's office. Otherwise the cops would have it and they'd be all over this too."

JP nodded his agreement.

I dipped a corner of French toast into the pool of Saskatoon berry syrup on my plate. "So, JP, you have to tell me everything you remember from when you looked in the file. You have to dig deep, and be as specific as you can."

"Oh man, that's gonna be tough. Like I said, I only went through it enough to get a sense of what was in there. I remember some newspaper clippings. There were a lot of references to a certain website. And there was a spreadsheet. That's what I remember the best, because it was so obvious what was going on."

"What sort of spreadsheet? What was on it?"

"It was kind of like a wishful thinking income statement. It looked like Lynette was detailing all the money she expected to collect as soon as her mother was dead. Insurance, proceeds from selling land and buildings and farm machinery, that kind of stuff.

But the best part was that, after the total income, she deducted something called FH Ending Fee." JP spelled it out for me.

"Do you have any idea what that was?"

He shook his head. "But over the phone one day, Jane told me she had figured it out. She said she didn't want to talk to me about it until we met again in person, and only when she was absolutely certain. But she did say she'd found out some shocking things. And that it didn't look good for Lynette Kraus."

"Was there anything else?"

Another head shake.

"Okay. Let's go back to the other stuff. What about the website? I don't suppose you remember the URL?"

"No. The only thing I remember about the website is that it had this crazy ass name, and had something to do with people contemplating suicide."

"Suicide? Where did that come from? Who was suicidal? Lynette? Her mother?"

"I don't know. I guess Lynette did kill herself in the end. Maybe that's why she had the gun in the first place?"

"Doesn't fit with someone who was wishing her mother dead so she could start living big."

"No, you're right, it doesn't."

"What do you remember about the newspaper clippings?"

"Not a lot. I didn't take the time to read them through. There were quite a few. There was usually a picture. Always an older woman."

"Are you talking about obituaries?"

"Yeah. Sorry, I guess I should have mentioned that up front."

"Were they all local deaths?"

"Local? You mean to Saskatoon?"

"Yeah," I said, getting up to refill our coffee cups.

"Oh no. These were clippings from all over Canada, and the United States too."

Oh great. That was going to make them even harder to track down.

"Do you remember any of the names, or maybe the dates of death?"

JP thought about this for a while. "I'm better with faces. I think if I saw the faces again I'd know them. The names, nah, I don't think I remember any. Damn, I wish I'd paid closer attention. But I didn't think I had to, seeing as I was taking the file with me."

I raised an eyebrow at his use of "taking with" as opposed to "stealing."

"The dates of the obits were over a long period; I'd say from the last five to seven years."

Terrific. How many old ladies could there be in North America, who died in the last seven years, anyway? Yech.

I sat down with a thud, searching for some way to excavate JP's head for the information we needed. Why couldn't he be one of those photographic memory types of PIs? But wait... "How do you know the women were from Canada and the U.S.?"

JPs eyes grew wide. "Friggin' right!" he suddenly shouted, hopping from the table.

Barbra and Brutus and I watched him disappear, and listened as his bare feet ran down the hallway toward the den.

I gave the dogs a look and said, "You're the ones who let him in here."

Brutus gave me one of his rare woofs.

"Do *you* know how he did it?"

No answer.

I cleaned up a bit in the kitchen, then picked up our coffee cups and headed into the den to see what boy wonder was up to. He was at my desk, busily tapping away at a laptop that wasn't mine. He'd put his clothes on, but the hair was still a piece of modern art.

"Thanks," he said absentmindedly, as I set his coffee next to him.

"So tell me," I said, pulling up a chair. "What's going on?"

"You're a genius, Russell. You see, I knew the women weren't local because the newspaper clippings were arranged alphabetically by the name of the city they'd lived in. Lynette Kraus must have been anal with a capital 'A.' Each clipping had a yellow sticky with the city's name written on it."

"Are you telling me you remember the names of the cities?"

"Well, a few of them anyway. A couple of others I can make a pretty good guess."

"So what are you doing now?"

"I have access to an obituary search engine through this genealogy website I'm a member of."

"Oh? You're into searching your genealogy?" Nerd.

He stopped tapping only long enough to give me a look, as if trying to determine whether I was being sincere or a jerk. I'm not sure what conclusion he reached, but he went back to typing while he answered my question. "No. I just thought this would be a good thing to have if I was serious about being a professional detective."

I had to give him that. "So what's your plan?"

"I'm going to see how many of these cities I can remember. Pull their obits for the past several years for any women over the age of seventy. See if there's anyone I recognize."

My eyes were sore just thinking about it. It's not that it was a bad idea, just a time-consuming one which had a high probability of netting no results. Better him than me. "Good luck."

"What are you going to do?"

"First, I'm going to take a shower. You might consider the same thing."

Without skipping a beat or bothering to look up, he shot back: "Sure. Just yell when the water gets hot and I'll be right in."

I turned my back and walked away. I didn't want him to see the big smile spreading across my face.

Chapter 8

Millie Zacharias answered the phone after three rings. As I was showering—alone—I got to thinking about the identity of Hilda Kraus's murderer. If it wasn't her daughter Lynette, as Millie had suspected, then whose car was it she saw sitting near and then in Hilda's yard in the days leading up to the death? Millie thought the car belonged to Lynette. Was she wrong?

"Mr. Quant, I'm surprised to hear from you," Millie said when I re-introduced myself.

"I hope this is a good time to talk."

"Sure, but I don't know what's left to say. I hear Lynette killed herself when they found out what she did. Sounds like case closed to me."

"The police were investigating her for Jane's murder, not Hilda's."

"Same difference, I suppose. Like Barb said, dead is dead: let's just leave it alone."

"Did you know that Jane believed someone else was responsible for actually killing Hilda?"

"What's that? Why'd she think that? It's obvious Lynette was guilty, isn't it?"

"Maybe. But Jane thought Lynette hired someone else to kill Hilda for her."

There was a break in the conversation. Millie had obviously placed a hand over the receiver, but I could still make out a muffled conversation with another woman, likely Barb.

"Is that right? Barb thinks..." A bit more muttering in the background. "I think that's a bit far-fetched. Don't you?"

"Actually, I don't. No matter what Lynette thought of her mother, to physically end a parent's life would be a very difficult thing to do. She knew she'd be coming into a lot of money after her mother was dead. So even if it was expensive, it would have been a lot easier to hire someone else to do the dirty work."

"I suppose. But in Saskatoon? Could she find someone like that in Saskatoon?"

"Ever hear of Colin Thatcher?" The Thatcher case had been big news in Saskatchewan. Thatcher, the son of a former premier, was a provincial cabinet minister until he resigned in 1983. Four days later, on a bitterly cold day in January, his ex-wife JoAnn was found bludgeoned and shot to death in the garage of her Regina home. The couple's divorce had been acrimonious. Rumours abounded that Thatcher was in some way involved and that he'd hired local men to help him commit the murder. He was found guilty, and sentenced to life in prison.

"So you believe the same thing, then? That Lynette didn't do the killing?"

"I'm having doubts," I allowed. "Millie, you told me that you saw Lynette's car near and in Hilda's yard around the time of the murder. How did you know it was Lynette's car?"

Without hesitation, she responded. "I didn't."

"Ding! Ding! Ding! Ding! Ding! Ding!" The discordant chimes in my head peeled. This is one of the reasons it is never a good idea to take over someone else's investigation. Things like this get missed.

"I only suspected, that's all," Millie told me. "I told Jane what

I thought. After I saw the car there two days in a row, and still couldn't get Hilda on the phone, I took down the licence number. Just in case, you know. I gave the number to Jane. She was pretty happy about that. Said she could use it to confirm it was Lynette's car."

"And did she?"

"Dunno. She never told me."

"Millie, you wouldn't happen to still have that licence number would you?"

"You bet. Hold on, I'll find the paper I wrote it on."

Hallelujah. Things were looking up.

By the time I'd called Darren and begged him to get info on the plate number I'd gotten from Millie Zacharias, JP was coming out of the shower. His hair was silkily wet, and somehow he'd gotten his face scruff back to the just perfect, slightly-unshaven length. He was wearing his own jeans, but had found an old Saskatchewan Roughriders sweatshirt that was one of my favourites for lazy Saturdays. I was about to protest. Until the jolt. It was just a little jolt. Somewhere in the region of my heart. It told me that I kind of liked him wearing my sweatshirt.

Instead of objecting to his wardrobe choice, I turned back to my computer screen, and said, "I'm trying my luck at finding websites on suicide. You said you'd recognize the name again if you saw it?"

"Yeah, I think so," he said. He plunked himself down on the den's couch, in front of the coffee table where he'd moved his own laptop.

"I'll write down the names I'm coming up with for you to look at. I've only just started, but this is a whole new world I didn't even know existed. Did you know there are websites that basically give lessons on the best ways to commit suicide? Some of them list all the different ways, then rank them in terms of overall popularity, ease of completion, associated pain, chance of success. There's even shopping lists for everything you'll need, depending on the choice you made. I found an advice column on selecting the perfect tubing for a successful carbon monoxide poisoning. There are articles comparing and contrasting different suicide methods by age, sex, geographical location. It's craziness. I had no idea this kind of information was out there."

"I'm glad to hear it. That you had no idea, that is."

For the next few hours, I learned more than I ever wanted to know about suicide. Meanwhile, JP continued—so far in vain—to locate at least one of the newspaper clippings he'd seen in the MOM file.

It was nearing noon when next we popped our heads up from our computer screen worlds, like two bleary-eyed gophers.

"What do you say we take a break for lunch?" I suggested. "I'll take you to my favourite spot downtown."

"Are you asking me out on our first date, Mr. Quant?"

I crooked my head to one side, thought about it, and answered. "I'd say yes, but doesn't a guy usually wait until *after* the first date before wearing the other guy's sweatshirt?"

JP stood, and with a deliberately slow movement, pulled the sweatshirt over his head and tossed it to the floor. "Okay. Now we can start all over again."

I looked at him, standing there, the lightly tanned skin of his muscled torso quivering with…anticipation? Cold? Doubt about how I'd react?

I rose and approached. I liked the fact that all evidence of cockiness and confidence had fallen away with the sweatshirt. His eyes followed my progress with a mixture of hope and nervousness.

I hadn't expected to see it so soon. But I knew. This was it. This was what I wanted. In a strange way—and uncharacteristically for me—I felt as if I already knew everything I'd ever need to know about this man. He was right for me, and I was right for him. My certainty was palpable. I felt pings of electricity zinging throughout my body. My head and my heart, with a fair bit of urging from my groin, were in favour. Everything I was feeling, everything going on inside my body, came to the surface in the form of the biggest, widest, possibly most idiotic looking stupid-ass grin since Jim Carrey in *The Mask*.

JP looked a little uncertain. "What's so funny?"

"With your permission, JP Taine, I am going to kiss you for a very long while."

Suddenly, we were both grinning.

Mary joined us at our table. It was well after two p.m., and the lunch crowd had pretty much thinned out.

"I love this place!" JP enthused, his eyes dancing around the Indian palace on the prairies.

"You haven't been here before?" Mary asked, her inquisitive, dark eyes carefully assessing JP.

I didn't quite know how to introduce him when we came in—mumbling something about us working together on a case—so Mary's antenna were up.

"No. I live in Regina."

"Oh," she said with a bit of a frown. "That's too bad. How long have you and Russell known one another?"

I waved at my friend. "Yoo hoo. I'm here too, you know. You can talk to me."

She made a "pshaw" sound, adding, "I can talk to you anytime."

"No way!" JP kept on, his attention now on the menu. "You have bison stew with bannock."

"My mother's recipe," Mary told him.

"I used to date this guy from Mistawasis. His mom made this killer bison stew. I think I might have to do a taste test, just to see if your dish holds up."

"Oh, a challenge. I welcome it. Care to add a wager?"

JP's eyes met Mary's across the table. "What do you have in mind?"

"If my stew wins, you tell me everything about how you and Russell met, and exactly what's going on between the two of you. I can find out anyway, but this will take less time."

"Hey hey hey." I wiggled my fingers between the two, to break up the eye kissing. "There's nothing to tell, so you..."

"It's a deal," JP interrupted. "And if your stew loses, our

lunch is free."

Mary smiled. I could tell she liked her opponent. "Of course."

"By the way," JP added with a wink. "There is *plenty* to tell."

Sensing that JP was someone she should get to know better, Mary decided to stay with us throughout our meal. I did my best to steer the conversation away from personal chit-chat by telling her more about the case we were working on. Jane's murder, and the suicide of Lynette Kraus, had been big news in the newspapers and on TV and radio, so Mary was enthralled with our side-investigation. She was particularly attentive when JP told her about the suicide website we were trying to track down.

"My head still aches from looking for that website this morning," I told her. "But JP didn't recognize any of the sites I came up with. So I guess it's back to the drawing board. I'm dreading it. You wouldn't believe the information that's out there related to this kind of stuff."

Mary looked thoughtful. "You know, guys, I might be able to help you with this."

I was taken aback. "Really?"

"Not me personally, but one of my staff came close to doing herself in last year." Mary noticed JP's surprised face. "Sadly, it comes with the territory. I hire a lot of at-risk people as wait staff; sexual minorities, gender variant, trans, drag queens, we got 'em all. This is one of the few places they can get a job and not have to pretend to be someone they're not. But, as you know, although Colourful Mary's may be a friendly place, the world isn't always. A lot of them have issues to deal with. Marushka and I, and the rest of the staff, try to help as much as we can. But it isn't always enough. Anyway, this particular story ends well. She—or he when she's out of drag—did a lot of research on how to end her life, and ended up—thank God—screwing it up. Now she's very vocal about what happened to her. She speaks at high schools, and to whoever else will listen. She wants to prevent the same thing happening to anyone else just like her.

"Tell you what. Let me talk to her about this. I wouldn't doubt if she had a compendium of every website around that deals with suicide. Maybe one of them is the one you're looking for."

"Mary, thanks," I said, giving her a quick peck on her cheek. "That would be very helpful."

"You're welcome. Now, JP, by the looks of the tongue marks at the bottom of your bowl, I'd say you enjoyed my mother's stew?"

With no argument to the contrary, JP recited: "We met when we tried to knock each other's block off at a murder scene in Regina. As far as what's going on between us, well, you Mary Quail, have just been present for our very first date."

Not often have I seen Mary speechless. Her olive cheeks turned bright, her eyes widened, and when she finally found some words, she began with a stutter. "Oh—oh my…why didn't one of you say something? Why did you just let me sit here, going on and on, and interrupting your date? Oh, gawd, I am so embarrassed." She lurched out of the booth, looking devastated. "Okay, I'm going to leave you now. I'll send over a bunch of desserts, and you can still have your date. Coffee? Maybe a bottle of wine? JP, would you like more stew?"

We laughed at her.

"Don't worry, Mary," JP soothed her. "This just gives us an excuse to have another first date some other time. After all, anticipation is sweet, isn't it?"

After paying the bill, and leaving the restaurant with a bag of cookies Mary insisted on sending with us as a final apology gift, JP and I parted ways. I decided I needed some time on my own to play Lone Wolf detective. He took a cab back to the house, to continue his online obituary search.

Constable Darren Kirsch does not have to look up a licence plate number for me. He also does not have to meet me for drinks on a Friday afternoon. But he did both. The reasons are complex. Especially given the fact that, outwardly at least, Kirsch is not a particularly complex individual.

At first we tolerated one another out of pure greed. We needed each other. I needed a contact in the police service. Kirsch needed a contact on the streets. Over the years, through twists and turns aplenty, we have wound our way into a relationship bordering on friendship. Although I can't quite identify what it is exactly, we seem to provide each other with that certain something unavailable from our closest friends or family. When I'm with Darren, I find myself telling raunchy jokes, laughing raucously, and—gulp—drinking beer. Sometimes, even draft. And Darren gets the opportunity to loosen the stick in his ass, let down his hair, and—gulp—drink wine that doesn't sparkle or have "Duck" in its name. I also know that, given the correct circumstances, Darren is not opposed to knocking off work around four on Fridays and having a drink. So when I called to suggest meeting, his arm needed little twisting.

Flint is a long, narrow, sleek, big-city type place with cool cocktails and hip servers. Not at all Darren's kind of place. Budding friendship or no, I still like to make the big dude uncomfortable for the fun of it. So I was rather surprised when he walked in looking like he'd just modelled for a Gap ad. Even his hair looked as if he'd spent more than two seconds on it with a pick axe.

He shoved his big frame into the chair across from mine, fitting in like GI Joe at a Polly Pocket tea party. I already had a dry, dirty, gin martini going. He ordered the same by wordlessly pointing at it when the chic waiter looked his way.

"Okay, you are definitely giving me an aneurism," I said. "What's with the Joe Cool outfit and smart cocktail?"

"I was glad you called, Quant."

Never—I mean never—have I heard those words come from his mouth.

He nattered on. "I was getting all antsy at work waiting for tonight."

I nearly choked on an olive. "Y-y-you mean coming here to meet me?"

He raised a dark eyebrow high enough to pitch a tent. "Yeah, I really wanted to know what you think of my new outfit." His tone was derisive. "Oh for frig sake, Quant, get a hold of yourself. Tonight Treena is making me...I mean, Treena has *arranged* for me to join her for a date night. Our first since...man, I can't remember when. Probably since Kylie was born."

"Kylie is your ninth or tenth kid?" I might have been exaggerating, but the Kirschs had *a lot* of children.

"Shut up, man." He took a slurp of his newly delivered drink, then: "So she sets up this whole 'date night' thing without me knowing a thing about it. I couldn't even go home after work. She said if I did, I'd probably land on the couch and talk her out of it."

"Smart woman."

"I had to shower and get dressed at work. She got me these new clothes and..."

"Wait! She buys your clothes?"

"Yeah. So?"

"Does she pack your lunch and make sure you wash behind your ears too?"

"Again. Shut up, man. I had to go to this Salon Pure place and get my hair cut. Even though I just got it cut last month. Then we're meeting at The Ivy for drinks, *then* going to someplace called The Victorian for dinner, and *then* to Calories for dessert. And after all that food and drink, she's going to expect hot sex."

I laughed. "And probably make another baby."

Kirsch downed another third of his martini. "Nooooooo way. We're done with that. As it is, I'll be working to eighty-five just to send all the kids we have to school."

"Well, you can always hope that at least two or three of them are just plain dumb."

"That's an inappropriate comment," he said. But he was smiling.

"As usual, I only offered to buy you a drink—and I said one, so slow down on that martini—to get information out of you. The licence plate. Any luck?"

"Yes, but you're not going to like it. The car belonged to a local rental company. Dennie's."

Crap. "You're right. Not good news. Maybe you can make it up to me by telling me if the investigative team has found anything unusual in Lynette Kraus's possession?" I thought if I stuck the question in real quick like, he might answer it before thinking too hard about whether or not he should.

No such luck. "Quant, if you think I'm going to reveal confidential information from an ongoing, province-wide investigation, you probably have too much dirty in your martini. Is this about you still thinking that there might be someone else involved in this whole thing?"

I shrugged noncommittally. I didn't want to share information if there was nothing in it for me. "I dunno. Maybe."

"What sort of unusual thing are you talking about?"

"Maybe a file." If the Saskatoon or Regina police found the MOM file—which JP stole from Lynette and believed she stole back—certainly it would induce them to look into the possibility that someone else had actually murdered Hilda Kraus.

Darren wordlessly shook his head back and forth, very slowly. "So far there's nothing in the facts to support that another killer was involved. Or that Hilda Kraus's death was even suspicious." He waited a beat. "Unofficially...?"

I nodded.

"Assuming—and this is a big assumption, Quant—but assuming Kraus's death was unnatural, the methods used in the two murders—gunshot and poisoning—are *so* different, I have to admit, I don't find your theory completely idiotic."

"Gee, thanks."

"And Quant, if you're still thinking about the fellow who attacked you in Jane's office, don't worry."

I hadn't told him about meeting JP. I didn't see a reason to. And I certainly didn't want to tell him about JP's ill-conceived evidence collection (aka stealing). I was in a bind. It was the contents of the MOM file—according to JP's memory of it—that would prove Lynette did not act alone. Without it, I had *bubkes*.

"We haven't forgotten about that guy," he continued. "We're making some headway."

Uh oh.

"Headway? What do you mean?"

"Aside from yours and Jane's, we found a third set of fresh prints in her office. We believe they belong to your assailant."

Phew. Okay, not much you can do with that, other than prove

there was someone else in there with me.

"And we got a match."

Shit.

"This is one interesting character. If I were you, Quant, I'd keep an eye on my back for a guy named JP Taine. Without a doubt, this guy is up to no good."

Chapter 9

After Kirsch left for his date with his wife, I sat nursing water, mulling over what I'd learned. Then I hit the cellphone. First I called in a favour from a pal who works with Dennie's Car Rental service. I gave him the licence number and dates in question, and asked if he could come up with a name for me. I'm sure it was against the rules and all that stuff, but what are friends who owe your favours for? He said he'd get back to me.

The next call I wanted to make was to JP. Had I unwittingly allowed a criminal into my home? Jeez, Quant, what was your first clue? The fact that he nearly knocked your block off in Regina? Or that he hog-tied you while you were sleeping? I'm generally not that much of a patsy. I couldn't be that wrong. I'd only known JP for a very short period of time, but something inside of me was telling me this was a good man.

But police records don't lie. The Canadian Police Information Centre had JP's fingerprints on file. Although Darren was stingy with the exact details, it appeared that JP had done some time when he was younger. More interestingly, after JP's last stint as a guest of Correctional Service of Canada, he seemed to disappear off the face of the earth. No driver's licence, no job history, nothing. Until two years ago, when he showed up back in Regina.

I dialled my home number. No answer. When I reached my answering machine for the third time, I started getting worried. I didn't think he'd hurt Barbra and Brutus, but would he make off with my good cologne and gatt sweaters?

Annabelle proved herself worthy against a buffeting wind, harbinger of a nasty winter storm set to arrive in the city by nightfall. By the time I pulled into the garage at the back of my lot, darkness had fallen on the City of Bridges. Snow had started to swirl around her like a crazy cyclone. When I opened the door into the yard that separates garage from house, it was clear that JP wasn't in the house. Every window was dark, giving the place a lonely, deserted look on a turbulent night. Shit. He'd lied to me. He was supposed to be here, trolling the Internet. Where else would he go? He had no car. No place to stay.

Trudging toward the back door, I bowed my head against gusts of arctic air, pinpricks of icy snow fighting each other for the chance to bite my skin. When I finally reached it and aimed my key at the lock, I noticed something attached to the door handle. Tied to it by a delicate pink ribbon, was a sterling silver stir stick. This was a Sereena Orion Smith calling card, if there ever was one.

It was a tempting invitation, but I had other priorities. I needed to assess what havoc had been caused me by JP Taine. I unlocked the door and entered my kitchen. Immediately I knew that he'd made off with two very valuable items.

Barbra and Brutus were gone.

After a quick rush about the house to see what else there was to see, I concluded that the dogs were the only things missing. What was this? Some sort of crazy kidnapping scheme? Who was JP Taine? What was he really up to?

I decided to go next door after all, in the vain hope that Sereena had perhaps seen or heard something that would tell me what had happened to my two dogs.

Sereena opened the door. She was wearing a black, slinky sheath that fell seductively off one shoulder, revealing the silky skin which had driven powerful men the world over crazy with desire. Me, not so much. Her dark hair shone with health, and her sparkling eyes relayed epic adventures without her ever having to speak a word. Behind Sereena were Barbra and Brutus. Their eyes told me they were happy and safe and recently well-fed.

"Come in out of the cold, Russell. I'm sure we can find you a few drops of something to warm you up."

Leaving my outerwear behind, Sereena led me to her living room. The expansive space would not have looked out of place in a New York City penthouse overlooking Central Park. Seated around a low coffee table, the lighting dim, the music soothing and big band-ish, were JP and a woman I did not know.

I gave the man whom I now knew to have a mysterious past an inquiring glance, and then shifted my attention to the woman.

"Russell, my love, I want you to meet Elena Petrokovich. She's the infamous crown princess of Novaskalyich, which of course you know from your history, was a major power annexed by the former Soviet Union. Until, that is, Elena's father, Victor, a charming man with a shocking reputation with the ladies, put down his foot and famously said 'Chairman Gorbachev, give me back my kingdom, or I'll have to sleep with your wife...again!' Isn't that right, Elena?"

Elena's laugh was throaty. She raised her left hand in such a way that made me think I should kiss it rather than shake it, and said: "Oh my dear friend, Sereena, you forget nothing. You have a true gift of making us all seem so much more interesting than we actually are." She then turned her powerful gaze upon me. "Russell Quant. How charming to meet you finally. Sereena has told me a great deal about you. And if she's done the same in reverse, I beg you, only believe half of it...well, maybe three-quarters."

I found myself unsure whether Elena truly was a crown princess, or Sereena's dry cleaner who'd dropped by for a snort. But she certainly looked the part. Elena was well into her seventh decade, and dressed in a loose tunic of deep rich colours, that somehow bestowed upon her an air of "to royalty born." Likely an attractive woman in her youth, she now bore no attachment to cosmetics or cosmetic surgery. Her face was pale and jowly, age spots dotted her temples and hands. Her fingers were twisted with arthritis, yet still she'd managed to don several sizable rings that sparkled with a vitality reflecting their owner's.

"My dreary children are thinking of deposing me this week," Elena proclaimed without a hint of a smirk. Her voice was deep, carried by a gurgle from somewhere far back in her throat. "So I thought to myself, what better time to visit my dear friend Sereena in Canada."

"Sounds sensible."

"Will you join us for a *caipirinha*?" Indicating JP, she told me, "I've just instructed this delightful young man how best to prepare one." She sipped from her own glass. "A skill which he's picked up rather nicely."

"What is it?"

"Only the toast of all Brazil; its national cocktail. It's made with *cachaça*, sugar, and fresh lime. Quite impossible to resist."

Giving JP a look he likely did not deserve, I responded with, "It seems no one can."

Likely, JP could sense I was not quite myself. But he simply smiled good naturedly, rose, and ambled over to the bar saying, "Why don't you try one, Russell? I think you'll like it."

I looked at Sereena. "You just happen to have *cachaça* in your bar?"

She swept past me to resume her seat. "Of course, darling. Doesn't everyone?"

Two *caipirinhas* and a rather long soliloquy on the life and times of Elena Petrokovich, crown princess of Novaskalyich, later (she wasn't big on two-way conversation), and still feeling the effects of my dirty martini with Darren, I needed to go home and put food in my stomach (Sereena rarely pairs food with drinks, especially if she has to make it herself). JP and the schnauzers followed.

In my kitchen, I let my eyes wander through the refrigerator, looking for something to soak up the alcohol in my system. Sensing JP standing behind me, I gallantly asked: "Are you hungry?"

"I stopped by the grocery store on the way home," he said. "When I heard on the news that a storm was coming, I thought it was the perfect time for you to try JP's chili. It's on the stove."

"I thought I smelled someth…" It was only then I noticed he hadn't taken off his coat or boots. I looked at the wall clock. Eight p.m. "Are you…going out?"

"I've booked a room at a motel. I think I've used up enough of your hospitality for the time being."

For a moment I was speechless. Indeed, I had been thrown off by Kirsch's revelations of JP's past. Coming home to find him visiting *my* neighbour, with *my* dogs, didn't help either. But all I really knew was that I didn't know anything. Rebellious youth get in trouble with the law all the time. The fact that JP seemed to have no life history for about ten years afterward was a little harder to rationalize. But looking him in the eyes, hearing his gentle voice—the man made me chili, for pity's sake—I just couldn't bring myself to conclude he was a bad guy.

"Oh, okay," I finally responded. "I'll get my coat and drive you."

"No, it's okay. I rented a car today."

Rented a car. Was it JP who'd rented the car Millie saw in Hilda's yard? God, Quant, get a hold of yourself. That's preposterous. Or is it? Sometimes I hate my detective's brain.

"You made all this chili—thanks by the way…"

"No problem. I hope you like it. I put a little molasses in it. Just adds a touch of sweet."

"Why don't you stay and have some with me? It seems wrong that you made it and don't have any. And the storm is really getting wicked out there. The roads will be a mess. Besides, we've got a lot of work to do if we want to get to the bottom of this case. You still want that, right? I've got a terrific Chianti I think will go great with your chili."

I was babbling.

I didn't want this man to leave.

So I said it. "JP, I want you to stay with me tonight."

He didn't move.

I didn't move.

Finally he began: "I know I come off all loud and confident and say things that I probably shouldn't. It's just…it's just the way I am. But most of it is just for show, you know. But this afternoon, when we kissed, I…I took that very seriously. More seriously than I expected to. And now I'm…I'm…" He laughed nervously and licked his lips and petted Brutus who'd nuzzled up next to him. "Now I'm feeling something weird. I feel…kind of stupid for saying all those inappropriate things to you about moving in and falling in love and now I…Jeez Louise...I don't know what to say."

Now he was babbling. We were even.

"How about this," I suggested with a calm voice, approaching him like he was a skittish deer who might bolt at any second. "Give me your coat. You heat up the chili. I'll open the wine…well, first I'm going to drink about four glasses of water to drown the *caipirinhas*…then I'll open the wine. We'll eat. Talk. See what happens. You can go to your motel any time you want. Sound okay?"

"Sounds perfect."

Several minutes later, we were sitting cross-legged on the living room floor, a roaring fire toasting our toes, and two big bowls of fiery chili with a hint of molasses.

"How did you ever end up at Sereena's with a Russian princess?" I asked as I poured the wine.

"I'm not exactly sure. I was out walking Barbra and Brutus. The next thing I knew I was playing bartender and listening to these amazing stories. Did you know Elena and Sereena were once charged with stealing some billionaire's yacht in Capri? Apparently they'd 'innocently' neglected to check if the guy was actually on board before telling the captain to head out to sea. Crazy stuff, right?"

I guffawed. "Knowing Sereena, I have no doubt every word is true…ish." I cleared my throat. "So let me get this straight. While I was working my fingers to the bone, you were partying it up?"

"Not true. I still managed to rent a car, go to the grocery store, make chili, walk the dogs, and identify Hilda Kraus's killer."

I leaned in closer, not sure if I'd heard correctly. "You what?"

"I made chili."

"JP, the part about identifying the killer?"

"Well, to be fair, I can't take credit for coming up with the name. But it's what I did with it that counts."

"What are you talking about?"

"The name of the killer. The credit goes to you and your friend—Roger is it?—at Dennie's Car Rental."

"Roger called back? You talked to him?"

"Of course not. I'd never answer someone else's phone."

"Oh no. You'd only break into their house and tie them up."

"You're never going to leave that one alone, are you?"

"Duh, no."

"He left a message. I was making chili and overheard it. He said the car with the licence number you gave him was rented by a woman named Frances Huber."

The name sat in the air between us like a dark, cold stranger who'd just entered the room. For a moment we said nothing.

"I did some checking. There are less than two dozen Hubers listed in the Saskatoon phone book. Fewer in Regina. None of the listings are for Frances or F. Huber. There are only a handful on Facebook. We have to assume she could be from anywhere. Tracking down every possible Frances Huber around the world will take a very long time, not to mention trying to contact them all."

"I need to call Roger back. Maybe he can give us an address..."

"I wouldn't bother. I already did."

I was about to blast him, until I realized that he'd done exactly what I would have in the same situation.

"He said she paid cash, bought no insurance, left a credit card impression, but no other personal information. And no, he was not willing to share the credit card information or anything else. He said he was already putting his tail in a trap for you. Colourful expression, don't you think?"

"Well," I replied slowly, already feeling weary from all the hours in front of a computer screen I could forecast were in my future, "we're just going to have to think of another way to whittle down our possibles."

"Well, while you were working your fingers to the bone…drinking martinis was it?...I got an idea. I figured it had to be serendipity."

"Serendipity? What?"

"Meeting Princess Elena had to mean something, right? I got to thinking that foreign royals and diplomats and all those kind of cats must have access to all sorts of information."

"And you know that because of why? You read it in a Robert Ludlum novel?"

"Maybe. Anyway, don't worry, I didn't tell her any real details. I asked her what she'd do if she were looking for someone. She loved the intrigue, and made some rather scandalous guesses as to why I needed to find Frances Huber. Then, bim bam boom, she called her assistant. The assistant said she'd have a list of every Frances Huber in Canada and the U.S. emailed to me within half an hour. Going farther afield than North America would take longer. But I thought it was a good place to start. It should be in my inbox now."

Like a dog on a bone, I jumped up, taking my chili and wine with me and headed for the den. "You couldn't tell me this first? What are we waiting for?"

JP was right behind me. Barbra and Brutus, happy by the fire, were not so quick to join us.

Resettled on the couch in the den, JP booted up his computer, found the promised email, and downloaded the list. Together we scanned the pages, our faces getting longer with each passing one.

"There's still got to be three hundred names on this list," JP stated, sounding a little deflated.

"It's a start, JP. You saved us a lot of time by getting this."

"Told you I rocked as a detective." The self-assured JP was back.

"I'll hold off on engraving the award until we find the real Frances Huber."

"Do you think she's our killer, Russell?"

"I don't know. But as they say in the police business, she's definitely a 'person of interest.'"

JP sent the list to my printer. As I went to retrieve it, JPs computer made a noise telling him he had an incoming Skype call.

"Russell, it's my sister. Why don't you come over here and meet her."

I returned to the couch and nudged up next to JP. Seeing Marie-Genevieve Taine's face pop up on the laptop screen was like seeing a softened, feminized version of JP, complete with blonde hair, green eyes, and dimples, sans the lantern jaw and five o'clock shadow.

"Marie-Genevieve, hey girl, I have Russell Quant here with me."

The young woman allowed a small smile on an otherwise serious face. "I can see you both," she said, her voice tinged with a francophone accent, similar but stronger than her brother's. "Hello Russell." Came out sounding like 'ello Russell. "Nice to meet you."

"Good to meet you too, Marie-Genevieve. I want to tell you how sorry I am about your loss. I knew Jane. She was a fine woman, and very passionate about everything she did. I admired that about her."

"You are a gentleman, and very tactful for saying so. I know she was a great pain in the ass a lot of the time too, right?" Marie-Genevieve said with a sudden smile and glint of a sparkle in her eye. "But I loved her for it."

What could I say? I only grinned and nodded.

"Russell, JP has told me that you have agreed to help him. To help us. Thank you so much. Jane would have wanted it this way. It would have driven her crazy to see a killer go free."

"We'll do our best, Marie-Genevieve."

"Are you okay, sis? Everything going all right? Is the car behaving?"

Marie-Genevieve looked at me. "My sweet brother gave me his car to use. In case I needed it with all that's been going on around here since...well since the other day. He wouldn't even take it back to get to Saskatoon. He took that horrible bus."

"It's not such a big deal," JP insisted. "It's a temperamental car anyway. It probably wouldn't have made the trip."

"Where's Joshua? Is he asleep?" JP turned to me: "Josh is Marie-Genevieve and Jane's son. He's the greatest kid. Almost a year old."

"Not quite. Barb is with him."

"Oh. Barb is there again?"

"Barb?" I interrupted. "Barb Harper? Millie's partner?"

"Yes," Marie-Genevieve confirmed. "She drove up all the way from Muenster again, to be with us and help out around the house. I feel so bad letting her do all of this. But I have to admit, it's nice having a friend here right now."

"Are things going okay?" JP sounded worried. "You look tired."

"Listen," I said, making to get up. "I'll leave you two alone to talk. Marie-Genevieve, it was nice to meet you. We'll do everything we can to make sure Jane's work doesn't go to waste."

She nodded, the shadowed look of a fresh widow falling over her pretty face. "Good-bye, Russell. And thank you again."

I winked at JP, picked up the papers from the printer, and left the room.

It was nearing seven a.m. when I woke up. The first thing I saw were two eyes, staring at me with unrequited love. Barbra. She'd finally forgiven me. When she saw that my eyes were open, she reached out with her tongue and gave me a few happy slurps. Rekindled love is a powerful emotion, even for a dog.

"Hello first born," I murmured to her, patting her exposed belly.

I felt the bed shift as Brutus, hearing action up above, jumped up to join the love in. I could see through a half open blind that although there still appeared to be a few flurries outside, the wind had died down. The storm had passed. It still looked bitterly cold though. Wrapping my arms around my furry bodyguards, I luxuriated in our shared warmth for several more minutes.

After I'd left JP in the den, Skyping with his sister in Regina, I'd settled into bed with the three-hundred-people-long listing of potential Frances Hubers. The information was good. It included name, last known address, and brief personal statistics. But still, it was three-hundred-people-long. I began reviewing each entry, not really knowing what I was looking for (inconveniently, none of them listed Killer as recent employment). Next thing I knew, it was morning.

Eventually I got up, put on my housecoat, and headed into the hallway. I stopped at the open door of the den and saw JP. He was fully dressed and fully asleep, on the couch where I'd left him last night. He looked like a little boy, clasping his laptop to his chest like a pillow or beloved teddy bear. Leaving him there, I made my way to the kitchen. After letting the dogs out, I prepared their breakfast, put on coffee, went to get the paper from the front yard, and whipped up two Gruyere cheese smoked ham sweet chili omelettes. With the dogs back inside, I took a tray with the omelettes, juice, and coffee, back to the den, where the kitchen noises and smells had gently eased JP into wakefulness.

"What time is it?" he asked all groggy and gravel-voiced.

I handed him a glass of juice. "Eight. What time did you fall asleep?"

He gratefully downed the juice. "Oh wow, this stuff is good. What kind of juice is this?"

"Apple lime. Did you get much sleep?"

"I was kind of worked up after talking to Marie-Genevieve, so I worked for a few more hours."

"Is everything okay with your sister?"

"Not really. Jane's family has descended. I don't know if you ever met them, but it turns out they are just as big assholes as Jane always said they were. They've basically told Marie-Genevieve that until they figure out what belongs to whom—including the money in their bank accounts—that she can't touch anything. Marie-Genevieve barely persuaded them to let her stay in the apartment. I think they agreed only because of the baby. Without Josh, I wouldn't doubt they'd have thrown her out in the street! In the middle of winter! Gawd, Russell, this makes me so mad!"

"But wait a minute," I said calmly, sitting next to him. "You said Jane and Marie-Genevieve were married. Jane's family doesn't have the legal right to do any of this."

JP rolled his eyes. "They didn't really get married. They just had one of those silly commitment things in their living room one Sunday afternoon."

"Why? Same sex marriage is legal."

"Marie-Genevieve got pregnant with Josh a lot quicker than they expected. So they wanted to tie the knot right away, without getting into all the legal hassle. They kept on saying they'd have time to do it the right way later on. I guess they were wrong."

"I see. So Marie-Genevieve's in trouble."

"I'm afraid so. I don't know what to do to help. I gave her whatever money I had. I put her in contact with a lawyer buddy of mine. But other than that, I just don't know. I think it helps her to know we're trying to finish Jane's last case. That seems important to her. But part of me just wants to be back in Regina, helping her get through this."

I rubbed JP's back. He was in a tough position, no doubt about it. "I'm sure you're doing everything you can. You're being a good brother. She knows that. I could tell, last night on Skype, how close the two of you are."

"We only have each other. No one else. No other family."

"You've got Joshua."

JP smiled, and it was as if light was finally allowed back into the room. "Yeah. We've got Joshua."

"Eat some eggs before they get cold."

JP pushed aside the plate and instead turned on his computer. "But first, you've got to see this." He tapped a few keys and opened a file where he'd saved a document. "Last night. I found one!"

"One what?"

He moved the computer onto my lap. "You read it while I dig into this. These eggs smell incredible, Russell. Thank you."

"You're welcome," I mumbled, as I began reading. The document was obviously a newspaper item scanned into digital format. The print wasn't completely clear, but legible enough to make out. I pulled in my breath when I saw it.

"Read it! Read it out loud!" JP enthused, mouth full of omelette.

"...left to mourn Agatha Dunwoody are her daughter Claudia Dunwoody, nephew Duncan Carlisle, niece Caroline Shaw, and her trusted caregiver...oh my god...her trusted caregiver Frances Huber."

Chapter 10

There was something deeply satisfying about seeing Frances Huber's name in the obituary found by JP. The two pieces of information together, or separately, still proved nothing against the woman. But the fact that a Frances Huber had rented a car seen at the home of Hilda Krause, and a Frances Huber was a caregiver for another elderly woman in Crestwood, Kentucky, both of whom were now dead, was finally something to hold on to. Something that, deep in our hearts, told both of us that we'd identified our killer. But now what?

Mary Quail had left a message on my machine asking us to come down to Colourful Mary's to meet with Onya Knees. Mary thought Onya, a part-timer at the restaurant, might be able to help us identify popular suicide websites. I wasn't sure what the connection was yet, but anything with the potential to lead us closer to Frances Huber was of interest to me.

We arrived just after ten a.m. The place was quiet. The regular, mid-morning Saturday coffee crowd was thinner than usual because of the unpleasant weather. Mary seated us at a table in a far corner, half-hidden by leafy palms and exotic carpet hangings. We ordered coffee and waited.

"Okay, bitches, shove over!" a booming bass voice ordered.

I looked up and saw a towering mass of Barbie-blonde hair, tinged with strands of Barbie-convertible-pink. Beneath the impressive up-do, was five-feet-two-inches of barrel-chested manhood-turned-womanhood. I thought it was a touch early in the day for a cowl-necked, pink sequin blouse, and too early in the season for a white leather mini. Then again, Anthony often reproaches me for being too conservative in my wardrobe choices.

JP and I did as we were told, allowing Onya to slip into the booth next to JP.

"Coffee will kill you," Onya announced with hearty Health-Canada-empowered scorn. "Try vodka. Doesn't stain the teeth, and it goes with almost anything." She laughed with the gusto of a drunken truck driver.

I was guessing that when Onya did work at Colourful Mary's, it must be the evening shift. She was simply too loud and boisterous for mornings.

"Thanks for agreeing to meet us," I said quietly, hoping to average out the sound wattage coming from our corner of the restaurant. "I'm Russell and this is JP."

"You two are better looking than a pair of Salvatore Ferragamos at Payless Shoes. I could just pour cream on top of you and have you for dessert. Interested?"

Both of us reacted with a shrug and our best killer smiles.

Onya shielded her eyes and pulled back. "Stop! Stop! The shine off all those teeth is going to burn a hole in my falsies!" She readjusted and leaned in, her voice dropping to a conspiratorial whisper. "Now listen up, you two. Mary told me what you're looking for. You have to understand a couple of things. First, what we're talking about today has nothing to do with Onya Knees. You got that? Onya is fabulous and loves life. Everyone wants to be Onya, or be with her. What we're talking about is all Steve."

"Steve?" JP asked.

Onya glanced down at her larger-than-life get up. "He's under all this somewhere, believe me."

We nodded our understanding.

"Second. While you're talking to Steve, I don't want none of that Pollyanna shit. Like: *"You'd never really consider killing yourself now, would you Steve?"*, *"We can help you, Steve."*, *"Let's make it all better together, Steve."*, *"Life is too wonderful to throw away, Steve."* Capiche?"

Again we nodded, a little less exuberantly.

"Steve don't need that shit. Steve may or may not be contemplating suicide right now for all we know. Whatever. It's none of your goddamn business. Got that?"

"We do," I promised.

"Third. No judgment from either of you."

"Deal."

"Good. Then we'll get along, and I'll try to help you. Mary told me all this has to do with the murder of some lesbian in Regina, is that right?"

I nodded.

"Okay then. Mary also told me you were looking for suicide help sites on the 'net."

"Well," JP said, "not exactly help as in needing help because you're suicidal. More like help because you're suicidal and would like to know more about how to do it."

Onya/Steve nodded. "I got that. I totally know the best ones. A lot of people might think these sites are repulsive. Evil even. But come on, people, face facts. Suicide has been around forever. Suicide will continue to be around forever. People kill themselves. Some for better reasons than others. I know that. But sometimes, it really is the only way out. And if people are going to kill themselves, doesn't it make sense they should have some guidance? Some help telling them how best to do it? Somebody to tell them this way is more painful but quicker, this way takes a while but is pain-free. This way has only a fifty percent chance of success, but this way is almost guaranteed. It's *Suicide for Dummies.* If we're going to do it anyway, shouldn't we know what our choices are? How else can we make informed decisions?"

Onya was asking some very deep and serious questions. I hoped she wasn't expecting answers. With answers came judgment. With judgment this conversation would be over. I decided the best thing to do was listen, and remain as impassive and stiff-faced as possible. I looked over at JP. He was attempting the same.

"Some of these sites are dangerous. I won't kid you about that. There are predators everywhere. Some of them are just bullshit. Filled with lies and bad information. I'm not surprised you couldn't find anything useful in just a few hours of surfing the web. Finding the best sites takes time.

"I don't give a flippin' burger if you two go sniffing around this world. But I have to warn you. There are some very dark places out there. You might wish you never went there. You ready for that?"

More nodding.

Onya reached into her bosom and pulled out a folded sheet of paper, laying it on the table between us. "Listen, I don't know exactly what you're hoping to find, or what you're looking for, and I don't really care. All I've done is jot down a list of several sites you might want to take a look at. They're the best...in my humble opinion. If you don't find what you're looking for here, then forget it, boys. Steve can't help you. And Onya never could."

With that, Onya left the table. On her way back to the kitchen, I saw her stop at a table of octogenarians having a late breakfast. Although I couldn't hear what it was she said to them, it was no doubt outrageous and totally inappropriate for both the audience and time of day. The three oldsters threw back their heads and had the best laugh they'd probably had in months. With a self-satisfied flourish, head tilted back, nose held high, Onya continued on her journey.

JP was full of piss and vinegar by the time we returned to the house. He thought he recognized one of the websites on the list provided by Onya, and was anxious to check it out. After taking the dogs for a quick walk in weather that was once again taking a turn for the worse, we did just that.

For hours. We sat in companionable silence—and frustration—in my den, me at my computer at my desk, JP at his on the couch, spending time in the bleak world of suicide.

After a couple of fruitless hours on *www.theendsociety.com*, and needing a break from the gloom, JP switched back to searching for obituaries that might have been in the MOM file. I stayed at it, paying particular attention to the associated chat rooms. During a case I had a few years back, I became quite familiar with chat rooms. And the danger that can lurk within them. The End Society website was exactly what Onya had described to us. It was an online community for people wanting to end their lives. I still had no idea how this tied in with murder or Frances Huber, but JP was adamant that this website figured prominently in the information Lynette Kraus had collected in her MOM file.

It was some time after I'd prepared a platter of finger food in lieu of a sit-down dinner—Asian dumplings, *pakoras*, cheese, and bread—when JP suddenly exclaimed: "Hey!"

I turned to look at him. "You find another one?"

"No, but I've been thinking."

"Glad to hear it."

"The website is called The End Society, right? Do you remember the accounting spreadsheet I told you Lynette had prepared? From the total inheritance she expected to get from her mother's estate she deducted something called FHEnding Fee."

"Yeah, so?"

"Ending, as in ending a life, right? A death. Supposed FHEnding was actually F-dot-H-dot-Ending Fee and FH stood for..."

I finished the thought. "...Frances Huber."

"Frances Huber Ending Fee! A fee paid to Frances Huber to end her mother's life."

"JP, that's good. You could be right."

"Russell," he said, his voice sinister. "We really need to find this bitch."

Revitalized, we went back to work, as if the impressive anger of nature, once again raging outside, was feeding our resolve to track down our quarry.

Within an hour, JP tracked down a second and quickly thereafter a third obituary that he was quite certain had been in the MOM file. Neither mentioned Frances Huber, but JP recognized the pictures of the deceased. One of the deaths took place near Seattle, Washington, the other in St. Paul, Minnesota. Both were women in their seventies. Just like the death in Kentucky. Just like Hilda Kraus. It was as if Lynette had collected the obituaries as references for Frances Huber's services. Services which, I was disturbed to realize, she was providing throughout both Canada and the United States.

Within the hour, we struck gold again when I became engaged in a conversation in The End Society chat room.

We finally had the rest of the story.

I'd begun each of my conversations with dwellers in the chat room much the same way. I'd ask if they knew how I could contact Frances, because I needed to speak with her *again*. Most of the chatters either ignored me or stated they didn't know anyone who frequented the room named Frances.

Until BlackPetals911.

I had engaged the dark side.

When BlackPetals911's eerie first line appeared on my screen, I felt as if I'd just swallowed a shadow, and its darkness was threatening to consume me from within. "How did it go last time?"

"JP," I whispered, as if BlackPetals911 could somehow hear me. "Come here."

JP pulled up a chair next to mine and studied the screen. "Holy shit," he whispered.

"Perfectly," I typed.

"Anyone suspect?"

"No. You too?"

"Yes."

My heart was racing. For a moment I didn't know what to do. For whatever reason, I sensed that BlackPetals911 was female. If I wasn't mistaken, she'd just told me she'd used Frances Huber to murder her parent. How do you move on from that?

I slowly picked at the keys to type: "How?"

For a moment there was nothing. Had I lost her? Had I gone too far? Did she somehow guess I wasn't who I was pretending to be?

Then: "A fall." A second later came: "You?"

I decided to go with what I suspected happened to Hilda Kraus. "Poison."

"Did you get what you hoped for?"

"Yes. You?"

"Peace," came the chilling answer.

JP let out a low whistle. We weren't aware of it at the time, but we were each sitting on the edge of our seats, staring almost without blinking at the unthinkable drama unfolding on the computer screen in front of us.

"Money," I typed back.

I waited a few seconds more, then added, "I need Frances again."

The response was jarring. "Does she do fathers?"

"Oh god," JP groaned.

"I need to find out."

"Money?"

I thought about this, and decided to appeal to a common desire. I wrote: "Peace."

"Good luck." And with that, BlackPetals911 was gone.

"No! No! No!" I screamed so loud, Brutus jumped up from where he was sitting near our feet, letting out a startled "woof."

"Don't go! We need you to tell us how to reach Frances!" JP beseeched the lifeless screen, knowing it was too late.

I threw myself back in my seat. I rubbed my computer-weary eyes for a good long time, moaning with exhaustion and aggravation.

"Come on," JP said, taking my hand and pulling me up off my chair.

"What are you doing?"

"We're going for a walk."

Barbra understood and was at our side in an instant.

"Are you crazy? It's almost ten at night. Not to mention that with the wind chill it's probably minus forty. And, in case you haven't noticed, it's snowing like mad out there."

"Perfect!" By this point he had me in the hallway, half way to the front closet. "It'll be good for all of us. The dogs too. We've been cooped up in here all day. We need a break, Russell. We need to rethink this. There's got to be a better way to get to Frances Huber. We're both exceedingly intelligent men, me in particular…" He shot me a quick grin as he pulled our jackets out of the closet. "We just need a vacation from the computer. We need to give our brains a chance to percolate on this without all the pressure from us, the Internet, or BlackPetals911."

He was right. I fished out a couple of balaclavas, and the extra warm Vancouver Olympics mitts my friends Jan and Paul had given me for Christmas a couple of years ago. Once we were suitably suited up, and the dogs were attached to their leashes, we headed out into the frosty fray.

We managed to get three blocks away. The wind was howling. There wasn't another soul on the streets. Not a single vehicle was moving within eyesight. And Barbra and Brutus were doing the Lipizzaner Stallion prance, which told me that ice was gathering underneath their nails and between their toes. We looked at each other through the frosted slits of our balaclavas, and nodded consensual agreement that we'd best hightail it back home.

Although short-lived, the late night icy adventure was just what we needed. The four of us ploughed through the mountainous range of snowdrifts that had accumulated in the front yard just in the short time since we'd been gone. We were falling over each other, scrambling to be the first to the door, the dogs yipping in playful delight. JP and I were laughing uncontrollably. Somehow the four of us squeezed through the front door at the exact same time, falling into a heap of parkas, scarves, and fur, in the gratifyingly toasty warmth of the foyer.

"Hot chocolate," the words came out sounding brittle through JP's near-frozen lips.

"With Kahlúa," I added. "God, what I wouldn't give to be back in…"

As the unbidden thought hit me like a punch to the brain, I stopped speaking.

"Russell?" JP asked, perching himself up on one elbow. "What's the matter? Frozen solid?"

"Why didn't I think of this before?" I yelled as I jumped up and ran for the den, not even bothering to discard my snowy boots.

All I could hear behind me was a trail of "What? What? What?"

By the time JP caught up with me, I was back at my desk, my eyes digging through the list of hundreds of Frances Huber's JP had obtained from Elena Petrokovich's assistant.

And there it was.

"Russell," JP pleaded as I stared at the page. "You have to tell me what's going on. Otherwise I'm going to make you go back out there."

Slowly my eyes rose to meet JP's. "When Jane called to ask me for help, I was in Zihuatanejo."

"I know," JP said. "You told me that already."

"She said: Quant, you are the only one who can help me."

"Yeah. So?"

"I thought it was weird she was calling *me* for help. And it was. That wasn't like Jane. She was a do-it-yourself kind of gal. Even hiring you must have been painful for her."

JP gave a slight nod, but said nothing, intent on hearing what was going to come next.

"But what was even weirder, was that she was calling me for help while I was in Zihuatanejo."

"I don't get it."

"JP, Jane wasn't calling me for help in Zihuatanejo. She was calling me for help *because* I was in Zihuatanejo."

"What? How can you possibly know that?"

I placed the piece of paper I'd been looking at in JP's hand. He looked down. Then he saw it too. About half way down the page. Frances Huber number one-hundred-and-twenty-three. Place of residence: Zihuatanejo, Mexico.

We'd found our murderer.

Part Two

Chapter 11

Some years ago, during a particularly fascinating dinner party, attended by some deep and weighty thinkers, someone asked this profound question: What do you wish you could un-know? At the time, my response was sadly uninspired and moribund; something about nearly running over a kitten with my bicycle when I was a boy. I didn't fully appreciate the question.

But now, I do.

There were times, during the past five weeks, when I deeply regretted my decision to catch Frances Huber. I wished I could turn my back, run away, and un-know her and all the terrible things she'd done.

Jane Cross was shot to death in her office by Lynette Kraus. But someone else was ultimately responsible for that death, and, as it turned out, many others. That someone was Frances Huber. As JP Taine and I laboriously sorted through sordid details and began to uncover the wicked ways of Ms. Huber, it became chillingly obvious that we'd found that thing that many believe only exists in fairy tales. We'd found a monster.

And so, I made a promise to myself.

I would do whatever it took to bring this monster to justice.

I knew it would take a great many resources. Particularly money and time, both of which I'd already been using up like water in a desert. Yet, in a way, this felt very right to me. There was a certain poetic justice to the fact that, after spending a year of nurturing myself, with this promise, I would pay the price.

So, no, it was not the giving up of time, or money, or any other sacrifice, now or in the future, that I regretted. What I regretted was becoming embroiled in the ugly, sad, unapologetically immoral particulars of Frances Huber's life.

The saying "knowledge is power" is no more true than when you are a detective planning a caper against a bad guy. Five weeks ago, JP and I had hastily pieced together bits and pieces of the events that we believed led up to Jane Cross's death, and Frances Huber's involvement in those events. But none of it constituted proof. The only potential proof had disappeared with the MOM file that was created and, we suspected, later destroyed by Lynette Kraus. I needed new information. I needed solid information. It was time to go into serious research mode.

It was also time to go into serious fundraising mode. If I was going to do this, I needed cash. To get cash, I needed work. My life for the next several weeks became focussed on two things only: making money and doing research. JP returned to Regina to deal with an increasingly difficult situation between his sister and Jane's family. He also reported back to his part-time job at Duncan's Shoes.

Although non-stop work and research may not sound exciting and glamorous to some...well, to most...those weeks turned out to be amongst the most creative, stimulating, and intense of my professional *and* personal life. I was crackling. I was making things happen with the satisfying, precise clicks of puzzle pieces fitting together with startling regularity. I was on fire. And not just when it came to life and work, but with the love stuff as well.

JP and I began to navigate the whitewater of a brand new relationship. This was done mostly via Skype, Facebook, e-mail, and good old SaskTel. None of which was without its trials. But as each stumbling block or seemingly impenetrable wall presented itself, I simply knew what to do to overcome it. Where did this wisdom come from? This strength? This unshakeable confidence? If this was what turning forty was all about, I pity those poor twenty- and thirty-somethings.

Over those weeks, I amassed several thick Frances files. Now fifty-four, Frances had been born and spent most of her adult life in Edmonton, Alberta. She never married. From the photographs I was able to collect, I would not say she was unattractive, but pleasantly plain looking. In candid, unposed pictures, her hair was usually a longish mass of unruly curls. She used little if any makeup. Her chin was weak, but her nose and cheeks were full, giving her the appearance of a self-satisfied chipmunk. Her wardrobe was unflattering. It consisted of clothes that were either much too loose or much too tight. Nothing fit just right, or at all complimented her figure. There were two or three posed, studio shots on Google image. They were taken to mark the launch of a short-lived career in real estate—and in those, a completely different Frances Huber emerged. The hair was dyed darker brown and straightened, giving her a more serious and surprisingly sophisticated look. Light makeup was used to great effect. It covered up sun freckles that usually dotted her nose and cheeks, and highlighted her grey eyes and Angelina Jolie lips. She covered up her heavy breasted, full figure with conservative business suits worn over turtlenecks.

Having compiled a list of former work and personal acquaintances, I visited Edmonton three times for face-to-face interviews. In these candid talks, one disquieting commonality soon emerged. Although only a few of the people I talked to knew one another, their experiences with Frances were startlingly similar. At some point, each had had some kind of relationship with her. Now these relationships were incontrovertibly, irreparably, and, from their perspective, thankfully, over.

The routine was always the same. Upon initial meeting, Frances would be super friendly, chatty, and typically quite amusing. First impressions were overwhelmingly positive, leading to mutually proposed future meetings. Frances would be exceedingly attentive and solicitous to her new friend. She would be the first to offer a helping hand if you were moving; she'd hop right on over with a needed hammer or cup of sugar. Unknown to the unwitting other party to the budding friendship, Frances would also be mentally keeping track. She knew by heart, each and every favour, big or small, she'd bestowed, and the manner in which the other person had responded. If there was no appreciation of an appropriate intensity, or symbiotic reciprocation, within a reasonable amount of time, a subtle shift would begin. The friend, to Frances's mind, was now beholden to her.

At this point, Frances would move into the passive aggressive stage. She would expect certain things from the friend to make up for the unspoken but obvious—to her—deficiency. If the friend did not deliver, or failed to meet Frances's expectations in some way—which was *always* the case eventually—Frances also kept track of these much more serious infractions. It only took a few violations of the friendship before Frances was firmly on the dangerous road of paranoia, spiralling ever downward. Every action, every outside relationship, every word spoken or left unspoken, every deed done or undone, became suspect. Frances would claim she only wanted the best from the friendship, but inside she fully expected the worst.

Frances would begin to look for that one thing, that one piece of irrefutable proof that her dear, good friend—to whom she herself had given all she could—had crossed her. She'd wait to be hurt, failed, disappointed, betrayed. All were inevitable.

At first the friendship would take a hit. The disoriented friend would be apologetic, contrite. Frances would bounce back and take the high road, being friendlier than ever.

And then the precarious circle of friendship would start all over again.

And again.

And again.

Each time, the period between point A, and the unavoidable point B, grew shorter and shorter. Until, finally, unable to take it any more, the friend would remove themselves from Frances's life for good. Such an act was not for cowards. Frances would respond with protests of betrayal and, to anyone who would listen, tales of deception, treachery, and falseness of a friend who was really a wolf in sheep's clothing. Fortunately, usually by the time Frances's anger was about to fall into violence, she'd have found a new friend and moved on in her super friendly, chatty, and typically quite amusing way.

Frances Huber did not have any long-term friends. As a young woman, Frances applied to the University of Alberta. She'd wanted to be a doctor. Unable to get into the Faculty of Medicine, she set her sights on nursing. After failing her first year, Frances moved on to other options in the field of health and welfare services. She earned certificates as a masseuse, a reflexologist, dabbled in acupuncture, and finally ended up hiring herself out as a caregiver / companion to the elderly.

Although I could find no particular training or education to back up Frances's career in social services, I expect she made good use of a cleverly worded resumé, embellishing her various other short-lived attempts at a caregiving career. If I didn't already know what I did about Frances Huber, I might have forgiven or even admired this steadfast determination to find some way to help others. But, ultimately, hers was not selfless motivation.

A developing idiom nowadays is that society is "greying." People are living longer than ever before. For Frances Huber, this was a good thing. With booming numbers of aging people, Frances was seldom out of work. Still, she rarely remained with one employer for longer than a year or two. I was unsuccessful at finding anyone who actually used Frances as a caregiver. But I did speak with two people, children of now-deceased clients.

The stories followed much the same narrative as all of Frances's relationships. At first, things generally went well: she got on with the oldsters and they liked her. They were simply happy to have someone to look after all their needs. It was an expensive alternative to government-funded institutional care, but worth it. *They* were not the problem, however. In due course, a son, daughter, neighbour, or well-meaning friend would enter the picture. At first, they too would think the world of Frances.

But sooner or later the familiar love/hate rhythm would play itself out. In the end, Frances would be let go to seek new employment. I can't imagine Frances came away from these experiences with many glowing references. If something hadn't happened to change things, I expect the job market would have, sooner or later, begun to dry up for her. But something did happen. And everything changed.

When Frances was forty-five, her mother turned eighty. Although generally healthy, Mrs. Huber's eyesight was failing and she couldn't look after herself anymore. It made sense for Helen Huber to move in with her only daughter, Frances. It would have been an equitable arrangement, with Helen paying Frances the same wage she'd have received taking care of anyone else. From what I could discover about Frances's financial situation around that time, I think she even managed a tidy raise. So whatever her personal thoughts on the matter, she made out like gangbusters. She probably thought her mother wouldn't know the difference. Besides, the money would be hers in the end anyway, so why not get some of it now?

The mother-daughter relationship was a little bumpy, but by all accounts, things seemed to go very well at first. As the months and years progressed, however, Helen Huber grew more infirm, requiring more and more of Frances's time. Unfortunately, this did not mesh well with what was happening in Frances's emotional life. With middle age came the deterioration in Frances's awareness of the line between good and very, very, very evil. Frequently housebound with her increasingly demanding mother, Frances discovered a new obsession. The Internet. But, according to Frances's ex-friends, she didn't go for the obvious. No online casinos or porn sites for her. Instead, she developed two very specific passions. One surprised me. The other did not.

The not surprising passion, was her love of various social media outlets—MySpace, Travbuddy, Facebook, Blogster, Fubar, Twitter; she tried them all—indulging in anonymous flirting, particularly with much younger men. Her more surprising pursuit was fine art purchased from online retailers such as eBay and Etsy. When her friendships were "on," she loved nothing better than to invite the chosen intimate over to show off her newest acquisitions. She relished telling extravagant stories about where each canvas came from, the style, and the medium. She'd rave about the artist as if she'd purchased the masterpiece directly from a private New York City gallery or she herself were the lucky painter's patron. Her friends, although not art experts, were usually underwhelmed by Frances's enthusiasms.

Falling deeper and deeper into her cyber world, Frances was not pleased with her mother's increasing demands on her time. She'd complain to whoever would listen that Helen was becoming progressively more quarrelsome and irritable. It didn't take a psychologist to deduce that this was likely due to her daughter's increasing neglect. The pair argued frequently. But Frances always backed down at the end. After all, she didn't want to kill the golden goose...or did she?

I corroborated reports from people in Frances's life at the time with various public health records I was able to catch a sneak peek at, thanks to a little help from JP's prowess on the computer and ability to get into places he probably shouldn't be. Helen Huber was indeed growing weaker. On the rare occasions she was seen in public, she was unsteady on her feet, and hard of hearing. She wore thick glasses and depended on an oxygen tank. One friend said that everything seemed to change after Frances's mother was hospitalized with a series of small strokes. Miraculously, the octogenarian survived, and even thrived under the care she received in hospital. But eventually, she had to go back home.

Although Helen had overcome the strokes, her reliance on Frances for day to day care was even greater than before. Frances grew morose and miserable and endlessly cranky. I guessed that this was the moment. This was the crack in the façade of Frances Huber. Her persona as caring daughter was slowly but surely slithering off to reveal the sociopath that hid beneath, like a snake shedding its scaly skin.

I allowed the dark side of my mind to travel where Frances led me.

It would be so easy. A wrong step on an icy sidewalk. Failure to look before crossing a street. Taking a tumble down a set of stairs. Mistakenly taking too much of the wrong medication. Allowing the oxygen tank to go empty. Lighting a match next to it. There were so many possibilities for getting rid of an ailing, elderly woman without causing undue suspicion. I shivered just thinking about it.

The official police report stated that at 7:47 a.m. on a Thursday morning in January, 9-1-1 received a frantic call from a woman identifying herself as Frances Huber. The woman could be heard wailing, and talking unintelligibly for several seconds. Then, quite clearly, she stated that she'd found her mother in the family car, which had been parked in an unheated garage behind the house. She feared her mother was not breathing. The police found eighty-three-year-old Helen Huber, dressed only in a light nightgown, having succumbed to hypothermia. The temperature, as forecast, had fallen to a low of minus thirty-eight during the night.

Frances made a formal statement to the police. She told them about her mother's growing problems with dementia and how the old woman would often wander off with no memory of why or where she was going. In a neat turn of self-censure, Frances blamed herself. Earlier that evening, her mother had asked her several times if they could go to Tim Hortons for a bowl of hot soup—one of Helen's favourite treats. Frances was worried about taking her mother out on such a blisteringly cold night. She convinced her to stay home with a cup of cocoa instead. Frances claimed that she put her mother to bed at eight-thirty p.m., as was her norm, then settled in for a *CSI* marathon before heading off to bed herself at eleven. She did not check in on her mother, for which she claimed she'd never forgive herself. It was not until the next morning, when she went to rouse her mother for her usual seven-thirty a.m. breakfast, that she noticed she was gone. Frantic and confused, it took her almost fifteen minutes to think to look for her mother in the garage.

My version of the story was a little different. Once Frances made the decision to knock off her mom, and how to do it, she waited patiently for the perfect night. She wanted a forecast that guaranteed her accommodatingly freezing cold temperatures. She invited her mother to go out for a drive to Tim Hortons for a nice bowl of hot soup. She benevolently escorted her mother into the unheated garage at the rear of their yard. On the way, Helen likely complained about the cold. She would have wanted a scarf and gloves and a proper coat to cover her flimsy nightgown. Frances insisted they continue on as they were, telling her the car would heat up quickly enough. There was no need to take all the time to go back to the house to put on layers of winter duds for what was only a ten-minute outing.

Once settled in the car, Frances probably gave her mother some fake excuse—like that she'd forgotten her wallet in the house—allowing her to leave her mother alone. She'd have claimed to be right back. Instead, she locked the garage from the outside. So even if she tried, her mother would have no possible way out. Frances headed back inside, where the rest of her evening and next morning progressed exactly as she told the police it did.

It took Frances Huber four months from the date her mother returned home from the hospital to work up the courage to kill her. The police, however, without the benefit of the extra information I'd now collected, did not see it that way.

What happened after Frances successfully got away with murdering her mother, I could only guess at vaguely. She collected her inheritance. Unlike Lynette Kraus, she was likely unimpressed by the amount. It was not nearly enough to finance a life of any great luxury. Around this time, Frances began expanding her online social network to include the suicide websites that JP later dug up with the help of Mary Quail and Onya Knees. Perhaps Frances did have a heart. Perhaps she did feel remorse. Perhaps her actions had driven her to despair, depression, and guilt. Perhaps she toyed with the idea of killing herself. Or maybe she was simply trying to find another pool of weak and needy victims to exploit. Whatever the reason, she parlayed her visibility in The End Society chatroom to create a brand new career for herself. Although we had nothing but circumstantial evidence, at last count, JP had connected Frances Huber to nine elderly women throughout Canada and the United States who had died from unnatural yet outwardly unsuspicious causes.

I could find no record of Frances Huber's ever being employed again. And yet, the woman was living in a lovely, art-filled home in Zihuatanejo, where she lavishly entertained handsome young men. I feared my nose was about to become permanently wrinkled. I smelled something very rotten down Mexico way.

Chapter 12

Checking myself out in the sunshade mirror of the coal black Lincoln Towncar I was "chauffeuring," I had to smirk at the image staring back at me. The look was pure eighties porn star. I was the hunky driver, replete with a jaunty chauffeur's cap, tight uniform, and an abundant Tom Selleck moustache. I was directing the big rental out of Zihuatanejo, onto the relatively new, four-lane, *Carretera Nacional 200* highway. The road would take us over the hill that separates the traditional fishing village from the more modern resort of Ixtapa.

My gaze shifted to the rear-view mirror. I adjusted it to get a better look at my passenger. Not surprisingly, Sereena had managed to embody her character perfectly. She was the vision of *Costa Grande* chic, a Mexican Riviera sophisticate. She wore a sleeveless, white linen pantsuit that showed off a devastating décolletage, while still maintaining an irrefutable veneer of elegance. She'd pinned up her dark hair into a mass of seemingly random tendrils, all held together with an appallingly expensive, bejewelled hairclip that regularly burst into mini-fireworks as the colourful gems reflected the sun. Her eyeglasses were of Jackie-O-on-a-yacht proportion. Her manner channeled *Ugly Betty*'s Wilhelmina Slater.

Inside, my heart was beating like Seabiscuit at the finish line. For in my mind, as soon as we crossed over the invisible line that took us from the charming, dusty, sometimes unkempt environs of Zihuatanejo, into the cool, sleek, contemporary Ixtapa, we were stepping into enemy territory. Frances Huber lived in Ixtapa. And, if everything went according to plan, this would be our first official contact with a killer of old women.

Like most people who came here, Frances focussed all her attention on Ixtapa, rather than its poor neighbour. Ixtapa isn't even a town. It's a planned tourist resort administered by a federal agency called FONATUR. Although Ixtapa and Zihuatanejo are only seven kilometres (about four miles) apart, in most other ways they are worlds apart.

The uninitiated and unadventurous usually stay put in Ixtapa. Some make the trip over the hill to check out the quaint, authentic Mexican village for a *cerveza* or two, then quickly head back. But if you dig deep enough, there is a whole other face to Zihuatanejo. This hidden face quite easily surpasses Ixtapa in terms of beauty, sophistication, and authenticity. Hidden in the bays and hills of the small city are some incredible small luxury hotels, ranked amongst the best in the world, and five-star restaurants with astounding views to match their menus.

From what I could gather, Frances first came to Ixtapa the year her mother died. It was a charter trip, direct from Edmonton, a short vacation with a now (of course) ex-friend. They stayed at the modest Dorado Pacifico hotel on Playa Palmar. They drank plenty of margaritas, attended the hotel's weekly fiesta, and had their hair corn-rowed on the beach. Frances fell madly and deeply in love with the area. It was the first of its type she'd ever visited, but she didn't need to see anywhere else. This was her place. She'd returned every year since, vowing to one day own a home there. She kept her pledge. Frances now owned a small villa in the hills, near Marina Ixtapa, with a sliver view of the bay. It appeared that, for Frances, business was booming.

Sereena and I said little to one another as I took the Towncar off the highway onto Paseo Ixtapa. After countless hours of planning, our scheme was set. Although I've never known Sereena to be nervous, the energy in the car was definitely wired. We passed the hotel zone and headed towards the marina. Once there, I again directed the car up a hill. The higher we went, the rougher and narrower the twisted road became. On either side of us, scruffy trees were dry and mottled; tourist properties gave way to modest apartments, then small homes, then larger homes. I knew exactly where I was going. I'd driven by several times before.

Senora Huber's residence was on a small, unpaved, cul-de-sac, with four other driveways leading to small *casitas* with undersized or non-existent yards. Up here, it was all about the view through the trees.

I checked my watch. (Oddly enough, Zihuatanejo and Saskatoon are in the exact same time zone.) It was 3:20 p.m. Perfect.

I positioned the car so that most of its rear end was across Frances's driveway. We were effectively blocking the spot she'd normally pull into after returning from her bi-weekly run to the local supermarket. She was, thankfully for me, a creature of habit. As were—I'd learned in my research—many successful serial killers.

I stepped out of the vehicle. I adjusted my cap and moustache, then lifted the car's hood. Sereena stayed put, assuming mock impatience. And doing very well at it, I might add.

Once again, my heart did a dance when, right on time, shortly after three-thirty, I heard the crunch of tires on gravel. Frances Huber was approaching.

Even though she couldn't possibly miss seeing the situation, Frances did not even attempt to park on the side of the road. Instead she pulled up to the driveway and nearly nose-kissed our car with hers, as if in a slow motion broadside. She gave her horn a little tap. When I didn't respond, she rolled down her window and called out: "Hey buddy, you're blocking my driveway."

I lifted my head from where I was pretending to toil on something I barely recognized; I think they call it a motor.

"Buenos diás, signora," I greeted in my best thick accent. Then I shrugged helplessly, as if to say: "I'm sorry, but I cannot start my car, and am working on it as fast as I can." In reality, I was more likely to be saying something like: "I'm sorry, but I know nothing about fixing cars. Do you have CAA?"

It was damned hot out, and I could feel the sweat on my lip begin to loosen the spirit gum holding my magnificent mustache in place. I ducked under the hood again, back to my manly pursuit.

A moment later, I heard Frances's car door open. I snuck a peek out of the right side of my aviator sunglasses. Frances was not dressed for company. Her hair was a blowsy mane, barely held in control by a sun visor. She wore a loose, sleeveless, white shirt that did little to hide her ample bosom but showed off a surprisingly slender waist. Her elastic-waisted, khaki, short-shorts were built to accommodate her made-for-waltzing hips, but not the skinny legs that held them up. Her dusty feet were encased in bright orange Crocs.

"What seems to be the problem, *amigo*?" she asked, sounding friendly enough. "I've got a couple of bags of groceries in the car." She added with a chuckle: "And they're as happy about sitting around in this heat as I am."

As Frances neared the Lincoln, the rear door swung open. Like one of those slow-motion gam-shots you often see in movies, out stepped glorious Sereena.

Frances stopped in her tracks to properly behold the vision.

"I'm sorry," Sereena began in a throaty purr, "but Manuel doesn't speak much English."

"Oh well," Frances replied. "That makes us even. I don't speak much Spanish."

Sereena babbled some Spanish at me that meant nothing to my ears. In response, I obediently went back to my work beneath the hood.

"I apologize for this, Miss…?"

Frances stumbled a bit over her words, but finally got out: "Frances…I'm Miss Frances Huber."

"Sereena Orion Smith," Sereena introduced herself, holding out a slender hand with sparkling friends on two of her fingers.

Frances shook, revealing a hand that was, unexpectedly, equally as slender and manicured.

"Wouldn't you know it? The car quit just as we were passing what I am now assuming is your driveway?"

"You got that right."

Sereena let out a sound that she meant to be a light laugh. I knew it was as authentic as Frances's French-tipped nails. "I'm afraid to tell you, we are entirely marooned. Would you believe it? My cellphone doesn't seem to work up here. We may as well be on the moon for all the good it's doing me."

"Not all American cellphones work in Mexico," Frances helpfully volunteered. "You have to get the kind that work anywhere internationally."

"Oh really? Well that's very good information to know. Thank you. Frances, I hope you don't mind my saying, but I love those shoes you have on. What a splendid colour. And so comfortable looking. Wherever did you get them?"

"Uh, they're Crocs."

"Crocs? Is that with a K?"

"C."

I could see out of the corner of my eye that Frances was beginning to look a little befuddled, not quite sure what to make of Sereena.

"Manuel," Sereena demanded my attention.

I popped up my profusely sweating head. She rattled off more words that ended up with her spelling out C-R-O-C-S to me in Spanish.

I nodded, committing none of it to memory.

"You know, it's getting awfully hot out here. If you want, you can come in to the house and use my phone," Frances offered.

"Really? Oh, you are a lifesaver, Frances. And Manuel will bring in your groceries." Without waiting for confirmation, Sereena ordered me in what I thought was a rather imperious tone of voice, to do exactly that. I shot my friend a quick frown. Hauling groceries was not part of the plan. Her reaction was an arched eyebrow and more unintelligible-to-me Spanish.

The good news was that, fortunately, I didn't think Frances was catching on to the fact that Sereena was actually translating everything she was telling me in Spanish before she even said it. It was the only way I could successfully come off as a non-English speaking Mexican chauffeur.

Frances wordlessly showed me where the bags of groceries were. Once I was loaded down, she led us up the driveway to her front door. As she unlocked it, I was glad to see that the locking device was a simple one. We stepped inside.

"Oh, Frances, it is so deliciously cool in here," Sereena enthused (something she rarely does in real life about anything). "However do you do it? You must spend a fortune on air conditioning."

"Nah, not really," Frances told her, directing me with a flip of her wrist to where I should deposit the groceries.

The kitchen was a long, narrow, dungeon of a room that ran along the road side of the house. It was a perfect place for me to be unobtrusive, yet still see and hear the women through a small serving hatch opening in the wall. It was also the perfect spot to watch Sereena handle Frances like a Hell's Angel handles a hawg.

"I spent a lot of money on window coverings that actually block the heat. And, up here, there is plenty of bush cover. Low-overhangs over the biggest windows do the rest."

"Brilliant, absolutely brilliant. It's quite obvious you've been local here for a long time."

Frances smiled, obviously delighted with the description. "Oh, no, not that long. But you learn things. And I didn't build the house. I bought it this way. Ixtapa is known for its sunshine and heat. Good for the tourists, but not so much for those of us who live here."

"So you live here all year round then?"

"More and more. I still keep a small place in Edmonton—that's a city in Canada, where I come from."

Sereena nodded as if fascinated.

Frances moved to the front of the room. She pulled aside her aforementioned window coverings to reveal an expansive wall of glass. "I'll just open these up so you can see the place a little better."

When the room was flooded with natural light, it did look quite impressive. Not huge, but nicely laid out. The windows made the most of a view that was trying its damnedest to catch a glimpse of Palmar Bay.

Sereena deserved an Academy Award. She dramatically pulled in her breath, as if overcome with delight at the room and its view. Then, without more than a moment's hesitation, she zeroed in on what we'd hoped we'd find in Casa Huber.

"Is this a Jose A. Soto?" she asked breathlessly, standing next to a rather large charcoal over an antique shelf.

Frances' smile widened as she slowly approached Sereena and the artwork. "You know Mexican art?"

I have to say, I was impressed too.

"Oh well, just a little. I've never seen a Soto up close before." Then her eyes darted to another canvas across the room. "Rufino Tamayo?"

"No, but close. It's a Franco Mondini-Ruiz, from San Antonio. Don't you just love it?"

"I do, I truly do. I should have known it was Mondini-Ruiz. I have one of his pieces as well in one of my homes." Sereena tossed in the last bit in such an offhand manner, it didn't even seem boastful.

"Oh well, then you must see the little Carl Hoppe I have in the hallway to the bedroom."

"Could I?" Sereena demurred. "Oh, but Frances, we've already taken up so much of your time."

"That's okay. I love talking about my art."

She was talking as if she'd painted them all herself.

"Tell you what," Sereena began. "If I could use your phone to call my mechanic first? Then, maybe, if you don't mind, I'd love to see the Hoppe?"

Sereena dialled a number and spoke into the phone, spouting all manner of lovely sounding words. When she finished, she said to Frances as if as an aside: "He says this often happens with this car in extreme heat like we have today. He says after a rest, it should be okay. I'll have Manuel go give it a try."

Inviting me back into the front room, Sereena repeated the same message to me in rapid fire Spanish. I gave her a curt nod and left.

Just in case Frances got a mind to watch me through the window, I made a good show of starting the car. I delivered a fist pump of happiness into the air when it caught, then exited the car to lower the hood. By time I was done my no doubt fantastic performance, Sereena and Frances were already at the front door, air kissing each other's cheeks. I opened the rear door for Sereena. She took her place without even resting an eye on me. Methinks she was enjoying her role a little too much. With some fluttery waves, we were off.

We each held our tongue until we were down the hill and near the marina. Only then did either of us dare to speak.

"So? Did she go for it?" As I asked the question, one half of my moustache drooped over my mouth. I pulled the entire thing off and tossed a hopeful glance over my shoulder at Sereena.

"Frances Huber has gratefully accepted my invitation to a private art show at the splendid home of *Senor* Toraidio Garza."

Another fist pump. A couple more of those and I betya I *would* be able to fix an engine. Phase 1 of "Taking Down Frances Huber" was officially a success.

Chapter 13

I will always regret being unable to accompany my mother, Kay Quant, on the occasion of her first airplane voyage. Instead, that "pleasure" went to my good friends Anthony and Jared. By necessity, I needed to be in Zihuatanejo much earlier than Mom did. So Anthony and Jared, who were also part of my grand scheme, agreed to ferry her down with them.

According to Anthony, it wasn't exactly a three-ring circus, but it came close. It began right at the Air Canada check-in counter in Saskatoon. Mom chatted up the check-in agent as if the woman was waiting there for no other purpose than to celebrate her first plane ride. Amid an impatient crowd of travellers waiting in line behind them, Anthony and Jared had to finally drag Mom away, all the while Mom promising to send the flabbergasted staffer a postcard to thank her for her help in taking care of her luggage.

Then came security. Although we'd gone over the many do's and don'ts in great detail, it was as if Mom thought the rules were merely suggestions. The bells and whistles began to shrill at the first sight of her. Firstly, the personal scanner detected several metal objects on Mom's person. According to Anthony, Mom began to describe to the security officer, in great detail, each of the operations she's had over the past decades to replace hips, knees, and various other body parts with metal facsimiles. This of course netted her a full body pat-down. She submitted to this quite good naturedly, saying loudly to anyone within earshot, that she'd rather have a massage from this nice young person, than some terrorist blow up her plane.

Oi.

Her carry-on was locked with a padlock. The kind she uses to secure the diesel fuel tanks on her farm. She could not find the key, and eventually acquiesced to the security inspector's request to cut it off with a pair of bolt cutters. Inside, they found a jar of borscht and a margarine container of still-warm perogies (for snacking on the plane, because she'd heard how little they feed the passengers), a full-size aerosol can of Aqua Net hairspray (I didn't realize they still made that stuff!), and another of Pledge (who knows why?).

All this, before even having left Saskatoon.

Most of the plane ride, first to Calgary, then direct to Zihuatanejo, went smoothly enough. Instead of being nervous or scared, Mom was apparently quite giddy over the near spiritual sensation of being lifted into the air above the clouds. She began a prayer of thanks, but soon resorted to silent mouthing of the words when she realized no one else was joining in. At one point, when most of the onboard service was completed, and things had quieted down, Mom leaned over to Anthony and asked if maybe they should start a sing-a-long to break the unsettling silence. Anthony managed to convince her that not many people would likely know the words to the Ukrainian ditties she had in mind. He suggested that maybe it was best to stick to watching a movie. She decided to forgo the onboard entertainment system in favour of cloud gazing and more praying.

Anthony, usually unflappable, found it quite disarming to realize that Mom was entirely non-plussed by the fact that he and

Jared had, as a treat, bumped her (and themselves), up to business class. Never having flown before, she wouldn't necessarily know the difference. But Anthony got the express feeling that somehow Mom would have preferred it in back, where people were a little noisier and rowdier. When the meal was served, Mom politely ate every last bite off her plate. She did, however, grumble under her breath about how nice a bowl of borscht would have tasted right about then.

It was late afternoon when the Air Canada flight pulled up to the Ixtapa-Zihuatanejo International Airport. Passengers descended a set of rollaway stairs directly onto the tarmac. It was at this point, when the first waves of glorious, radiant heat, tasting of sunshine, saltwater, and desiccated vegetation first caressed the skin of sun-starved passengers as they disembarked. It was also at this point that my mother's legs began to cramp.

Mom grabbed onto Jared's arm, yanking him to a standstill.

"Kay, what's wrong?" Anthony asked, alarmed.

"Oh, eets notting. Just my legs. Here, hold da bag, *proshu*."

Anthony held on to Mom's carry-on, while she dug around in her purse. Passengers coming behind them, desperate to either get out of the heat, out of their long pants, or into a bottle of tequila, hurriedly zigzagged around the stalled trio, and headed inside the small terminal building.

A guard, armed with a rifle, approached, making a motion with his non-arms-bearing hand, encouraging them to keep moving.

"*Si,*" Jared said, explaining in passable Spanish that his "mama" needed to get some medicine for her sore legs.

Little did Jared know that the "medicine" Mom was searching for was a small tin, filled with white powder, which looked suspiciously like cocaine.

The guard's eyes widened as Mom wetted her forefinger, dipped it in the powder, and put it to her tongue. Immediately he began some speedy Spanish rant that, even without a translator, told Anthony and Jared that he was more than a little upset.

Jared, at first a bit discombobulated by what was happening, demanded to know what my mother was doing. In Spanish. She looked at him, confused, and answered back in rapid-fire

Ukrainian. All the while, the excited guard continued to rail.

This went on for a few bewildering seconds, until both Jared and my mother converted back to English. Jared quickly understood that mother's "medicine" was actually three or four packets worth of McDonald's salt, which she'd poured into an old Anacin pill tin. She'd heard on TV—Dr. Oz or some such expert—that having a blast of salt as soon as you felt cramps, quickly relieved the pain. As it turned out, the cure worked for Mom. She was fine.

The guard was not.

It took Jared a full two minutes to convey to the guard what Mom had done, ending up with offering him a taste of the white powder. Surprisingly he took some. Eventually satisfied that Kay Quant, international drug fiend, was actually just another pale Canadian tourist, he let them go.

It took another ten to fifteen minutes in the long, snakelike waiting line to get through Customs. On the other side, the three quickly found their luggage, and headed straight for the final obstacle in what was quickly turning into Mom's *National Lampoon's Vacation* Inaugural Flight.

Only in Mexico have I seen this system of luggage screening. It is a wholly random process, whereby all passengers entering the country must push a button that will either light up green or red. Greens go through. Reds are searched. Mom approached the button. Anthony and Jared were close behind her, whispering in her ear what to do. As her arthritic forefinger reached for the button, both men fully expected a blindingly red light to fill the room with the intensity of a lighthouse beacon.

Instead, Mom smiled at the attendant, used her newfound command of the Spanish language by saying: "Bwenee Day-o, Senyoka," pushed the button, and sailed right through on green. She moved directly into the waiting area and my arms with a "Bwenee Day-o, *Sonsyou!*"

Anthony and Jared were rewarded for their many hours of caregiving with two reds in a row.

Later that evening, in a very *Ocean's Eleven, Twelve,* and *Thirteen* way, we all gathered on the balcony of Errall's condo for a welcome dinner and to review our plot to bring Frances Huber to justice. While Mom and I were staying with Errall, everyone else was bunking with Sereena at the large home of her friend, Toraidio Garza. (I'd long ago realized that Sereena has friends pretty much everywhere in the world. This comes in handy more often than you might expect.) The arrangement worked out well. Errall's place, although big as far as beachside condos go, couldn't accommodate many more people than the three of us. More importantly, it was always a good idea to keep my mother and Sereena separated as much as possible. The two women mix about as well as ketchup and Coke.

Errall's condo was located right on Playa la Ropa, with panoramic views of Bahia de Zihuatanejo (Zihuatanejo Bay). Designed in part by a well-known local architect, Enrique Muller, the complex's buildings were craftily constructed on the side of a hill above the beach. It gave the place a unique look, as if the apartments are cascading down the slope. Each building has a different colour scheme that coordinates perfectly with its natural surroundings. Smoky violet. Sandy maize. Rusty orange. Chilled avocado. The condos are an open-air design, with handcut tiles and river rock flooring. Palapa roofs hang lazily over large decks, and tactile fabrics cover the chairs and beds. Local artisans handcrafted each piece of furniture, which included great wooden chests and tables, and wide, well-padded lounges for the deck. All of it had been carefully selected to reflect the rich culture of the region. My favourite features of all were the private cool-water dipping pool and outdoor shower. My mother was not too keen on either.

There were seven of us in all. Errall had the management bring up a special table and extra chairs, so she could serve dinner on the expansive balcony. It was, as usual, a perfect evening, cooling off just enough to allow us to dine outdoors in comfort. We gathered just as the sun, following a hard day's work, began its slow descent into the sparkling Pacific. Everything in the dying sun's path was thrown into the otherworldly golden glow of approaching dusk. Errall distributed margaritas with salted rims. Lime and chili flavoured peanuts were our amuse bouche.

Much later that night, with dinner gobbled up, along with some lovely Casa Madero Chardonnay, the group divided into smaller clusters throughout the condo, chatting and drinking coffee. Errall approached me, contemplating the dark near the same railing I'd stood by so many times during my earlier stay there.

"Peso for your thoughts," she said.

"I'm just thinking about the next few days."

"Worried?"

I tried a smile that probably more closely resembled a grimace. "Are you kidding? What could go wrong?"

Errall wasn't buying my flippancy. She never did. I don't know why I tried.

"Is this going to work, Russell?" Her tone was uncharacteristically uncertain.

I turned to look her in the eye. I uttered the words I'd said to no one before. Not even myself. "I really don't know."

Toraidio Garza was one of those men who flirt with everyone. Old. Young. Fat. Skinny. Women. Men. He didn't care. In any situation, he was happiest when oozing charm, like juice from an overripe peach. Somehow, he pulled it off, the object of his attentions never doubting his sincerity, even long after he'd moved on to someone else. Hours later, you'd find yourself smiling, your cheeks heating, recalling something he'd said to you. It was an art, and he an indisputably skilled artiste.

Toraidio was a near perfect doppelganger for the Cuban American actor, style icon, and "confirmed bachelor," Cesar Romero. Unlike Romero, however, I was quite certain Toraidio was straight. Comfortably into his seventies, Toraidio took care of himself extremely well. Still svelte, he kept his thick white hair combed into a luxuriant pompadour, and favoured smoking jackets, ascots, and tassled loafers with argyle socks. He was often spotted wearing a beret as he promenaded around the streets of Zihuatanejo.

Errall, Mom, and I arrived at Toraidio's stunning hacienda intentionally early the evening of the art show. Although we'd been rehearsing our roles for days, I wanted one last chance to go over everything before the unwitting guest of honour, Frances Huber, arrived.

If I do say so myself, our assigned roles suited us perfectly. This was a good thing, as I was discovering that my mother was about as good an actress as I am a ballet dancer. She was playing Kay Quant, my widowed mother. She was stinking rich, as the result of the death of my father, an obscenely wealthy Russian industrialist. Best of all...she could not speak English. All the better for keeping her from engaging our quarry with conversational gambits like "Why you keel all dose nice ladies? You go to hell for dat!"

I was playing her son, Russell, disgruntled to have received no monies upon my father's death. Dependent on my stingy mother, I was being ground into bankruptcy by my addictions to gambling and other pursuits. Errall was my unhappy wife (can't imagine why), and solidly distained by my mother. Anthony and Jared would be patrons of the arts. They would mix in amongst the cast of friends invited by Toraidio to fill up the space. Sereena would be the only one with a prior relationship with Frances, as well as close acquaintance of the evening's host.

I had little fear that Frances would recognize me as Sereena's chauffeur, even if she saw us together. Yes, my disguise was that good. (Plus, it helped immensely that Frances hadn't once looked me in the eye the entire time we were in her house.)

We went a little overboard with Mom's costume for the night. I learned that even fake jewels and furs can cost a pretty penny. But it was worth it to see my conservative, Ukrainian, farm-woman mother, all dolled up, befitting her character for the night. She was in a fitted blouse, covered in sequins the colour of wet sand, and silk, off-white palazzo pants that just swept the floor (and hid the horrifying flats she insisted on wearing…something about bunions). Despite the heat, we'd wrapped a faux fox stole around her sturdy shoulders. Her freshly manicured fingers were encrusted with cubic zirconium. Her ears are not pierced, so we had to go with chunky matching clip-ons. At the last minute, we added a small tiara to top off her new teased-out do. This was quite a departure from my mother's usual get up of a freshly pressed, plain housedress, worn beneath a flowery apron, thick nylons, a tightly permed coiffure, and black, horn-rimmed glasses.

Errall, too, pulled out all the stops. She brought out her inner lipstick lesbian grandeur, with a tight, peachy-raspberry hued sleeveless tunic. It looked drop dead gorgeous with her dark tan, and hugged every angle of her well-toned physique. She balanced precariously atop suicide stilettos, and she'd let her glossy hair dry naturally, leaving it all pointy and pokey around her chiselled face. I was no slouch myself, in a ginger coloured jacket, off-white trousers, and a turquoise open neck shirt that somehow made my eyes appear the same colour.

A diminutive maid invited us to enter the house through large wooden doors with wrought iron inlays. Already the house was alive with music and the smells of Spanish tapas cooking in some far off kitchen. Like many Mexican houses on the beach or near water, this one was made up of a sequence of integrated interiors and exteriors that casually flowed from one to another. We were led down a wide hallway through a repeating series of archways, the walls a rough stucco. At the end was a massive rotunda that was half indoors, half outdoors. At its centre were three trees, their gnarled yet graceful-looking roots intertwining like an artistic snarl of snakes, reaching from half way down the thick trunks to a hole in the tiled floor. Here the walls were a muted adobe, but the solid, chunky furniture and the room's varied accessories, including pillows, ceramics, and chair cushions, were an explosion of typical Mexican colours: magenta, orange, blue, yellow, red.

"Well, well, well, *bonita senorita*!" came a deep voice, rich with texture and age.

From the midst of a gaggle of guests already arrived and tittering over cocktails, emerged Toraidio Garza. He approached, arms outstretched, as if begging for my mother's hand in marriage. His eyes were sparkling, his neat white moustache curled up at the edges where his toothy smile forced it to do so.

My mother's cheeks reddened as she stared at the man, unmoving, uncertain what to do. Toraidio helped her out by reaching down for her hand and, placing it firmly against his lips, whispered sweet Spanish nothings in her general direction.

I was certain Sereena had briefed our host on our plans, but just in case, I said, "I'm sorry, Senor, but my mother only speaks Ukrainian."

"Then we shall speak the universal language of love!" he pronounced.

Oh gawd.

"Tell me, Madame, what is your favourite song?" he turned his face sideways to me, as if asking me to translate.

I sighed, turned to my mother, and feeling more than a little embarrassed, asked her the question in my rusty Ukrainian. This was especially discomfiting, given that I knew full well that she understood every word he was saying. Well, the English ones anyway.

My mother actually giggled, and shrugged her shoulders.

Toraidio took it in stride. "Then perhaps a little something like this…"

And that was when he began to croon "That's Amore" to my mother. He actually sounded pretty good. Like Dean Martin.

When he was done, he gave my mother a big hug and topped it off with a kiss right on the lips.

Let me say it one more time: Oh gawd.

Toraidio next turned his charms onto Errall, who, although polite, was less bowled over. This did not sit well with our host. He leaned in and whispered something in her ear. When he was done, Errall stepped back, gave Toraidio one of her arched eyebrow looks, and smiled enigmatically. She grabbed my mother's hand, and with a "We need to find drinks," led her off in the direction of the bar.

I, too, was taken aback when suddenly, Toraidio took both my hands in his, and, squeezing them tightly, gifted me with a kiss on each cheek. He pulled back and said, "So, you are the Russell Quant my Sereena has told me so much about."

Just then, *his* Sereena pulled up next to us. She was ravishing in a lingerie-style, lavender, Elie Saab dress. "I see you two have met."

He laid an affectionate arm around Sereena's shoulders and gave her a surprisingly gentle peck on the cheek. "Oh, my beautiful girl." He gave me a serious eye. "The one that got away."

Uncharacteristically, Sereena said nothing.

"And it was not for a gentleman's lack of trying, I should tell you," the man told me in earnest. "But she was always so busy. Flitting from here to there, like a gracious angel, bestowing the gift of her presence on all who loved her."

I tried to recall, but I was certain Toraidio featured little, if at all, in any of the tales I'd heard my neighbour tell. I suppose she might have mentioned him in passing, something like: "...and then I weekended with my Mexican lover, before heading on to Lisbon for the summer regatta." I searched Sereena's face for more, but it told me nothing.

A server came by offering champagne, which we all accepted.

"I must tell you, Russell," Toraidio said, "Sereena doesn't believe me in this, but the paintings you had delivered here for tonight, are actually quite good."

Champagne bubbles up the nose are as uncomfortable as they sound.

A server was immediately at my side with a cloth. I used it to clean off my spritz. What was this man talking about? Over the past few days, I had tasked my mother with filling the two dozen or so blank canvases I'd purchased from a shop in town, with whatever she wished. If we were hosting an art show, we needed art. Mom was happy to have something to keep her busy and out of the sun. I set her up in a shady corner of Errall's condo with some paint and brushes and let her have at it. To be truthful, I hadn't even given them much of a look before the delivery men came to pick them up. My mother had no artistic talent as far as I knew. But I wasn't worried. I'd seen pieces which I would not have been surprised to hear were painted by a three-legged, blind Border Collie, sell at auction for great sums. I didn't need Frances to love the art. I needed her to want it. Two very different things.

"Come," Sereena ordered us.

We followed as she headed to the opposite side of the room, dodging crews of new arrivals to the party. Despite the quickly filling room—I guess Toraidio had plenty of acquaintances who never missed an opportunity to attend a fake art show—I found Errall and shot her a look. It was still early, but I didn't want to miss the arrival of Frances Huber. Errall shook her head, then went back to conversing with a rather muscled-looking woman in a skimpy jumpsuit. I didn't have time to wonder where she'd dumped my mother.

Sereena stopped in front of one of the largest paintings, all of which were displayed throughout the room. It was so big, it rested on two separate easels.

"This piece in particular," Serena told me, "has Toraidio ready to prostrate himself in front of it."

"What she says is true, Russell," he proclaimed, his eyes fully engaged with the swirling colours on the canvas.

I said nothing, taking a first close look at my mother's handiwork. For a moment I couldn't make heads or tails out of it, overwhelmed by the bright masses of colours (Ukrainians are much like Mexicans in their love for strong primaries). I stepped back. If I bent my head just right, and squinted a bit, I began to see what I could only describe as a gathering of clouds—but without a single cloud-like colour in use. What made it intriguing, was that Mom had primed the canvas using dark and dirty pigment before layering on the candy-like confections. The contrast was jarring, yet oddly compelling. At the bottom right-hand corner of the canvas, in gold lettering, was the signature: a single K.

I couldn't make up my mind about the piece. Maybe I was too close to the artist. "Are you serious, Toraidio? You actually like this?"

"No," he said, quite seriously. "I love it."

Still befuddled by what I was hearing, I felt a tug on my sleeve. In my ear I heard the words that brought me rushing back to reality: "She's here."

Chapter 14

As if meticulously choreographed, from our various corners of the room, thrumming with the noise of about sixty guests, Anthony, Jared, Sereena, Errall, Mom, and I exchanged looks of…worry? Anticipation? Excitement? Although imperceptible to everyone else at the party, everything in the room had just changed. Frances Huber had arrived. It was time to engage the enemy. But before that happened, I had one very important task to take care of.

Leaving Sereena and Errall with Toraidio, I stepped into the outdoor section of the rotunda. There were quite a few people milling about and admiring (really?) my mother's art here as well. I needed privacy. I pushed aside an Aztec pattered drapery covering a nearby archway that led into another open-air room. Although much smaller than the rotunda, the space was equally inviting. There were large chairs surrounded by striking painted gourds, terracotta urns, baskets, and earthenware pots. Rustic tin wall sconces and religious art decorated the walls. I sidled over to the farthest edge of the room where the sound of the party was least invasive. I pulled out my cellphone and dialled a number. As I waited for an answer, I enjoyed a stunning view of Playa Las Gatas, far below the rough-hewn hilltop that held aloft Toraidio Garza's grand house.

"Russell?" came the answer.

I smiled at hearing the familiar voice. "It's me, JP."

JP was the seventh member of our team. His role, in many ways, was the most important. And the most dangerous.

I had vociferously argued against JP's taking the responsibility he now had. I was the trained professional. I had the most experience with this type of thing. I was the one who had planned this whole escapade. It stood to reason that if anyone should be in peril, it should be me. I was ultimately defeated by logic.

JP argued that he had as much, if not more, motivation to want to see Frances Huber brought to justice. Jane Cross was not only his employer, but also his sister-in-law, and the mother of his nephew. Although he didn't admit it, I knew he still believed that if he'd made an extra copy of the damning MOM file, none of us would be doing what we now had to do. All that was true. But it wasn't enough to convince me. His final argument did.

As far as I could tell, Frances Huber had three weaknesses. Fine art. Young men. And a deep craving for respect. She was the ultimate wannabe. Frances had come from nothing. Now she wanted it all. And she would do anything to get it. The money she'd gotten as a result of her mother's death turned out to be not nearly enough to buy herself the life she so desperately desired. So she found a way to make more. Murder. It probably only took a few jobs before she began rolling in the green. But her penchant for the good life, fine art, and male suitors, left her constantly requiring cash infusions to maintain her addictions. I knew that to catch this woman, my plan would have to be well thought out, elaborate, and multi-pronged. I would attack from every angle. If one way didn't work, I'd get her from another, until I pierced her soft underbelly, with my sword of retribution! Okay...maybe that's a bit too *Clash of the Titans*, but my intent was no less true.

To make this work, I'd have many irons in the fire. I'd involved all my friends and even my mother. Someone needed to keep a close watch on the entire operation from a bird's eye view. And, most importantly, someone needed to keep an even closer eye on every move our quarry made. It only made sense that that someone be me. And as the person who knew the most about this (next to me), JP knew it. He insisted I would be much too busy, and that he be the one to search Frances Huber's house. What to do?

This new Russell Quant I'd discovered over the past year, was less foolhardy. He was more apt to make sound decisions, based on intelligent consideration, rather than rash ones based on foolish pride or masculine bravado. So I did what needed to be done.

I told JP to bugger off. I was searching Frances's house.

But then he enlisted the support of our other team members. They agreed with him. I was lost. Only after much discussion, and rehearsal of what to do, how to do it, and when to bail, did I relent. Unhappily.

There was one more thing.

I was very concerned about the safety of this man.

Because this was a man I was most certainly falling in love with.

JP was waiting outside Frances's house in Ixtapa. He carried with him a knapsack, which held a portable scanner and a laptop with an external hard drive for electronic storage. Although he likely would have seen Frances leaving for the party, we agreed he wouldn't make a move until he heard from me, confirming that that she was five kilometres away, with us in Zihuatanejo.

"It's a beautiful night for a break-in," JP's voice rolled into my ear. It was his attempt at breaking the tension that, most definitely, was hanging in the air like a polluting smog.

"JP..."

"I know, I know, but say it anyway."

"Be careful."

"What could go wrong? I got my scanner. I got my James Bond balaclava. I got my wonderpants on..."

What did I just hear? "Your what?"

"My wonderpants," he responded easily. "You know, the pants everyone has. They always feel comfy; they're always in style. And let me tell you, Mr. Quant, if you could see me from behind right now, you'd faint dead away."

What? Could it be? Wonderpants belonged to me. Well, at least the term did. Or I thought it did. But wait. This guy was a known thief. Did he...did the bugger actually steal my word from me too? "Hold on a second," I began, sounding quite harsh, I'm sure. "Did you hear me talking about wonderpants, and now y..."

"Over and out, amigo." And he was gone.

He hung up on me! To be fair, we did have more important things to worry about at the moment than wonderpants. *Slightly* more important.

It was time to jump into the fire.

It was a heated argument. And not very private. I would say something to my mother. She would reply back. All discourse in Ukrainian. With each volley, our voices grew louder and angrier. In reality, we were discussing last year's crops near Howell. Howell is the town near where Mom still lives on the family farm. She was also telling me, in excruciating detail, what she was planning to plant in her oversize garden this coming spring. She had high hopes for cucumbers this season.

I was taking a chance that no one in the room understood Ukrainian. I was feeling confident. It was mostly full of well-to-do Mexicans, who spent time in Zihuatanejo, but most likely came from Mexico City or one of the other inland metropolises. Even so, I was only really concerned with one person—whom I'd ensured was within listening distance before beginning the squabble. Every so often, Errall, sitting between me and my mother on a low-slung couch, would ask me—in English—what the "old hag" was saying.

"Oh, she's making a big deal about the cost of dinner at Tentaciones." Tentaciones was an elegant establishment perched atop a hill in the Zihuatanejo hotel zone.

"What? Did she want us to come to this thing without eating?"

"She didn't think I should have chosen such an expensive restaurant when she could have cooked for us at home for a fraction of the price."

"Bah! Has she tasted her own cooking?"

Even though Mom knew this was all an act, she couldn't help frowning at that last comment. Mom prides herself on being an excellent cook, especially when butter, lard, or a deep fryer are involved.

"You'd think with all her millions, she'd stop acting like a pauper," I complained bitterly.

"Well I don't care about that," Errall responded with a sniff. "But why should we have to live like paupers right along with her?"

Mom began another tirade. This time she told me about her tabby cat named Mittens, who, yet again, looked as if she was pregnant. If history proved repetitive, the cat would likely deliver at least six new kittens before summer. Mom wondered if Barbra and Brutus might enjoy a kitten as a sister.

I turned to Errall, and said with no shortage of exasperation, "Now she's asking how much the wine was, and why we couldn't just drink water like she did."

Showing fine form as the incensed daughter-in-law, Errall glared at Mom. She muttered something not very nice under her breath, raised herself off the couch, and stormed off towards the bar.

I glanced up to check if we still had Frances's attention. We did. Catching her eye, I gave her an embarrassed smile. She did a little empathetic eye-roll of understanding, before meandering away. Perusing the room, I quickly found Sereena. I touched the side of my nose. She made her move.

"Frances, I'm so glad you made it," Sereena slid up next to the woman, weaving her thin arm around Frances's. I followed at a discreet distance.

"Oh, Sereena. Thanks for inviting me. I had no idea these kind of homes even existed way out here."

"Oh? You mean up in the hills?" Sereena asked innocently, as they slowly walked together through the crowd. Frances didn't know it, but Sereena was doing more than directing the conversation.

"I mean here in Zihuatanejo." She pronounced it "see wah tah nay JO" instead of "see wah tah nay HO." "I always thought this place was..." She glanced around to make sure no one was close enough to overhear. I hurriedly looked away, as if entranced by another conversation. Satisfied, she continued on in a conspiratorial whisper. "...a bit of a backwater. It's so grimy and dirty in town. And that marina compared to the one in Ixtapa, like night and day, right?"

Over the years, Sereena had perfected a seething smiled that fooled most people. She used it now.

"That's a lovely dress," Sereena commented. "It really sets off your skin tone."

Frances glanced down at her outfit. She'd obviously gone to some trouble to look especially good tonight. The dress looked fresh out of the store. Her hair, piled on her head in a slightly old fashioned bun, looked like she'd come to the party straight from the old-lady salon. Although Frances Huber could afford the money for good clothes, she knew little about dressing for her body type. I couldn't help wishing I could sic Anthony on her. Was it wrong to want my serial killer to have a bit more fashion sense?

Speak of the devil. "This is bloody fantastic, Toraidio." Anthony's more upper-crust-than-usual British accent punctuated the air. He and the evening's host were standing nearby, studying the same large painting of my mother's that Toraidio was in love with. "Why haven't I seen this artist's work before? Are you hiding him from me? Keeping him all to yourself, are you?"

"Actually, my dear friend, the artist is a woman. A beautiful woman at that."

"Is that so? Well, where is she? Come on, old chap, trot her out. I will meet her. I want to discuss this piece. And the price."

"What do you think?" Sereena whispered in Frances's ear, as

they neared the painting. "Isn't it extraordinary?"

Frances missed less than a beat. "Yes, it really is. Who painted it? Do you know?"

"Oh god, yes. It's a K."

"K?"

"She doesn't reveal her full name to the public. Very mysterious. Only those of us who own a piece are let in on the secret."

Frances's eyes widened at this. She stared at Sereena's powerful profile. "You know then?"

"I do."

"What is it? What does K stand for? Who is she?"

Sereena let a small chuckle tumble through her dark-ruby lips. Her head moved slowly into position, only stopping when she was nose to nose and eye to eye with the other woman. "Oh Frances. If I told you that...I'd have to kill you."

For a millisecond, Frances looked alarmed. But she quickly relaxed and smiled. Realizing that Sereena was not about to break the stare, Frances was the first to look away. "I've collected so much art over the years. Maybe I have one of her pieces and don't even know it."

"Look around," Sereena instructed. "Her style is very distinct. Besides, the price of her work is significant. I don't think you'd have forgotten buying a K."

"Oh. I suppose not."

"There is something particularly thrilling about tonight's show," Sereena said in a stage whisper.

"Oh? What? Can you tell me that?"

"Look at the size of these pieces. You rarely see a K anywhere near these dimensions. Obviously the prices will be even higher, but my god, Frances, to have one of these...well, I'm not surprised to see Mr. Gatt here."

"Who's that?"

Sereena indicated Anthony with a tick of her nose. "Anthony Gatt is one of the most renowned and respected collectors of modern art in the U.K. I'm not surprised he's got his eye on that particular piece. It's quite obviously the crown jewel of the lot."

Frances took a step closer to the canvas. "Oh, well, for sure. I love it too. What's this one called?"

"Korova," Sereena told her, rolling her "r"s like a czarina.

I shook my head. We asked Mom to give each of her paintings a title. Time was running short, as was, I guess, her creativity. She decided to name each one after an animal. In Ukrainian. *Korova* was cow. Nearby, I could see *Svenya* (pig), *Skoons* (skunk), and *Kachka* (duck).

"Korova," Frances repeated slowly. "Interesting." She waited a beat and shot Sereena a questioning look. "Will you be bidding on it?"

Sereena sighed. "If only." She let out another small laugh. "Alas, my art budget for the year has expired. If only I'd known about this piece before I bought the Juan Luna in Manila last month."

"Oh poppycock, Garza!" Anthony was spouting nearby. "Why all the pretense? Let me write a cheque this minute, and you can be done with it. Besides, you have all these other pieces to worry about."

Frances leaned into Sereena. "You would have bought this one instead?"

Sereena let out a sound as if she were about to dig into a particularly good bit of dessert. "Oh yes, most definitely."

At that moment, carrying a half-full glass of champagne in her hand, Errall approached the two women. She held out a hand to Sereena. "You're Sereena Orion Smith, aren't you?"

Shaking unenthusiastically, Sereena gazed at Errall with little apparent interest.

Errall kept on. "I saw the feature they did on you in *Better Homes and Gardens*. You have a beautiful home. Well, it's more like a castle isn't it?"

Sereena answered with a curt: "It is."

"The artwork in particular. I was blown away."

"Well, thank you, Miss...?"

"Strane. Errall Strane."

Sereena nodded to Frances. "I don't know if you've met. Errall, this is my friend, Frances Huber. Frances, Errall Strane."

Errall's mouth dropped open. "Frances...Huber?"

Even from my vantage point behind a particularly leafy palm, I could see a shade of alarm enter Frances's eyes. The two women shook hands, the entire time, Errall studying Frances's face as if preparing to sculpt it.

"I know you," Errall finally said.

Frances abruptly pulled her hand away. "Oh, I don't think so."

"Are you an art collector too?" Sereena suggested helpfully. "Perhaps you know each other that way. You see, Frances is a major patron of the arts."

Frances smiled at Sereena, bathing in the compliment.

"No," Errall replied, never taking her eyes off Frances. "You did some...work...for my sister a few years ago, and...I guess, indirectly, for me as well." Errall said the words slowly, in a way that communicated more than the words themselves meant.

Frances's face grew rigid. She began to fidget.

"I want to thank you again for...your good work," Errall continued. She might as well have added: "Wink, wink, nudge, nudge."

I had to give it to Errall. She was yanking Frances's chain quite nicely. Sereena was building her up, and Errall was ripping her down. It was perfect. I wanted Frances Huber to feel as uncertain and wobbly on her feet, as if she were standing in Lima during earthquake season.

Frances gave Errall a tight smile, then turned back to Sereena. "I think I need to visit the little ladies room. Do you know where it is?"

"Of course, darling." Sereena pointed out the way to *el cuarto de baño*."Shall I keep an eye on the painting for you?" she added with a knowing smirk that only fellow *patrons of the arts* would understand.

Frances hesitated, then said, "please," before hurrying off. She was just about at the archway that led to the washrooms when Errall called out her name.

Frances turned, frowning when she saw who it was. "I'm sorry, but I don't know who you are. I'd appreciate it if you left me alone."

"I understand," Errall said. "I only have one question for you."

"What's that?"

"Are you still in the business?"

Frances appeared temporarily mute.

With a show of disdain, Errall flicked her head toward the main part of the rotunda where most of the guests were, including her argumentative "mother-in-law." "As you may have surmised, I'm in dire need of your special services."

Still silent, Frances's eyes grew narrow as she focused on Errall's face.

"Tell you what," Errall said brightly, reaching into her purse. "Let me give you my card. It has my phone number on it. If you're interested, call me." She handed Frances the card.

Without looking at it, the older woman palmed the card and walked away.

Errall spun on her heel, and did the same. She found me doing my Peter-Sellers-*Pink-Panther* bit behind a nearby potted plant, winking as she passed by.

Chapter 15

Once upon a time, Jared Lowe was the toast of Manhattan, Milan, and Madrid. He was a rarity. A male supermodel. Generally male models are seen as little more than accessories to their more flashy and sought after female counterparts. Yet, for a brief time, Jared worked as many jobs and made as much money as Claudia Schiffer, Naomi Campbell, or Kate Moss. Jared was smart enough to know that time was not his friend. Age and tastes would soon catch up to him. Building a healthy nest egg along the way, he and his husband Anthony lived the good life, planning to mine the fashion industry for every ounce of adventure and gold until the magic carpet ride was over. Tragically, a deranged psychopath brought the joy ride to a dead stop sooner than expected. Love, to this deranged man, meant tossing acid into his beloved's face. Into Jared's face.*

**Stain of the Berry*

Although the piercing golden-green eyes and lion's mane of copper curls remained unchanged, many years and surgeries and therapists later, Jared was left with a face considerably less perfect than it once had been. When people first met him, Jared saw the struggle in their eyes. They strove to appreciate the beauty left behind—for that is what pleases us all. But the still-visible scarring couldn't help but distract them. They tried in vain not to give in to their flawed concept of what true beauty is. Inevitably, pity and sadness would cloud their faces. They would try to talk around it, ignore the obvious. Poor Jared was left with the burden of trying to make *them* feel comfortable. It was a burden he accepted as his new reality.

Until he met Frances Huber.

As I watched the goings on in the active rotunda of Toraidio Garza's house, I was surprised to see that it was Frances who approached Jared. Jared had been standing on his own. He was leaning against the outdoor railing, watching the far-off twinkling lights of the hotels along Playa la Ropa. The plan had been to eventually dangle me or JP in front of Frances, hoping she'd find one of our carrots tasty. But as I neared the two, and heard what was transpiring, I knew that something wholly unexpected was occurring instead.

"Those are quite the scars you've got there," Frances bluntly pointed out. "Car accident?"

Jared gave her an appraising look before answering. "Something like that."

"You don't have to be uncomfortable around me," she assured him in a kindly tone. "I used to be a nurse. I've seen burns before. Yours aren't so bad. And you're lucky."

"Lucky? How do you figure that?"

She eyed him with a small smile on her lips. "I don't want to offend you by saying this."

"Go ahead."

"You're the kind of man whose scars only make him sexier."

Jared smiled. It was the same smile that had incapacitated countless people over the years. Including me.

"I hope your wife thinks so too," Frances added, not a bit of coy in her.

I bit my lip. We had a three-pronged plan. We were going to reel Frances in using her weaknesses against her: art, respect, and a hot hunk. Jared knew the plan as well as anyone on the team. JP or I was meant to be the hot hunk, but now…?

"Actually, I'm single."

He did it.

Frances moved in a bit closer. "I can't believe that."

"Disappointingly, not every woman has a *Beauty and the Beast* fantasy," he said light-heartedly.

Frances answered with a small smile. Her hand rose to his face. She touched the most pronounced of his scars, the one that ran along the sharp line of his jaw.

"What would you say if I told you *Beauty and the Beast* is my favourite movie?"

"I'd say '*I want to do something for you...but what?*'" Jared recited, using his best Gaston-like voice.

Frances played along beautifully, following through with the memorable quote from the movie: "*Well, there's the usual things: flowers...chocolates...promises you don't intend to keep...*"

They both laughed. I thought I might throw up a little. I turned and caught Anthony in the distance, also watching this unforeseen development with keen interest. His brow was puckered, his mouth tight. For a moment, I enjoyed the rare sight of our aging matinee idol in discomfort. The man was jealous.

"How about lunch instead?" Jared asked.

Wordlessly, Frances reached into her purse and pulled out a pen. She drew close Jared's hand, palm out, and began writing her phone number there. When she was done, she stood on her tippytoes and kissed him lightly on the same scar she'd touched, then walked away. Not a bad exit, actually.

I came out from behind the movable screen I'd been hiding behind. I shot Jared a pointed *WTF!* look, and followed Frances back inside.

By time I caught up with her, I saw that Frances had re-joined Sereena. What I saw next made me shudder, as if icy water were suddenly diffusing throughout every inch of my body.

Frances Huber's cold, dark eyes were solidly locked on one thing.

My mother.

Oh God. *What have I done?*

I fought an impulse to run over to the couch where my mother was innocently seated, and get her out of there, away from Frances Huber's murderous gaze. Instead, I counted to five very slowly, allowing my brain to catch up with my heart.

I felt a stirring in my pocket, and realized my cellphone was vibrating. Perplexed, I pulled it out while I searched for a quiet spot amongst the crowd, which seemed to have doubled in the past hour. With the exception of JP, everyone who had this number was in this room. And JP wasn't supposed to be calling me. I was to call him, only when it looked like Frances was heading home.

"Hello?" I answered.

"Russell, it's me." JP's voice. I could barely hear him.

"Is something wrong? What's going on?"

"Well, I have good news and I have bad news. Which would you like to hear first?"

I was not in the game-playing mood. "JP, just tell me what's going on. Are you okay?"

"Good news it is. I'm fine. And there is a ton of shit here, Russell. All sorts of papers and records that I think might help us once we have time to go through them all."

"Okay, so what's the bad news?"

"I'm trapped."

Errall was at my side, trying to get my attention.

The room had gotten loud with revellers who'd been filling up on the free flowing champagne. I turned away from Errall, putting a finger to my free ear in an attempt to block the noise and hear JP better.

"What do you mean you're trapped?"

"Russell!" Errall was tugging on my sleeve.

"JP, I can barely hear you."

"Russell, you need to hear this," Errall insisted.

I turned on her like a viper on a tree frog. "Not now!" I hissed.

"I don't want to talk too loud." This from JP. "Can you hear me now?"

"Yes, now!" Errall nearly screeched. "Frances is gone!"

My heart skipped a beat as I stared at Errall and processed the information.

"She left, Russell. She's probably on her way home. You have to tell JP it's time to get out of there."

My eyes travelled the room in hopes of seeing the woman. But it was no use. The place was too full. I dashed through the crowd, heading for the same private room I'd used before. Errall was close on my heels. As I ran, I yelled into the phone, "JP, you have to get out of there. Now!"

He said something I couldn't hear.

Thirty seconds later, Errall and I were in the quieter room behind the curtain.

"What's he saying?" she asked.

"JP? Are you still there?"

"Of course I am," he replied, sounding frustratingly calm. "Like I said: I'm trapped." Mercifully, I could hear him much better without the background noise of the party.

"What do you mean you're trapped?"

"There are two guys with guns standing watch over the front of the house. I can't leave."

I felt my cheeks drain of blood. Damnit! I knew it was too dangerous to send him in there. Why did I let him do it? "How can that be?" I asked. A stupid question, but I needed to say something while I thought about what the hell to do to help.

"I've been checking the front every fifteen minutes or so. Just in case." Smart move. "Suddenly they were there. I didn't worry at first. I thought maybe they were a neighbourhood patrol or something like that. I assumed they'd eventually move on. But they didn't, Russell. They've been out there for the last forty-five minutes. They're not going anywhere. And the front is the only way out of this place."

Shit, shit, shit, shit, shit. Shit! JP was right. There was only one way in and out of Frances's house. By the front. The back of the house sat perched on the side of a jagged-toothed hill that led to nowhere but the sea.

I should have known Frances wouldn't leave her home unprotected. Mexico isn't exactly the most law-abiding place in the world, and she knew it. Plus, she had valuables she was willing to pay to protect. Ironically, the valuables she was protecting—her art—was not what this particular thief was after. But none of that mattered.

This was my fault. I'd spent hours canvassing Frances's lifestyle, her neighbourhood, and her home, trying to get a sense of her habits and regular movements. When she left, I would always follow. I should have—at least once—stayed behind to see if she had hired guns to look after her property while she was gone. Dumb mistake. And now JP was about to pay the price. Our entire plan was about to blow up in our faces. All before it barely got off the ground.

Taking the time to give myself fifty lashes wasn't going to help us now. I needed to think of a way to get JP out of that house before Frances came home.

"Russell, what is going on?" Errall wanted to know.

"Hold on, JP," I said into the phone.

"Oh, sure, I'll just hang out here for a while," he replied with a bit of sarcasm meant to give me a smile. But he couldn't fool me. I could detect a tremor of trepidation in his voice.

"He can't get out," I hurriedly explained to Errall. "Frances has hired guards manning the front of her property."

"Oh fuck."

"Nicely put, but not very helpful."

She shrugged. "Okay, well, how big are the guards? If we hurry, maybe we can get there before Frances does. Between you, me, and JP, we could take them down."

"They're armed with big guns. And I don't think getting into guerilla warfare in the hills of Mexico is exactly the best idea right now."

"Suit yourself."

"JP?" I called into the phone.

"Uh huh?"

"Here's what I want you to do. I want you to go out the back."

"Russell, over the back rail is nothing but straight down."

"I know that, JP. But you have to get out of there. There's no other choice. The hill isn't as steep as it looks. If you're careful and go really slow, I know you can make it down to the water's edge. Watch out for loose gravel and jagged rocks and..." I was about to add snakes, but thought better of it. "...go as slow as you need to. Once you're safely out of the house, there's no rush. There's no reason for Frances or her goons or anyone else to look down there. As long as you leave everything the way you found it, she won't be suspicious."

"And what do I do when I get to the water?"

"Just wait. I'm going to find a boat." I had no idea how in the world I was going to do that, but he didn't need to know it. "I'll come get you. Don't worry. You'll be okay. Just wait for me there. We better not use cellphones though. I don't know how much sound travels up the hills from the water."

"Okay, babe. I'll be watching for your yacht. Get the champagne chilling."

I couldn't help but smile. "JP, I'm so sorry I got you into this."

"Are you kidding? I'm having a ball! This is even more exciting than the time I sold a pair of loafers to the Finance Minister of Saskatchewan on budget day."

"You goof. I'm going to see you very soon. Okay?"

"Okay. Over and out."

I hung up and looked at Errall with what must have been a crazed expression. "I need a boat. I need a boat driver. I need a flashlight. I need a ride to Ixtapa. I need to have my bloody head examined!"

"I could have told you that. Come on, let's go find a boat."

I considered selling Sereena into servitude as a sexual slave, in exchange for what Toraidio Garza did for us that night. Within minutes of explaining the dilemma we were in, Errall, Jared, and I were in Toraidio's chauffeur-driven limousine, speeding toward the Ixtapa Marina. He'd arranged for his boat captain to take us out to sea. As it turned out, JP would get his wish after all. We were on Toraidio's yacht.

When the craft arrived at the spot in the water near the hill where Frances lived, we were confronted with one big problem. The boat was too big to get near shore. Although it was risky, I asked the captain to use his searchlight to scan land to see if we could spot JP. And indeed, there he was, waving with joyful abandon, as if he was Gilligan and we were a rescue boat.

I texted him, explaining what the problem was, and that we needed a few minutes to figure out a solution. Before we knew it, JP dived into the water and began swimming toward the boat. The distance looked unbearably far to me, the dark water too unsafe. My own swimming skills were of the panic-stricken-dog-paddle variety. I'd been tested in this before. In particular, one horrible night, several years ago, in the hellish waters off the coast of Sicily*. I survived. But only barely.

All we could do was watch and wait.

And then there he was, his muscular arms reaching up out of the water for mine reaching down to him. I cannot remember the last time I was so happy to see someone.

Unlike the rest of us who were in Zihuatanejo, JP was staying in a small hotel room in Ixtapa. He needed to be as close to Frances Huber's house as possible. Whenever an opportunity arose for him to break in, he needed to be nearby, at-the-ready. That was where I took him as soon as our hearty captain brought us back to shore. I did feel a little uncomfortable leaving Errall to explain to my mother why I wasn't spending the night in the condo. But really. I was a thir...aw crap...a forty-year-old man. I could do what I wanted. And I wanted to take care of my boyfriend.

As soon as we got to the hotel room, I stripped off his still-soaked clothing and put him in a steaming hot shower. Even

* *Tapas on the Ramblas.*

though the outside temperature was balmy, the waters of the Pacific were not. When he was sufficiently warmed up, I put him to bed, closed all the blinds, crawled in next to him, and cradled him in my arms. For once, JP Taine was quiet. And then he fell asleep.

And then I woke him up.

I'd had a hard time getting to sleep. My brain was racing a mile a minute, trying to figure out what the night's happenings meant to our plan. A horrible thought struck me. I needed to talk to JP right away. I tried nudging him gently at first, but the guy was a sound sleeper. I finally resorted to a shake. Then a more forceful shake. Then: "JP! Get up!"

He opened one eye, and said in a sleep-slurred voice: "You've just totally ruined a very nice Sleeping Beauty dream."

"JP. I just remembered. Your knapsack! Where is your knapsack? The scanner...you didn't leave it in the house did you?"

He sat up and rubbed his eyes lazily. He glanced at the bedside clock. It was close to three-thirty a.m. "You know, since you woke me up from a perfectly good sleep, you're going to have to put out."

"JP! If you left anything behind in your rush to get out, Frances is going to suspect...not to mention that everything you've collected so far is lost...this could all be over!"

"Russell, it's okay," he said, giving my bare forearm a comforting rub. "I didn't leave anything behind."

"But where's the laptop and scanner? You didn't have them with you."

"I couldn't very well swim to the boat carrying them, could I? Electrical equipment and sea water don't mix very well."

True.

"When I realized the boat couldn't get to me, and I had to get to the boat, I knew I'd have to leave the equipment behind. So I hid it. I thought it would be pretty safe there. That's a pretty unfriendly piece of terrain. Not as if there'll be a bunch of sun worshippers running around there tomorrow, stumbling over it."

Also true. "We'll have to go back for it somehow."

"I've been thinking about that."

"You have? When? You fell asleep in like two-point-five seconds."

He smiled. "It's a gift."

"So what's the idea?"

"Earlier this week I was thinking about renting a boat to go fishing. I chatted up these guys down by the marina. For not a lot more than the price of this hotel room, I can rent a good size fishing boat."

"Uh, are you telling me you're quitting all this, and going fishing?"

He sniggered. "Not yet. Actually, I was thinking that instead of living here, I could live on the boat. I'd anchor it off the beach by Frances's house. Whenever you give me the coast-is-clear, I'd row a small kayak to shore—keeping me and the scanner dry—crawl up the hill, get into the house, do my thing without the Incredible Hulks in front knowing a thing, and I'd leave the same way. There's a lot of stuff there, Russell. I don't know yet what's useful and what's not. So we gotta get it all. At an hour here, and an hour there, this is going to take more than one or two visits. Especially if we want to make sure we have enough to send her away for good."

This—could—work. "You know what?" I said, bringing my face very close to his. "You were right."

He lay back, pulling me with him. "Oh yeah? About what?"

"You are good at this."

"And if this was some cheesy forties movie, right about now I'd say something like: I'm also very good at something else. And then I'd kiss you."

"I always liked those movies."

We shared a smile. Somehow it seemed more intimate than any kiss.

"Your hair," he began in a quiet voice, lazily running his fingers through it. "It's exactly the same colour as mine."

I hadn't noticed it before. But he was right.

"And your hands," he kept on, "they look just like mine."

Some men are into butts, or breasts, or legs. I like those

things...well, the butts and legs, anyway. But mostly, I am a hand man. I love a nicely shaped, well-tended, strong, man's hand. JP knew this about me. I took one of his hands in mine and stared at it, as if for the first time. It was a good hand. Just the right shape and size, the skin was soft, yet tough, the fingers long but thick. It was a caring hand. A hand you could imagine cupping a newborn's head, yet masculine enough to handle a stick shift or baseball bat. I opened my palm and placed it against his. They were a perfect match.

There was so much about JP that was different from me. His impossibly thick butterfly eyelashes, his devilishly cherubic facial features, the way his body moved when he walked, the way his lips always seemed to be partially upturned in a smile. But we were also alike. The biggest way of all was that we were two men, two blond men, with the same hands. I suddenly felt very close to him. I was so in love with him. I wanted to wrap him up in my arms and squeeze him forever, to somehow eat him up, to cover every inch of his body with my own. The latter was probably the better option.

Rolling on top of JP, I entwined my hands in his and threw them above our heads, bringing us face to face, pelvis to pelvis, toe to toe. For a long time, we just stayed that way, only interrupting the communion with light kisses, or by licking the tip of an ear or nose. Finally we curled up into each other, and made love until we couldn't.

Chapter 16

I've always loved it when detectives on TV or in movies go undercover wearing disguises. In practice, however, I have found my career sadly lacking in opportunities to indulge in the same activity. But Mexico was changing everything.

First there was my stellar turn as the Spanish-speaking, grocery-carrying, chauffeur. And now, I was going for long-haired hippie to Errall's psychedelic lovechild. We were having lunch at Beccofino, one of the best pasta joints at Ixtapa Marina. Although it doesn't look it, Ixtapa Marina is Mexico's largest. It has two large basins, with capacity for over six hundred boats.

Like most of the waterside restaurants here, Beccofino is split in two, divided by a sidewalk that runs the length of the marina. One half of the restaurant is indoors, the other—outdoors—was made to look as if you were sitting on the deck of a boat floating in the marina waters. We were on the faux boat side. We weren't here dressed like Sonny and Cher circa 1970 just because we enjoyed looking silly or were feeling a little peckish. This was work. Intentionally seated at a table within listening distance, was Jared, waiting for his date: Frances Huber.

Errall blew away an errant strand of long black hair that seemed intent on lodging itself in her mouth. "This wig is fucking hot," she spit out along with the hair. "It's already eighty degrees, and with this get up it feels like ninety."

"Think of it this way," I told her, trying to ignore that my own false hairpiece was also causing me to work up a good sweat. "At least you aren't sitting over there as bait for a serial killer."

"I thought the plan for Jared was that he was going to start sorting through all the scanned documents JP is bringing back."

I nodded. "That was Plan A. But flexibility and spontaneity are a detective's best friends. Frances got the hots for Jared, before JP or I could put ourselves on the market. So it's on to Plan B."

"This was Plan B?"

"It is now."

She studied our friend. "He looks so calm."

"Oddly enough, he seemed pretty happy to have his responsibilities shifted from office grunt work to himbo. The wardrobe is much better too."

"I hope he does better than I did. I haven't had a call from Frances yet. I don't think she bought my scam."

I shrugged. Part of me was glad of it. The way Frances was assessing my mother at the art show had made me think twice about setting her up as a potential new victim for Frances's little business operation. "The good news is that she did buy Sereena and Anthony's shenanigans."

"Really? She's going to buy your mother's painting?"

"Well, not quite. But before she left the party, she told Sereena to ask Toraidio not to sell it to Anthony until she had time to think about it."

"My god, Russell, your mother could actually become an internationally recognized artist out of all this."

"Oi."

"Double oi."

"Oh oh, keep it down, Cher. Here she comes."

I watched Jared stand up to greet Frances like the perfect gentleman he was. They cheek kissed and he held out a chair, inviting her to sit down. I immediately texted JP to tell him to get to work. He texted back a confirmation. We ordered lunch.

Over the next forty-five minutes, not much of note happened at either table. We enjoyed a delicious Catch of the Day at our table, and Frances inhaled several sangritas (a tomato-based cocktail with tequila) at theirs. Things started getting more interesting when Frances, quite obviously enjoying Jared's charming company and not wanting it to end, suggested a chilled bottle of Duckhorn Sauvignon Blanc as the dessert course.

"Oh, Frances, it's a lovely idea, it really is," Jared replied. "But...well, I'm embarrassed to say this..."

"What? What is it? Spill it. Come on, you and me are old friends now."

"I invited you to lunch, but...well...the Duckhorn isn't exactly in my budget today."

I grinned at Errall. Nice play, Jared.

"Oh, who cares about that? Dessert's on me!" she laughed a little too loud for lunchtime.

"No, no, no, I can't accept such generosity. And, if I buy the wine, I won't be able to afford to take you out for dinner," he added suavely.

Frances's eyes ogled. "Dinner? As far as I know, I don't believe I've been properly invited."

"Is that a yes?"

"Only if you let me buy us some liquid dessert. Besides, it's so nice here, isn't it? I don't feel like going home yet. Do you?"

"Absolutely not." Jared was turning out to be a surprisingly accomplished liar.

Frances waved a hand at a server who was attending to a nearby table. Not getting anywhere, she finally whistled, and said, "Hey waiter, can you take our order over here, please?"

The waiter graciously complied, with more civility than I could have mustered. I could only hope they'd leave him a real big *propina.*

"Do you come from a less-than-well-to-do family too?" Frances asked Jared in her typical disarmingly candid way.

I winced. I wasn't sure how prepared Jared was to make up an entirely false background.

"Actually no," Jared told her. "My family was pretty well off until..."

"Until what, sweetie?"

Jared touched his face. "Until this."

"What do you mean?"

The waiter returned with their wine. Frances made a to-do about having Jared taste it.

"Is it good, hon? Would you rather have something else?"

"It's very good," Jared replied after the ceremonial sniff, swirl, and sip. He smiled up at the waiter. "It's great, thanks."

The waiter filled glasses and left.

"You see, I'm from Canada...," Jared began.

"No kidding! Me too! A lot of people here in Mexico are, you know. It's so cheap. To live here. To buy a house here. If only it was cleaner. Or if more of them spoke English. Then it'd be perfect."

Jared nearly choked on his wine.

Frances took a large gulp of hers. "Sorry, sweets, I interrupted you. So you're from Canada...?"

"When I had my accident, I was travelling in the United States. Like an idiot, I had no travel insurance. You know how it is. When you're young you don't believe anything bad can happen to you."

Frances nodded, seemingly very intent on hearing the story.

"Of course, my Canadian health insurance didn't help me unless I could get back to Canada. But the accident and my injuries were so severe, they couldn't risk flying me home for several weeks. In the meantime, the medical bills just grew and grew. My parents were by my bedside the whole while. I was out of it for a long time at the beginning. When I finally came to, they just told me all I had to worry about was getting better. So I did. I had no idea that the cost was skyrocketing. By the time I was well enough to be transferred to a hospital in Canada, my parents were near bankruptcy. I had no money of my own. We were broke. As soon as I realized what had happened, and that it was all because of me, I stopped all further treatment and surgeries."

"Surgeries? What kind of surgeries?"

"Oh, you know," he lied with bashfulness. "Reconstructive procedures to…well, to make me look like I used to. Even though I was back in Canada, they were considered cosmetic, so insurance wouldn't pay."

Errall and I exchanged gloomy glances. I couldn't imagine what it cost Jared to say those words. In reality, he and Anthony had travelled the globe visiting every specialist and spending great sums of money to do just that. To restore his former beauty. But the damage had been too great. What Jared was left with today, was the best it would ever be.

As I sat there, listening to Jared reel in Frances like an expert fisherman bringing in a hooked shark, I couldn't help but wince from the twisting and grinding of the twin monsters residing in my stomach—guilt and doubt.

JP being in continuous danger, my mother set up as bait for a killer, now Jared suffering emotional indignities; my family, friends, my boyfriend, were paying high prices for what was happening here in Zihuatanejo. For what I was making happen. What right did I have to ask them to put their lives and emotional health in jeopardy? Had I made the biggest mistake of my career? My life?

I watched in distaste as Frances reached across the table and touched Jared's scars, just as she'd done the first night she met him.

"My father used to beat us," she said in a casual way.

I almost lost my wig when I heard the unexpected admission. I knew a lot about Frances Huber. But I didn't know this. I resisted the urge to pull my seat closer to their table. What sort of game she was playing now by uttering such seditious words?

Apparently Jared was not quite so jaded. He reached over and laid his hand atop hers. "Us?" he asked tenderly.

"Me. My brother. My mother too. It was his thing."

"Frances, I'm so sorry to hear that."

"Yeah, yeah, well we all have crap in our past, don't we? Here, let me refill your wine."

Jared had hardly touched his, but she used the offer as a handy excuse to refill her own near empty glass.

"Is everybody…okay?" Jared asked her.

Frances took a long swallow, then carefully laid down her glass on the table top. She eyed Jared warily, as if trying to decide if she could really trust him. After a beat, she answered. "Not really. My brother got the worst of it. Especially after my mother got smart and started hitting the bastard back. Dad was a coward. Like all men who hit women and kids. I think she got in a few good shots one night when he was too drunk to defend himself. He got scared of her. So I guess he decided that me and my brother David were easier targets. Which we were."

"Didn't your mom try to stop him?"

"Nah. She was just happy not to be the one to wake up the next morning with a bloody nose and black eye."

"Oh Frances, that's terrible."

"Well, I shouldn't blame her completely. By then she was a pretty good drunk herself. She was usually passed out by time it got really bad. They say it's a disease, you know."

"Alcoholism?"

"Yeah. But I don't think so. She didn't have a disease. She had a self-induced ticket out of hell. If I could have, I'd have done it too. I should have, come to think of it. I should have just gotten drunk. I probably still would have gotten beat, but at least I wouldn't have cared. Or remembered."

It wasn't until I looked down, that I saw I was clenching my fists so tight, my fingernails were digging painful dents into the skin of my palms. Frances was telling the truth. I just knew it. By the look in Errall's eyes, so did she. I shifted uncomfortably in my chair, steeling myself. I didn't want to feel sorry for this villain. I couldn't allow it.

"How did it end?" Jared asked.

"He gave David such a good licking one day, we had to take him to the hospital. After that, the police got involved. Dad went to jail. I never saw him again. He died there."

"And David?"

"He died too."

There was silence at their table. If Frances had been paying attention, she'd have noticed a curious hush at our table as well.

It was Frances who spoke first. She sounded surprisingly jubilant, perhaps fuelled by all the wine she'd consumed. "Something good always comes from bad. I learned that the hard way. Don't you forget it, sweets."

"What good possibly came out of all that?"

"My mother. It was like a wake up call for her. She totally turned her life around. She got sober. She became one of those enter-pree-noors. She made loads of money. Even left me some when she died. And look at me. Here I am, living the good life in Mexico. Having a delightful lunch with a beautiful man."

But Jared was smarter than Frances Huber. He did not forget what he was meant to do at this delightful lunch. "Oh well, that's nice of you to say, Frances. But you don't have to. I know my days of being a beautiful man are long over."

She looked at him steadily. "They don't have to be."

"What do you mean?"

"How's your wine? Want some more?" she asked, holding up the three-quarters empty bottle over his still-full glass.

"Oh, no, I've had too much already. You go ahead."

Frances empted the rest of the wine into her glass.

"What I mean is that I could help you. I could get you those surgeries you need."

Jared looked appropriately taken aback. "Frances, what are you saying?"

"We're friends now, right?" Her hand covered his, as if she'd just taken possession of a new purchase. "Right?" she repeated.

"Of course."

"Friends help friends, right?"

"If they can."

"How much do these surgeries cost? Come on, tell me. Give me ball park."

"Frances, this is ridiculous. We're talking about $75,000 of procedures. Never mind all the pre- and post-care costs."

She whistled through her teeth. "Okay, okay, so what, a hundred grand in total? One-twenty-five maybe?"

Jared nodded haltingly. "I guess."

Frances pulled herself forward in her chair. She leaned over the table and kissed Jared lightly on the mouth. When she pulled back, she smiled, her cobalt eyes shining. She said, "Let me see what I can do."

Frances Huber went home that afternoon and made two phone calls. The first was to Sereena. She asked the price of the painting named *Korova*. Sereena told her that Anthony Gatt had a standing offer of $50,000 on the work, and was anxiously waiting to hear back from Toraidio about when he could take delivery. The second was a business call. To Errall Strane.

Chapter 17

The coal embers that were Frances Huber's eyes grew even darker when she saw that Errall was not alone. An extraordinarily beautiful hostess led Frances down the steps and into the sand where Errall and I were already seated at a candlelit table. The setting, La Marea beachside restaurant at The Tides resort in Zihuatanejo, was exquisite. The sand, the candlelight, the sound of the ocean crashing not twenty metres away. Much more suitable for a cozy, romantic dinner, than for our purpose: Buying Death.

Frances plunked herself down into the chair held back by the hostess. She barked at Errall: "What's he doing here?"

"He's my husband," Errall replied calmly. "And he knows everything I know."

"Oh yeah?"

"Besides," she added with a hint of a smile. "It's Russell's mother we've come to...discuss."

About then a trio of waiters descended upon us. They offered cocktails, cool water with our choice of condiments (sliver of cinnamon, frozen cranberries, lemon rind, a sprig of cilantro, and on and on), and to discuss the menu and specialties of the night.

Once they were gone, Frances asked me with a pointed directness, as if daring me to say something she didn't like: "Tell me what you *think* you know."

"Well," I began with a show of hesitation. "I don't know if you'll remember this exactly. About five years ago, you...helped...my wife's sister with the problem of their mother." If she asked for particulars, JP and I had researched enough of Frances's handiwork for me to bluff my way...but only so far.

"Like I told you when we met, we really appreciated what you did for us." Errall sounded exceptionally sincere. She even convinced me. "I want to thank you again."

I could see Frances bob her head. Just a tad. She was not immune to back patting. She probably didn't get much of it in her line of work. I could imagine that, typically, when she finished her business, the client wanted nothing more than to pay the bill and see her backside.

"So everything...worked out for the best then?"

"It did," Errall let her know with a sedate level of enthusiasm. "My sister and I could not be happier. Well, let me rephrase that. My sister is happy. I still have my mother-in-law to deal with."

"I see," she responded slowly. Her eyes narrowed and her brow furrowed as she studied both of us with great care.

"Maybe you heard my mother going on about things at the art show the other night?" I prodded.

She tilted her head in the affirmative. "A little, yes."

"Well, she's simply become impossible. My father—he was a multimillionaire Russian industrialist—left her with scads of money. Yet she keeps me—and Errall—on a ridiculous budget. As if we're still children, and need to be told what we can buy and what we can't. Do you know we still have to live with her in one of *her* houses? We're not *allowed* to buy our own. She won't even give us enough money to buy separate vehicles. We always have to use one of hers. And of course we have to tell where we're going and when we're coming back, because we're using *her* car! Can you believe that? I mean, what choice do we have when she won't give us the money to buy our own? It's complete idiocy!"

Errall carried on. "She regularly goes through my closets to make sure I haven't bought anything new that she doesn't know about. If she finds anything she didn't approve—even something as small as a Gucci scarf or Louis Vuitton handbag—she accuses me of stealing!"

We went on like this well into the service of our wine and main courses. It was actually quite a lot of fun.

"I hate going on and on about her like this," Errall said with a sniff when her motor ran down. "I mean, it's not like she's my mother. But I just worry so much about Russell. Dealing with her every day is giving him ulcers. I know what relief you gave me and my sister. And it's not as if Kay's enjoying her life. She has three homes and hates every one of them. The whole time we've been here on vacation, all she does is complain about the food, the heat, the language she can't understand. Wouldn't you agree, Russell?" Errall patted my hand in an icky way, meant to communicate her so very deep caring for my well-being. "She's miserable. She really has no quality of life anymore."

Frances very patiently listened to our story. It helped, I suppose, that while she did, she was also gobbling up every last morsel of the expensive meal and more than her fair share of two bottles of wine.

"So what do you think?" I asked plaintively. "Can you help me too?"

"Well, first off, I need to explain to you how my business works." Even though the nearest occupied table was a good four metres away, Frances spoke in subdued tones. "The event is called an Ending. We would arrange it very much how you might arrange a funeral for a loved one. I insist on dignity and respect for the loved one, both during the planning period and, of course, during the actual Ending."

"Oh, of course, of course," we both readily agreed.

"This is a business. I provide a service. You will pay a

prearranged Ending fee once the service is provided."

We nodded our understanding.

"Although there are no formal signed agreements, as I'm sure you can both well understand...?"

"Yes, yes, we understand."

"Like any other business, I do have my insurances to guarantee collection of my Ending fee. But I'm certain we don't have to discuss that sort of thing in this case?"

We shook our heads. I think we'd just been threatened. Pay up...or else.

"Good, then. Here is how I prefer to proceed. Once we have agreed on the Ending fee, I will begin with my research on the loved one in question. I will visit her place of residence, study her habits, routines, identify the areas of her regular day-to-day life that may be open to, shall we say, mishap, mistake, or misstep. Once I have done that, I will select what I feel is the safest, most humane, pain-free, and efficient method of carrying out the Ending.

"Now, be warned. This may take days. It may take months. It really depends on the kind of life the loved one lives. The circumstances that affect my work can be many and varied. I only act when I am absolutely certain I can carry out my duties in a way that is satisfactory to all parties involved, including myself."

"Will you tell us when you'll do it?" I asked.

"And how?" Errall added, sounding quite intrigued with the repulsive feats of horror being described to us.

"Not necessarily. Sometimes, the best opportunity presents itself in unplanned moments. If you insist on knowing these things, it would, I'm afraid, affect the price."

I looked at Errall as if pretending to gauge her feelings on the matter. Inside, I was thinking: there is no way in hell, lady, that I'm going to give you carte blanche to wipe out my mother without telling me first. It was really the only way I could guarantee Mom's safety. It was the only way I'd go ahead with this.

"Money is no object," I said. "I would prefer to know. It's not that I don't appreciate and trust your methods and decisions, I'd just...I would like to know when and how it's going to happen for my own private reasons." I felt sick to my stomach saying the words.

Frances nodded her assent. "I can understand that."

"Thank you."

"So what do you charge for something like this?" Errall asked.

"Two hundred and fifty thousand dollars," she told us, looking straight in our faces without blinking an eye.

Let's see: Jared said his surgeries would cost $125,000, the painting an extra fifty. After paying for assured nookie in the sack with a grateful boytoy, and contributing to her reputation as a patroness of the arts, Frances was still managing to build in an extra seventy-five grand pure profit. Minus whatever expenses she might incur in doing her "research." Not bad, if you didn't care that you had to knock someone off to earn it.

"That's pretty steep," I said.

"You have my number," Frances said quite tranquilly, making to get up from the table. "Feel free to contact me if you'd like to go ahead."

"No! No, wait!" Errall almost yelped, giving me a pleading look. "Russell, what's the problem? A quarter million is just a drop in the bucket of what's coming to us. Don't you remember how...miserable...she is...with life. We're doing her a favour, really. And Frances is a busy woman. Right, Frances?"

Frances sat back down. "I am."

I waited a respectful thirty seconds, then said, "Okay. So what do we do now?"

"Maybe a little more wine?"

We arranged another bottle, and fell further into the dark hole of planning The Ending of my mother. Also known as: her murder.

"You said she has three homes. Where does she spend most of her time? Or better yet, where will she be going after this vacation?"

This was tricky. There was no way I was actually going to let Frances Huber start investigating my mother. First of all, everything we'd told her about her was a lie. Second, learning that her new "loved one" was an elderly Saskatchewan woman, just like Hilda Kraus, her most recent victim, would likely send up some red flags for her.

"Actually, we're going to be here in Zihuatanejo for another couple of weeks. Do you think…?"

Frances smiled. "You want things to happen sooner rather than later."

"Yes!" Errall heartily established.

I said. "I know you mentioned that sometimes this can take a long time. But if you could just try…? Just see what you think."

She nodded. "Oh good. The wine is here."

As disgusted as I was with Frances Huber, and having to spend an evening with her, the good thing was that JP, busy at work in her house, was getting plenty of time to collect data to send this sociopath to hell.

That evening, when we were finally done with Frances, I began what would become a nightly tradition. I headed down to the Ixtapa Marina. Fresh from his evening of information thievery, JP was waiting for me in his kayak. The same kayak he used to get back and forth from his temporary fishing boat home and the coastline below Frances Huber's house. I—albeit a little nervously—got into the kayak. We rowed ourselves back to the little fishing boat that bobbed up and down in Bahia del Palmar like a cork. Once there, we cuddled under a blanket of stars, and fell asleep to the gentle sound of water lapping at the wooden edges of our oasis in the sea.

I was back in my chauffeur get-up when Frances arrived at Toraidio's house the next morning for her appointment with him and Sereena. As the maid led her into the rotunda, I was making busy as if packing up paintings to be shipped back to the artist or new owners. Astoundingly enough, nine of mom's paintings sold to Toraidio's friends who'd attended the party. *Korova*, the largest of the bunch, and subject to a minor bidding war between Anthony and Frances, remained un-wrapped. It still sat atop its double easel.

Frances was wearing a beige pants suit that would have been more appropriate at a business meeting. One taking place somewhere a lot cooler. And about fifteen years ago. She'd tied a Hermes scarf around her neck. Instead of looking jaunty, it seemed to swallow up her already disappearing chin.

"What loveliness is this?" Toraidio exclaimed, making nice work of gliding the distance to greet his visitor. "Mademoiselle Huber, isn't that right?" He reached for her hand and held it up as if to kiss it. "I must admit, I barely recognize you. How do you do it?"

Frances couldn't hold back a girlish giggle. "Do what?"

"How do you manage to look younger and lovelier each time I see you? Before you know it, you'll be nothing but a girl in her petticoat."

Oh groan.

Sereena joined the fawning man and his helpless conquest.

"Frances, how good to see you again. Toraidio is right. You do look wonderful."

"I understand you've come to see *Korova* again?" Toraidio said, leading her down the steps into the rotunda proper, still holding her hand as if it were his fondest possession.

"Yes. Sereena was to tell you not to sell it. You haven't, have you?" she asked, as she allowed herself to be positioned directly in front of the huge, bright canvas.

"Your request was highly unusual, I must tell you. But for you, mademoiselle, anything."

Frances was warming nicely to the attention of Toraidio, basking in it like a walrus on a sun-baked rock.

"I understand the price is at fifty-thousand..." she smiled at him with her best naughty ingénue look, "...and one dollar?"

"Fifty-*one*-thousand!" the voice reverberated around the rotunda like a struck bell.

All of us swivelled our heads to watch Anthony as he made his grand entrance. He was wearing a truly splendid royal blue jacket, over white pants and shirt, and a pair of plum-coloured suede Donald J Pliner slip-ons. And, for some inexplicable reason, he carried a magnificent walking stick with the head of a

Crested Caracara, Mexico's national bird. What a guy.

"Mr. Gatt, how nic..." Toraidio began, but was ruthlessly cut off.

"Garza! How dare you pit me against another bidder without telling me? Fifty-one-thousand. That is my new offer!" He glared at Frances, then back to Toraidio for a decision.

Toraidio gave Frances a distressed look. "I'm so sorry, Mademoiselle Huber. I did not know he..."

Now it was Frances's turn to cut him off. She was no dummy. Although I hated to admit it, she was proving herself a shrewd businesswoman. "You can stop right there. I know you knew that both of us would be here at the same time. You want the best possible price for the painting. The higher the price, the higher your commission, am I right? I get it. You don't have to double talk on my account."

To keep things smooth, Sereena slinked her way to Toraidio's side and slid an arm through his. She looked up at him, as if beholding an adorable scamp, and said, "Oh dear Toraidio, I think our Frances has your number."

Frances pumped up her already impressive cleavage, glad that Sereena acknowledged her judiciousness. She also enjoyed being referred to as "our" Frances. She gave Anthony a silent, measured look, then turned back to Toraidio. "I'll give you fifty-five."

Anthony made a sound, as if he'd just swallowed a canary.

Toraidio's eyes lit up.

She'd read Anthony perfectly. If he had money to burn, his counter offer would have been something much more significant than a one thousand dollar increase.

Toraidio looked at Anthony with an inquiring look.

"This is a travesty!" Anthony railed. "I simply cannot raise that kind of money with no notice. Certainly not while I'm in Mexico. Give me ten days and I'll see..."

"In cash." Frances stated. "By the end of the week."

Toraidio seemed to be hovering on a heavenly cloud. He smiled sweetly, and confirmed: "Cash?"

Frances nodded, agreeing to the terms.

Anthony huffed, puffed, then turned on his heel and stomped out, all the while pounding the heel of his walking stick violently against the floor with great effect. I was certain that as soon as he turned his face away from us, he'd be smiling all the way to the front door, congratulating himself on a bravura performance.

When he was gone—or nearly so—Toraidio and Sereena spontaneously broke into applause, calling for celebration. The look on Frances's face was nothing less than rapture. She was a hawk with its mouse, Salome with John the Baptist's head on a platter, Matthew McConaughey with an Academy Award. She had won, over a mighty foe, not only the painting, but the respect of two people whose admiration she coveted.

As Sereena and Toraidio collected champagne and glasses, Frances moved into a quieter corner and pulled out her cellphone. Although she was blissfully oblivious to me, a mere employee, I couldn't very well move along with her. But I did hear a few snippets of a steamy one-sided conversation. If I didn't know any better, I'd say Jared was in danger of being wined, dined, and bedded by one very happy murderer.

Chapter 18

That afternoon, while everyone else was off doing their own thing, JP and I ensconced ourselves on his boat, with a cooler full of cold drinks, some junk food, and a mound of paper. JP had been working hard. During the hours when he was not inside Frances Huber's house collecting data, he was burrowing into her life, analyzing it. He'd invited me on board to show me what he'd come up with so far. He seemed pretty excited about it.

"Okay," he began, donning a pair of spectacles I'd never seen him wear before. They made him look unaccountably sexy. And smart. "You know how I was able to find nine obits or newspaper articles about dead old ladies that matched the ones I saw in the MOM file?"

"Yeah."

"Well, take a look at these." He handed me a stack of files. He had a big, Winnie-the-Pooh-eating-honeycomb smile on his face.

"What are these?"

He grabbed the top file back from me, and opened it on the makeshift table top in front of us. The fishing boat wasn't exactly decked out for business meetings, but an ice cooler did the job just fine. Inside the file was a ream of paper. He sat back, arms crossed, eyebrow cocked. With a tick of his chin, I understood that I was to start reading.

The first document was a copy of a newspaper article. It recounted the long life, and eventual death, of Constance DeRochers (née Ballyntyne). She was ninety-one at her passing, and a longtime resident of Aliso Viejo, a city in Orange County, California. The article was written from the perspective of a warning, informing elderly readers about the many dangers of living alone. Apparently, a weak and sickly Constance had been found drowned, in her own bathtub. She wasn't discovered until two days after she'd expired. I'd seen the article before, and quickly moved on to the papers accompanying it. Here was the gold.

The other pages in the file were all copies of documents JP had found in Frances Huber's home, scanned, then later printed off at a shop in town. The first was a duplicate of Constance DeRochers's obituary, listing her date of death. Then came an Aeroplan statement. It detailed Frances's flight to John Wayne Airport in Orange County, just a little over two weeks prior to the death and then a return flight the day after. Added to that, he'd found a VISA statement showing payment for the same flights, car rental, hotel, and meals in and around Aliso Viejo for the same time period. Next was a copy of Frances's bank statement from the month immediately after the death. It showed a deposit of $175,000. Phone bills for the months prior to and after the death, showed multiple calls made to an Orange County residential phone number, as well as to several other Orange County businesses. JP had done some follow up. He'd learned that the residential phone number belonged to Alicia DeRochers. She was the sole daughter of guess who? The recently deceased Constance. He went even further. In the months immediately after her mother's death, Alicia purchased a brand new Jaguar, and paid for a five-star trip to St. Lucia.

I glanced at JP. He was now stretched out on a nearby platform that did double duty as a storage chest and couch. His shirt was off, and he looked as if he had nothing better to do than soak up the rays of an intense Mexican sun. But I wasn't fooled. He was alert as a leopard, his eyes fastened on me like salsa on chips. I winked, then returned to studying the files.

Each one was much the same as the last. They varied only in the victim's name (always an elderly woman), manner of death (accidental this, accidental that), and location (spread across North America). But in every instance, Frances Huber was there. Sometimes only for a few days, sometimes for a month or more. Then, as sure as a drag queen kicks off her heels once out of the limelight, as soon as Frances returned home, a big, fat cheque would land in her bank account. From just these cases we knew about—who knew how many more there were—Frances had made well over two million dollars in less than seven years.

More than two hours had passed by the time I'd finished reviewing the files. I checked and double-checked details and facts, made sure dates and times meshed. JP had done an extraordinary job. I was both impressed and proud of him. And I was excited. We had her. When I looked up, I was surprised to see that at some point, JP had changed into a fetching pair of swim trunks. He'd covered himself in Ombrelle 15 SPF, and had fallen asleep in the sun, like a hunky June bug.

I didn't have any swimwear with me, but I didn't care. We were bobbing up and down on the ocean, with no other boat nearby. I stripped down to my underwear. They were Le 31s that I order online from Simons Department Store in Montreal: orange with bright blue piping. Cute as any Speedo, in a pinch. (Not that I'm promoting Speedo wear by anyone, other than a few blessedly perfect men.) I lay down next to JP, so that my head was at his hip, and the same in reverse. My feet dangled off one side of the boat, his off the other.

"You're really something," I said into the air, letting the words float about on a lacy breeze.

"I know." He was awake.

I elbowed him. He sighed.

"I can't take all the credit," he said after a minute. "I was just doing what you told me to. This was all your idea. You told me what to look for. I just did the grunt work."

"JP, those files are works of art. That's more than grunt work. Much more."

If it's possible, I think I heard him smile.

"I brought you a cold bottle of water."

He reached over and took the bottle, downing half of it. His eyes were behind classic aviators, but I knew he was watching me closely.

"Thank you," he said quietly, when he was done with the water.

"There's more where that came from."

"I meant for the compliment," he said. "Coming from you, that really means a lot. I know we josh around, but I respect you, Russell. You're a good detective. And an even better man."

I didn't say anything for a bit. My throat seemed to have something in it.

"And you can't fool me, Russell. I know you're worried about all this. About us."

My only response was to run a finger along the side of his face, around his ear.

"I know you're worried about our safety. You think you talked us into this, and now you're second-guessing yourself." He waited a bit, then kept on. "I can't talk for your mother, Russell, but for what it's worth, I think she's safe enough. You'd sooner die than let anything happen to her. Hell, she's probably safer here with you in Mexico playing bait for a murderer, than living alone on that farm of hers. And the rest of them, Russell, well, I think it's kind of like hypnosis."

"Hypnosis?" I didn't get it.

"You can't make anyone do anything they really don't want to do. Errall, Sereena, Jared, Anthony, Toraidio…they're having the time of their lives. They get to help you out, bring a killer to justice, avenge Jane, work on their tans, and drink margaritas, all at the same time. Sounds like a good deal to me."

"I know you're right," I relented, glad to be talking about this out loud with someone other than the voice in my head. "But I can't help but feel responsible for what happens to them."

"Russell, they're your friends, not your children. I love that you care so much. But that's as far as it should go. Love them. But accept their decisions as their own. We're a team in this. We're not your subjects, your royal highness."

"Oh har har." I made light, but I felt immeasurably better. "And what about you, JP? You haven't talked about yourself."

"That's different. I *am* your loyal and faithful subject, happy only when doing your bidding." Funny guy.

"Good. As long as we have that clear."

He added after a beat, "I'm in this for me, Russell. You know that. The danger I accept is mine to take on. I want nothing more than to bring this bitch down. For Jane. Hear me roar, Quant, because I'm the new PI around town. Like it or lump it. It's your call."

I groaned. "Aw jeez, are you getting ready to belt out Helen Reddy or Mariah Carey?"

He laughed. "Nah, I'll save that for another time."

"So you're a full-fledged detective now, are you? My competition?"

"Yeah. Why not?"

"JP, I have to ask you something."

Silence. Of all the times I'd thought life should come with a musical score—and there've been a few of them—this had to be in the top ten. Perhaps something low and dark, like the dull, rumbling drum beat of an impending storm.

"Shoot," he finally said.

"Where have you been?"

"Did you mean to end that sentence with: ...all my life?"

"JP...before you showed up in Regina, before you started up at the shoe store...where were you?"

I was glad we were lying the way we were, that our eyes were protected by sunglasses, that we weren't looking directly at each other. It was making the difficult turn in the conversation a little easier to navigate.

"You've been checking up on me," he said, no hint in his

voice about what he thought about that.

"The cops were. You know they found your prints in Jane's office."

"What else do you know?"

"That you did some juvie time as a kid. After that, it's like you disappeared. Until two years ago."

"You sure you want to hear this?"

Oh boy. What did I get myself into this time? I'd already dated a murderer once before, a few years ago.* Certainly that particular lightning wasn't going to strike me twice, was it? "Yeah," I whispered, not sure I was telling the truth. "I do."

There was silence for a while. I hoped he was using the time to figure out how best to tell me the truth, rather than how to get the hell off this boat. Finally, he began.

"I was an unruly kid, that was for sure. My poor parents. They didn't know what to do with me. I don't know why I was the way I was. I mean, it wasn't anything horrible. I wasn't running around knifing people or anything like that. But I had some issues. Mostly with drugs, and taking things that weren't mine. It was petty stuff, but still not good. Eventually, it caught up with me. I did a stint at the correctional facility. You know, there are a lot of people who complain about our justice system. They say it doesn't work. They say it ruins kids. They say it makes criminals, rather than rehabilitates them. But I don't get that. For me, it totally worked. I got turned around in there."

I held my breath. I could feel a big "but" coming up.

"It was more than getting clean and getting my life back together. I found something new."

"Something new?"

"God. I found God, Russell."

I'm ashamed to say that I felt myself stiffen at the words. A holy roller? This was most definitely a new one for me. Then again, there was Father Len, a really cute priest I'd met on my first big case several years ago.** I liked religion. I liked religious people. Look at my mom, after all. Then again, she was a seventy-

* *Tapas on the Ramblas*

** *Flight of Aquavit*

year-old Ukrainian lady. I think being religious was in her DNA. You kinda expect it with someone like her. But a guy like JP? No way. I tried keeping my breathing even, my mind open, my mouth shut.

"We used to go to church every Sunday when I was a kid," he continued. "But I didn't think anything of it. It was just something we did. I wasn't really paying attention. When I was locked up, I started having these regular sessions with a spiritual counsellor. I realized I had these feelings. I didn't know what they were at first. It's hard to explain. It was like I was in love…with God. I wanted to be with him, to work with him, or for him, or something. I didn't know what was going on. It was so confusing for me."

"How old were you?"

"Just barely in my twenties. In my head though, I think I was still a teenager. Painfully immature."

"What happened to you then?"

"When I got out of Corrections, I went to stay at a halfway house in Vancouver. It was run by these monks. Around that time, my parents were killed in a car accident."

"Oh God, JP. I'm sorry. I didn't know."

"Yeah, yeah, thanks. It was terrible, for sure. It was a long time ago."

I squeezed his hand.

"When all that was dealt with, I found myself suddenly thrust into the real world. But I didn't belong there anymore. I had no real life. I went back to Vancouver. I couldn't live at the halfway house anymore; it was against the rules, or I probably would have. But I did go back to visit the monks I'd made friends with there. We'd have these long talks. Sometimes for hours at a time. A year later, I joined their monastery, this very cool place, up north in rural BC."

I sat up. Sunglasses off. "You're a monk?"

JP sat up too. He slipped off his aviators and looked at me with those soft, kind, beneficent, monk-like eyes…

Okay, maybe I was just seeing things.

"Yeah, I was."

"For how long?"

"Seven years."

OMG.

"But I struggled. The whole time I was there, I was struggling."

I bet.

"It wasn't the devotional life. It wasn't the periods of enforced silence. Or the bad food. I mean, come on, a little sauce isn't gonna kill anyone!"

We laughed. Uncomfortably.

"So the struggle was about you being gay?"

"No," he answered. "The struggle was about me wanting to act on it."

I nodded. Big difference.

"I was on one of my furloughs from the monastery, when I finally realized it was a battle I wasn't going to win. I was twenty-eight when I finally made the decision to leave. It was one of the hardest things I've ever had to do. It was like…it was like getting a divorce from someone you still really, really love.

"For a long time I doubted myself. It would have been so much easier to stay. Imagine, coming back into the world at twenty-eight. I had no friends. No support system. No resumé. My only work references were monks who'd taken a vow of silence!"

Another chuckle. This time we were more at ease.

"What did you do?"

"I roamed about aimlessly for a while. Two years ago I came back to Regina. To be with Marie-Genevieve. She was the only family I had left in the outside world. The only…anything. She agreed to take me in. I'll never be able to thank her enough for that. She helped save my life. Ever since then I've been trying to find my path, make a living…sell shoes…Then I met Jane. As soon as I learned what she did, I knew this was what I was meant for. The day she agreed to give me a chance was the best day in my life. Until I met you, that is."

I laid a big fat kiss on him.

"Thank you for sharing this with me. I had no idea."

"Of course you didn't. And I know it's a little...unusual. But unusual is good, right?"

"In this case," I said, giving him another peck on the cheek, "most definitely."

We each fell back onto the deck, drinking in the sun. In my case, sighing with relief. Our hands curled into each other.

"You know," JP started up after a minute of quiet contemplation, making a sharp left turn back into business, "I think one more visit tonight to Chez Huber, and I'll have it all."

"There's more?"

"There are a couple of boxes I haven't gone through yet. I think there may be correspondence in there. Wouldn't it be great if we could find a letter or some sort of communication from one of the people who hired her?"

"What you've got is terrific. Surely enough to get a major investigation started. If you found all that in just a few days, who knows what the police can dig up if they really get into it."

JP let out a satisfied sigh.

"How she got away with it for so long is what baffles me," I commented, taking a long drag from my water bottle. "And not only the obvious; escaping suspicion of police and family and friends. She's pulled in millions of dollars over the years. How does she get away with having all that cash and not attract some attention?"

"I know how."

I sat up again, surprised. At this rate, I'd be able to skip my sit-up routine for a week. "You do?"

"I've got copies of her tax returns for the past five years. I know you want to believe she's a master criminal, and therefore stupid. But Frances is not stupid, Russell. She's really thought this through. She doesn't get caught by CRA because she doesn't hide anything from them. Well, not exactly. She claims all her income. Every cent of it."

"What? You've gotta be kidding me. Does she fill out Form T666 as an evil, self-employed murderer?"

"Kind of. Except she calls herself a Self-Help counsellor. She reports all her revenue. And expenses: the travel, rental cars, meals, on and on. CRA loves her because she never claims a loss. She actually pays quite a bit in taxes every year. So they leave her alone. No need to audit a golden goose, I guess."

I was back on my back, head next to JP's firm hip and thigh. We were silent for a long while. My mind wandered. I began to think about those people you hear of, the ones who go away on tropical vacations and never come back. They leave well-paying jobs, family, friends, and live in beachside hovels. They set up little businesses, teaching surf lessons or selling beaded necklaces to tourists. All so they can have oodles of spare time, to sit in the sun, and doze the day away. That was me—in a way—all of last year. Sure, it sounded good in theory. But for me, life needs to be about more than that. I was glad to be back.

"JP?"

A garbled sound was his response.

"There's one more thing I don't understand."

"Whazzat?"

He sounded a little groggy. Good. "How the hell did you get into my house that day and tie me up without Barbra and Brutus making a fuss?"

The only reply was light chuckle, before he fell back into a lazy day slumber.

I wouldn't get my answer today. Even lulled by the sun, he was on his game. I felt myself slide toward sleep too, luxuriating in the company of a wonderful man, gentle waves lapping at our heels, the day's setting sun painting us bronze. It was bliss. It was an afternoon I'd always remember.

Set high above Zihuatanejo Bay, Amuleto is a sumptuous enclave seemingly created from the very rocks and greenery of the natural landscape that surrounds it. Like Toraidio Garza's home not far away, the aerie has a spectacular view of the roaring ocean, calming itself as it kisses sister beaches La Ropa and Las Gatas. The boutique hotel offers only six suites, each exquisitely decked out with furnishings and decorations of elemental stone, ceramic, and wood, and its own small infinity plunge pool.

A thirty-seat restaurant, open to the public, is accessed from the side of a twisting, gravel corniche necessary to get to it. When you first arrive, a bougainvillea-laden path leads you to a thick wooden door. Behind, a small taste of the remarkable view greets you, as a hostess escorts you down a steep set of steps into the open air dining area.

It's a cozy, unusual space. At one end, a miniscule cocktail lounge serves up first-rate martinis. Next to the lounge is an open-style kitchen, under the control of one of a long list of famed guest chefs anxious for the opportunity. Glass trinkets hang low from tree branches and umbrella stands, meant to scare off birds.

It was here that Frances decided to take Jared for dinner. To Jared, and whoever else might care, the stated purpose of the dinner was to commemorate Frances's acquisition of *Korova,* the much sought after painting by the mysterious artist, K. Frances, no doubt, was also celebrating her new job. Not only would it allow her to pay for the painting, but I was also pretty sure she intended to use some of the proceeds to buy a little love from her date.

It was an understandable coincidence—what with our shared appreciation for fine restaurants that my mother pretended she couldn't afford—that Errall, Mom, and I, should also be dining at Amuleto the same night.

"Isn't this a pleasant surprise?" Errall proclaimed, as we swept in, not five minutes behind Jared and Frances.

Jared, ever the gentleman, stood up to greet us with a gracious smile. Frances remained seated, with a plastered-on smile of her own.

"I'm not sure if you know my date, Jared Lowe?" she said with a wave of her hand. "You may have met at the art show the other night. That's where we met, isn't it, sweetie?"

Jared was a born actor, sharing an intimate wink with Frances, before shaking hands with us. "No, I don't think we did. A pleasure to meet you."

In Ukrainian, Mom suggested that it looked like rain. I scoffed and said *sotto voce* to Frances: "She wants me to ask you if this place is expensive."

Frances chose to ignore this, and wished us a pleasant evening.

That was our cue to move on to our own table. So we did.

I texted JP, telling him the coast was officially clear. Shortly after the ordering of food and wine was done, Jared excused himself to find the washroom. While he was away, I caught Frances slipping an envelope onto his side plate, where he couldn't miss seeing it. Awwww. Young love. How sweet. She was planning to surprise him with something.

When Jared returned, he made a great to do about the card. He opened it and feigned immense surprise. I suspected he'd just received a sizable cheque. Frances leaned over to say something. Although I'd tried for a seat as close to their table as possible, I still had a hard time overhearing her. But it was something like: "And soon you'll have your perfect face again. Are you happy, honey?"

Jared acted thrilled. There was much clinking of wine glasses.

From there, the evening progressed pleasantly enough. I was straining to hear everything I could from the exchange between Jared and Frances. Much of it was painful-to-listen-to banter, loaded with sexual innuendo and goo-goo eyes. I don't know how Jared stood it. I was glad his husband, Anthony, wasn't there to witness it. In defence of my own sanity and gag reflex, I myself began to tune them out, and focussed on enjoying my delicious grilled dorado.

Some time later, I noticed that my mother, who had left the table for the washroom, had been gone longer than she should have been.

"Where has she gotten to?" I asked Errall. "She can't still be in the bathroom, can she?"

Errall shrugged.

Something wasn't right.

My eyes shot to Jared's table.

Frances was gone.

Oh god.

Mom.

I jumped from my seat, my face flushed with fear. I rushed to the edge of the dining room. The restaurant overlooked the hotel's diminutive pool area, accessed by a short stairway near the bar. Another set of precarious steps from the pool area led down the side of the hill to the washrooms. My eyes fought the dark, trying to find something to hold onto. The sun had set long ago, and the provided lighting was meant more for atmosphere than practical use. At first I didn't see them. Then my heart jumped into my throat. Frances Huber and my mother were together. They were standing next to each other, near the far end of the infinity pool, where the water seemed to pour over the edge into vast nothingness. They seemed to be checking out exactly where the water was going, leaning slightly forward, peering into the abyss. With a burning dagger tearing into my chest, I realized that all it would take was one shove, not even a very forceful shove, and Frances could make good her verbal contract with me. The one where I asked her to kill my mother.

"Mom!" I cried out, much too shrilly for the until-now, pleasant dining environment. I could feel the stares of the other guests dig into my back like claws. They were here to enjoy an intimate dinner in one of the most beautiful spots on the Mexican Riviera, not listen to me scream out for my mama. I didn't care. I rushed toward the stairs and took them two at a time down to the pool level.

When I got to the spot where my mother was standing companionably next to Frances Huber, I screeched to a halt, like Wile E. Coyote.

"Mom!" I burst out again, sounding out of breath. "I was worried about where you'd gotten to."

Mom released some Ukrainian verbiage. Unbeknownst to all around us, she was wondering whether or not Mexicans can grow potatoes all year long, seeing as there is no Saskatchewan-style winter.

Frances gave me a steely-eyed smile. "We were just getting to know one another. Turns out your mother *does* know a word or two in English."

"Oh?" I cringed. Did my mother ruin her cover?

"Goot and okay." Those were the two words. Phew.

I gave Frances a sickly smile. It was the best I could manage.

Mom said something else and tottered off. Frances and I

watched wordlessly as she navigated her way up the steps, back to the table.

I turned back to Frances. She wore an expectant look on her shadowed face.

I began, haltingly, "Is this…is this a good place then?"

"You tell me."

"B-b-but I mean, for what you…what you have to do."

Frances made a show of tossing another assessing glance over the brink.

Nothing but a sharp, rocky decline, straight down to the ocean.

She turned back to me. "I think it could be. Maybe at lunch time, though. When there are fewer people around."

I swallowed. I couldn't believe what I was about to say. "Tomorrow?"

She thought about it for a moment. Then nodded. "One o'clock."

"She'll be here."

"Well then, you'll have to excuse me for now. My date and I have a romantic rendezvous at home." She smiled and left.

I stood there for many moments, thinking about what I'd just set in motion. Part of me wished I'd never said what I just had. Was it too soon? No. I'd played this out in my head a million times already. It was time. It was most definitely time.

I almost startled myself when I realized I'd been so busy considering what was coming next, that I'd forgotten to call JP to tell him to get out of the house. I pulled out my phone and hit the speed dial number. It rang.

And rang.

And rang.

JP wasn't answering.

In that instant, I knew with a crushing certainty, that something had gone very wrong.

Chapter 19

It took only one quick, frantic call to bring Toraidio and his sea captain to my assistance once again. Within moments, Toraidio's large town car pulled up outside Amuleto. There was no time to get Mom back to the condo, so she and Errall slipped into the back seat with me. Toraidio was driving; Sereena sat next to him in the front. With tires churning up a cloud of dust, the car began its speedy descent down the mountain towards the marina. Toraidio was not a particularly good driver, but he was a fast one. Tonight, that was fine with me. Along the way I repeatedly re-dialled and texted JP's cellphone. He never answered.

The boat was ready when we arrived. The five of us climbed aboard, and began the journey out of Bahia Zihuatanejo. We sailed past Punta Godomia, Punta Esteban, the more remote and less touristy Playa Majahua, and Islas Blancas, an area popular with divers. But there would be no divers now. Not this late at night.

As it had been for days, I knew JP's boat was anchored near Playa Cuata. We were still a fair distance away when the captain raised an alert. Even though he was speaking Spanish, I knew what he was saying could not be good. All of us rushed toward the front of the boat, wind tearing at our hair and clothing. The captain was staring at something through binoculars, all the while keeping up an excited dialogue with Toraidio.

"What is it?" I demanded to know. "What's going on?"

Toraidio gave me a look I wished I hadn't seen. It looked suspiciously like pity.

"Toraidio!" I barked to get him to snap out of it.

He said nothing, but raised his hand and pointed an unsteady finger to somewhere in the distance. My eyes followed.

At first I saw nothing. Just black. Black water. Black sky.

Then I saw a speck. It looked like nothing more than a lone firefly, flickering in the distance. As the boat rushed ever closer, the firefly grew larger and larger.

It was…a fire?

On water?

How could that be?

I heard troubled murmurs from the others as they too caught sight of the unlikely thing, all of us trying to make sense of it. I rushed to the captain's side and pulled the binoculars from him. I quickly found the bizarre light in their magnified gaze.

My stomach contracted, then plummeted to the ground. My heart pounded so loud, I was certain I could hear it over the roar of the boat's speeding engine. My head felt as if it would explode if I didn't scream, or yell, or find some way to release the horror of what my eyes had delivered into my brain.

It was JP's boat.

Aflame.

"*Más rápido! Más rápido, por favor*!" I screamed at the captain.

I could hear people call my name, saying things to me, but none of it made any sense. Everything was garbled. My brain was spinning like dough in a mixer. I put all my remaining focus into willing the boat, my body, everything and everyone around me, to speed up and get us to JP as soon as possible. I didn't care if laws of physics needed to be broken to make it happen. We had to get there now!

Then I heard a cry. The sound was unimaginable. I'd never heard such beseeching grief. It took me a few seconds to realize that the hollowed out, dark-to-the-depths-of-hell screams belonged to me. I'd reacted to what I suppose I worried might happen, but refused to believe it would.

JP's boat exploded.

With a resounding thunk, the binoculars fell to the floor of the boat. Someone grabbed them up. We were still too far away to see exactly what was happening. I heard people making dreadful noises. Shock. Fear. Sorrow. And, again, damnable pity.

It was hours before we all returned to Toraidio's house in the hills. Anthony and Jared were waiting for us. Someone had called ahead and told them what had happened. Earlier in the evening, Anthony had been tasked with saving Jared from Frances's amorous clutches. He waited for just the right moment, then burst into her casita. Disregarding Jared's presence, he demanded Frances relinquish the *Korova* painting to him, in exchange for the inflated price he was now willing to pay. In the melee, Jared excused himself, claiming a headache. He hid down the street until Anthony was able to pick him up.

"Oh, Puppy," Anthony cooed as he reached out and pulled me into his arms. Jared encircled us both with his own.

After a moment, we pulled apart. I looked Anthony in the eye, and said, "It will be all right. JP will be all right."

"What?" Anthony uttered, sounding understandably surprised. "Have you heard something new? I thought the police had searched the water and...?"

Errall pressed a glass into my hands. It was tequila. Straight. I downed it.

"They did," Errall told Anthony. "They found only bits and pieces."

"Bits and pieces of the *boat*," I added, more sharply that I probably should have. "Only the boat."

Anthony led me to a couch and sat next to me. The others gathered near. They were looking at me as if I was some poor soul, rendered unstable and unreasonable by a sudden shock. I did not like it, but I understood.

It was true. I was rocked by what had happened that night. But I could not bring myself to believe what I knew each of them did. That JP Taine was dead. Killed in the explosion that destroyed his boat. Every fibre in my being told me it wasn't true. I don't know why or how. I knew it went against everything we'd seen with our very own eyes. But somehow JP had survived. He would walk into this room any minute now, with his big, lopsided, beautiful smile, his blond locks charmingly dishevelled. Maybe he'd have a bruise or two. His clothes would be torn, scuffed up a bit. But he would be fine. Absolutely fine.

"Something must have gone wrong tonight," I told the room. "Maybe the guards who watch the house caught sight of him through a window. Or maybe they heard a suspicious noise from inside and decided to check it out. They must have seen JP. He would have managed to escape. And now he's laying low. Waiting for things to cool down."

"Yes," Anthony murmured assuredly. "That could be."

"But why would they blow up the boat?" Errall, always the logical thinker—damn her—asked no one in particular. "How would they even know it was out there? Or that it belonged to JP, if he escaped like you say he did?"

I could see the others peppering Errall with scathing glares. They didn't like her bursting my delusional bubble. But I knew they were all thinking the same thing: She was right.

Uneasy glances were being exchanged. Well, to hell with them. It wasn't my job to convince them of what I knew to be true. JP had said it best. I could love them, but I wasn't responsible for them, what they did, or what they thought.

"Somehow...I guess...they must have known the boat was his," I said, my voice sounding a bit croaky. "Maybe Frances figured out he was sneaking documents out of the house and storing them on the boat. She knew how damning they'd be. So she ordered her goons to destroy it."

"But Russell," Errall noted, ignoring all the "would you shut up, already!" stares, "there's no way Frances could have been back at her house by the time the boat blew up. She only left the restaurant minutes before we did. Considering how fast Toraidio got us to the pier, and the speed of the boat, she couldn't have gotten to Ixtapa, figured all this out, and arranged an explosion. There wasn't enough time. Besides, Anthony was there. His grand rescue of Jared wouldn't have gone down the way it did if Frances had been busy dealing with a thief. Everything must have happened before she and Jared got back to the house. She didn't have a clue what was happening. At least not then. Anthony, isn't that right?"

He nodded his agreement, but said nothing, not wanting to fuel Errall's unappreciated fire.

"Then it was the guards," I shot back. There had to be a good explanation to fit my scenario. The scenario where JP got away safely.

"Can't we talk about this another time?" Anthony requested of the room, eyeing me worriedly.

Errall hit her forehead with her hand. "Oh shit! With everything else, we didn't even think about what was on the boat. Fuck, Russell! All the papers! The laptop, the scanner, all the information JP's been collecting. Every shred of proof we had against that bitch. It's all gone. It all went down with the boat."

There was shocked silence in the room. No one wanted to think about that. Not when it also presumed JP was dead. But, of course, they couldn't help but be stunned by the horrible truth. All that we'd worked for, the months and months of planning. Gone. All gone. Somewhere at the bottom of the Pacific Ocean. Maybe one day, some diver off Islas Blancas would find an electronic data device. He'd wonder what was on it; what poor sucker lost it over the side of his boat.

I stood up and announced that I was going back to Errall's condo. "JP might be waiting there for us right now."

No one argued. Errall and Mom came with me.

It was a horrible night.

There was still no sign of JP by the next morning.

I had gotten no sleep. I'd dialled his number every fifteen minutes, all night long. No answer. Still, I was undeterred in my belief that the man I'd fallen in love with was alive. Powered only by the strength of that belief, I knew the rest of our shattered plan, or what was left of it, had to go ahead. At a minimum, I was, more than ever, determined to exact at least one small pound of flesh from our detestable killer. I made short work of getting ready and returned to Garza's house

Frances arrived exactly on time. Sereena and Toraidio greeted her with their usual round of enthusiastic bon mots and compliments.

"Do you have any idea how hard it is to get your hands on fifty-five thousand dollars in a matter of days?" Frances asked. They'd settled on the couches in the outer rotunda, freshly made mojitos in hand. I was well hidden behind a column. No mojito.

"However did you do it?" Sereena wondered aloud, shaking her head in mock admiration.

"Well, keep this under your hats," she said, shooting a look in the direction of the just departed maid and mojito-maker as if she might be a potential thief. "I always keep some of the green stuff handy. You know, just in case. This is Mexico, after all, right? You never know what might happen. Or when you might need some cash to buy your way out of here. If you don't already, you two should really do the same."

Toraidio's face froze in a rare show of distaste for a female in his company. He quickly rallied, and gallantly said nothing.

"Oh dear," Sereena moved in to cover the awkward silence. "I hope this doesn't leave you too short."

Frances smiled. "Fortunately, I've just landed a lucrative new business contract. My coffers will fill up very soon."

"How nice for you."

"Speaking of crazy things happening in Mexico, you won't believe it when I tell you what happened last night."

The air in the room seemed to disappear. What's this? Did she know something? Did she suspect Sereena and Toraidio were involved?

"That Gatt fellow came charging into my house!" she crowed, thrilling herself with the telling of the story. "I don't even know how he knew where I live. He might have been stalking me, for all I know."

Phew. I watched Sereena and Toraidio's faces visibly relax.

"He wanted me to sell him the painting! Can you believe that?"

"Well," Sereena said smoothly, "it just goes to prove what a good decision you made to buy it. And what a good deal it is. Imagine, your purchase has driven a world-renown collector to such extremes. Not many people can say that, Frances."

"Yes, *Senora*," Toraidio agreed, somewhat recovered from his earlier revulsion for the woman. (Although I noticed he was now using the more matronly *senora* instead of the youthful and playful *senorita.*) "You should be very pleased by this."

Frances puffed out her chest and congratulated herself with a healthy swig of mojito.

A short silence, with Sereena and Toraidio both looking at Frances expectantly, led to Frances pulling a thick envelope from her purse. She handed the package to Toraidio. He accepted it with a small bow of his head.

"Are you free for lunch?" Sereena asked. I smiled to myself. There was nothing Sereena wanted less than to have lunch with this viper. But she already knew that Frances Huber was otherwise engaged.

"Oh darn. I'd like that. But I already have plans for lunch. My life is just so busy right now, you know. But how about dinner? Tonight? Maybe someplace nice and clean, in Ixtapa?"

Sereena smiled. "Of course." She rose, signalling an end to the meeting. "Call me later?"

And with that, Frances left to kill my mother.

Chapter 20

It was a rare cloudy day in Zihuatanejo. The temperature was still in the high seventies, but something about the sombre colouring of the sky and a flicking wind made the early afternoon feel considerably cooler. We were back at Amuleto. There was only one other table for two finishing up lunch. A lone hotel guest sat at the bar nursing a cocktail. Mom was down on the pool level, alone, near the precipitous edge, pretending to admire the foliage. No one from the dining level could see the pool area. And because of the weather there were no sunbathers. The setting was perfect for murder. All Frances Huber would have to do was give Mom a quick and forceful shove. Down she'd go, rolling down the rocky cliff, likely ending up bloody and broken near the hill's base, or lost in the roiling waters of the Pacific. Of course, I would never let any of that happen.

At ten minutes after the appointed meeting time of one o'clock, I was getting worried. Was she not coming? Had she found us out? Had something else gone wrong? I could see that Mom was getting a bit antsy. It was tough pretending to look at flowers and greenery when you knew that a murderous hellcat was scheduled to jump out of the bushes and push you off a cliff. But she was doing okay. Mom was, if nothing else, a tough old bird. I'm pretty sure that if I left her to her own devices, she'd take on Frances Huber without hesitation. Who exactly, between the two of them, would end up at the bottom of that mountain, was not exactly a given.

And then she was there.

The devil in a blue dress. Frances had dressed up for the event. How thoughtful.

I was taking no chances. Just as she made her appearance, so did I.

"Frances," I called out to her.

Her eyes whipped away from my mother and hooked into me, like a prowling hyena distracted from its prey. She gave me a surprised, questioning look. My mother turned around and said something in speedy Ukrainian. Although Frances didn't know it, Mom was complaining about her bunions, telling me her feet were sore, and wondering if she could sit down soon?

"Frances," I said again, ignoring my mother. "Could I talk with you? Please?" I dosed my tone with sufficient urgency to get her attention.

She simply stared at me, then my mother, then back at me.

"Just for a minute. Maybe over here?" I indicated a narrow pathway that led away from the pool area toward the guest rooms.

Frances gave my mother an icy smile. Although my mother rarely uses profanity, she took the opportunity to smile back and describe a female dog (in Ukrainian).

Oblivious to the insult, Frances followed me into the passageway. Once there, she immediately jumped all over me. "What do you think you're doing? We had a deal. If the situation was right—which it is—I would fulfill our contract today. Now look what you've done. You've messed everything up. There's no way I can go ahead with things now."

"I think...I think I may have changed my mind. At least for now. I'm just not ready for this yet."

"In case it wasn't clear, Mr. Quant, I don't do this for fun. This is a business. I provide a service. I get paid. I was fully prepared to provide that service today. I expect to be paid for that. Today."

"A business...?" I needed Frances Huber to say more than she was. All this talk about contracts, business, a service, would mean nothing to anyone. I needed her to say she was there to kill my mother.

"That's right. A business."

"You call what you do a business?"

"What would you call it?"

Uh uh. That wouldn't work. "I can't pay you for nothing."

"Then wait right here," she said, an ugly pitch in her voice. "Where did your precious mother get to? Maybe I'll just go finish what I came here to do after all. I expect you to be waiting here with a cheque when I get back."

"No!"

Frances crossed her arms over her prodigious chest and stared at me.

"I need to go over this again. What will you do? To her. Exactly."

Frances sighed impatiently. "We've talked about this. I don't like being dicked around. Is this happening or not?"

I hesitated, trying to think of a way to steer her into an admission of what she did for a living.

"Tell you what, big shot. I'll give you two choices. Either (a) we postpone and I try again at a later date. But that will cost you more, just because you pulled this little stunt. Or (b), I'll call it off, for a reduced fee. So, which is it?"

"How much are we talking about?"

"You pick (a) and it's going to cost you two-seventy-five..."

"To do what, exactly?"

Frances stepped back. Oh jeez. Had I gone too far? Her piglet eyes were burning into me. Either she thought I was trying to frame her, or that I was a mindless wing nut who couldn't remember exactly what our original deal was.

"Are you fucking with me?" she finally asked.

"Of course not. I just want to make sure I understand the deal. I'm a businessman too."

She snorted. "Somehow I don't think your mother would agree with that assessment."

I frowned at the insult, but said nothing to defend myself.

"If you decide to go with (b), which I'm guessing you will..." She said it as if I was much less of a man for calling off my own mother's murder. "I'll take two-hundred and we'll call it a day."

"Two hundred! That's only fifty less than what you were going to charge me in the first place."

"Then consider it a down payment, should you ever decide to resurrect this little arrangement."

"You mean...you'd consider killing my mother again?" Someone had to say the "k" word.

And in the worst timing known to man, that is when Saskatoon's finest, Darren Kirsch, along with several of Mexico's finest, came bursting into the passageway from both ends.

Stupido! Stupido! Stupido!

I almost had her! I almost had her admitting that she was going to kill my mother. That's why the men in blue (or in this case, a dirty brown) were hiding in the wings in the first place. We needed Frances to incriminate herself. With all the information we had tying her to the other murders she'd committed having been lost—somewhere at the bottom of Bahia del Palmar—this was all we were left with. And now we had nothing. Not once during our confrontation did Frances say anything that made it sound like she was doing anything more than selling Mary Kay cosmetics.

We were foiled.

And by the look on Frances Huber's face as she took in the situation, she knew it too.

"What's all this?" she asked innocently of the authorities who had surrounded us. "Is this man in trouble?" She meant me. Ballsy, I have to say that for her.

"Frances Huber," Darren said in his tough guy voice, a voice that sends shivers down most women's and some men's spines. "I am Detective Darren Kirsch of the Saskatoon Police Service. I must inform you that I have no jurisdiction here, but my colleagues are allowing me to translate for them until an English speaking police officer can attend the scene."

"The scene? What scene?"

"Frances Huber, you are under arrest for suspicion of the murders of Sally Ann Coontz, Agatha Dunwoody, Mary-Jane Johnson, Mary Anne Knoble, Gertrude Steinbock, Constance DeRochers, Delores Schenectidy, Pramila Chopra, Henrietta Tannin, and Hilda Kraus."

As Darren sang out the names, each louder than the one before it, although I did not personally know any of these women, my heart soared. Justice. Justice was being served here today in Zihuatanejo. In memory of these ten elderly women. Women to whom fate had delivered evil children who caused them to be murdered in cold blood by an immoral woman named Frances Huber. As an added bonus, with each name recited, I had the joy of watching the smugness on Frances's face slide away, to be replaced first by disbelief, then horror, then fear.

As I witnessed the drama unfold in front of me, I pushed back with all my might the one feeling that threatened my rejoicing. The feeling that maybe, just maybe, Errall and the others were right.

There was one more victim of this horrible woman.

JP.

If this past year of meandering the globe, deep introspection, trying to understand the world and my role in it, had taught me anything, it was that sometimes bad things happen to good people. As they had to me when my new family of Ethan Ash and daughter Simon were pulled away from me. You had to grieve it. Learn from it. Move on.

But I couldn't think about that now. I simply wouldn't be able to hold it together. And now was a time when holding it together was of paramount importance. Yes, bad things happen to good people. But right now, bad things were happening to a very bad person. I wanted to be fully present for that.

Yet, there was something else concerning me. How could Darren Kirsch be making such lofty accusations? Our proof had disappeared with JP. The police had jumped the gun. What did we really have to prove Frances was guilty?

By this point our large group had moved out of the tight quarters of the corridor. We were in the bigger pool area, which had the added benefit of giving my mother a front row seat to all the action. I know she was thinking this was finally good payback, for her having to miss her daytime soap operas to be here in Zihua.

"I don't know what you're talking about," Frances said, regaining some of her bravado. "I don't know any those women you just mentioned. You must have the wrong person. I'm a consultant."

"I'm afraid we have compelling evidence to the contrary," Darren calmly responded. "Evidence pointing to your presence at each and every…Ending…event."

Frances bristled at the use of her self-coined term. If he knew that, what else did he know? "That's ridiculous," she announced, sounding more confident than the quivering hem of her blue dress attested to. "And, I must warn you Detective, if what you're talking about has anything to do with papers or documents stolen from my home last night, well, I'm not sure how it works in Mexico, but in Canada and the United States, I'm pretty sure the police cannot use *stolen* evidence to obtain a conviction against anybody."

I suspected Frances watched too many episodes of *CSI* and *Law & Order*, but she was also probably right. What the hell was going on here?

"Stolen?" Darren responded, sounding a little confused by the very idea. "Who said anything about anything being stolen?"

"I did! Just last night my security guards chased down a petty thief who was rifling through my *private* papers in my *private* house, which sits on *private* property! That, in case they didn't teach it to you in police school, is against the law."

Darren shook his head sympathetically. "Well, I'm sorry to hear about that, Ms. Huber. Did you report the incident to my friends here?" He indicated the Mexican police, surrounding the area like a wagon train circle.

"No, I did not."

"Why is that?"

"That's none of your business."

"I see. Well, that aside, as I already said, I know nothing about any stolen documents or papers. The information we received was volunteered to us. By a man who was in your home by invitation."

"A man? What man?" she demanded to know.

"Your boyfriend, Ms. Huber."

"My boyfriend? I don't have a boy..." Her words died off as Jared appeared next to Darren. "What the fuck are you doing here?"

Jared only shrugged.

Her eyes moved from Jared to Darren like a claw scratching across a chalkboard. She spit out: "This man is not my boyfriend. I barely know him. He's nothing but a two-bit hustler who tried to solicit funds from me to fix his face. I told him no, and sent him on his way. I've had nothing to do with him. He certainly was not welcome in my home!"

Again, Darren appeared unperturbed. "Oh, I see. Well, we have sworn statements from witnesses who recently saw you with Mr. Lowe at several restaurants and social events in both Ixtapa and Zihuatanejo. They certainly intimated that you and Mr. Lowe were more than just strangers. We have another statement from a Mr. Anthony Gatt. He told us he happened to be in your home at the same time as you were...entertaining...Mr. Lowe. And, Mr. Lowe has shown us a cheque, signed by you, dated this week. So, I'm sure you'll understand if we have some doubts about your stated relationship with Mr. Lowe."

I thought Frances might become apoplectic. Her face was turning bright red at the cheeks and tip of her nose. By drastic contrast, the rest of her skin had gone deathly pale. She was wringing her hands so ferociously one of her French tips had snapped off.

"B-bu-but I was a consultant to those women. That's all!

Nothing more. You can't prove anything more!"

"We've already begun preliminary discussions with your actual clients—the children of the deceased women—and it seems your stories don't quite match up. As such, Ms. Huber, we're here to invite you to be our guest in a very nice Mexican jail."

I'd never been as impressed with Darren Kirsch as I was at that moment. Although I'd never admit it to his face, I always felt he was probably a pretty good cop. Now I knew how wrong I was. He was an *excellent* cop.

With more than a little pleasure, I watched as Frances Huber resisted arrest. She cursed, shouted and flailed, and finally blubbered and pouted as they fixed the cuffs around her wrists.

With my arm around my mother's shoulders, we were the last to leave the area. We mounted the steps to the dining room, not far behind the criminal and her captors. Ahead of us, we could hear a renewed commotion. When we reached the top step, I could see the cause.

Frances was standing in the middle of the dining room. All the staff and paying guests had long ago been evacuated. But waiting for her, like a jury convened to witness her downfall, were Errall, Sereena, Toraidio, and Jared, now in the arms of Anthony. Mom and I joined them. For a brief moment, Frances locked eyes with each one of us, painfully taking in the extent of our betrayal and treachery. It wasn't, to be truthful, a happy moment, but it was deeply, deeply, satisfying.

When it was just us left in the room, silence descended like a shroud. My mind was racing, trying to understand what had just happened. The next voice I heard spun me around like a top.

"I don't know about any of you, but I need a stiff drink. Do you think the bar will reopen now that the murderess is gone?"

JP.

"You did what?" Marie-Genevieve Taine asked her brother.

"I'm the one who set the boat on fire."

"JP, I always suspected you were a little on the cuckoo side, but this proves it!"

We were gathered in my sunny living room, the nearby front door left slightly ajar to let in a stream of unusually warm spring air. There was still snow on the ground, but the steady *dwop dwop dwop* sound of dribbling melt water off the roof, was a sure sign that winter was on its way outta here. It was the first day since we'd returned from Zihuatanejo that we were all together again. The occasion was extra special because JP's sister, and Jane's year old son, Joshua, had driven down from Regina to join us.

We were celebrating many things. Topmost were the successful completion of Jane Cross's final case and the incarceration of Frances Huber. Sharing top billing was the fact that JP was, contrary to popular belief, still alive and kicking.

"You call it *cuckoo*," JP said making the most of his lilting French accent, "Some call it *éclat*!"

Some of us tittered; others only smiled at the dark memory of the night we thought we'd lost him.

"Tell me, *mon frère brillant*, just how does exploding your own boat make any sense?"

"I was in that woman's house, like I told you. There were guards outside. I must have made a noise or caught their attention somehow, I don't know. I saw that they were intending on coming inside to see what was up. I grabbed my stuff, jumped out the back, and scrambled down the hill, which was my regular escape route. Maybe not the best idea, but I had nowhere else to go. I could hear them shouting at me to stop. I made it down to the kayak I'd left at the shore. I got in and started paddling for my life. I was feeling pretty good about things at that point: I had all I needed from the house. If only I could get to the boat, pull up anchor, and get the hell out of there fast, I'd be all right."

"Something went wrong?"

"Oi, you poor, poor boy. Dat's so bad for you," my mother interjected, as if hearing the tale for the first time.

"I knew they'd try to find a way to come after me. What I didn't expect was for them to get in the water so fast. I don't know where they had it stashed, but before I was even at the boat I hear the roar of a Sea-Doo."

"*Oh merde,*" Marie-Genevieve murmured.

"Vhat's dat?" Mom asked.

"It's nothing, Kay," Anthony assured her, not even looking up from the baby, blissfully asleep in his arms. "Just a French expression of concern."

"Okay, den."

"Then it got even worse. They had guns. They started to shoot at me."

"*Oi merdey*!" my mom said in her best French.

Marie-Genevieve gave Mom a sweet smile, and me an apologetic one, before returning her attention to her brother.

"I was in a bad spot. They were coming fast. There was no way I'd get to the boat, ready her to sail, and get away from these guys without being shot and probably killed. I knew I had to get out of there. But after everything we'd been through, I just couldn't leave them all the stuff we'd collected on Frances. Plus, I knew I'd need a distraction to have any chance at getting away."

"Ahhhhhh, so you started the boat on fire. Now I see."

"Yeah. And then I swam like hell."

"Which was about the time we were approaching in our boat," I told her. "We saw the fire. Then boom!"

"We thought…" Errall hesitated, looking at me, "Well, some of us thought, JP had blown up with his boat."

"When he hadn't shown up by the next morning," Anthony added, "I have to say, we thought the chances of his having survived were pretty slim."

"So where were you? Why wouldn't you have called your friends? You must have known they'd be worried to death about you," Marie-Genevieve pointed out.

"Well, a lot of things happened at once," JP explained. "I was a little too close to the boat when it went off. A flying board hit me in the head. I was hurt, and bleeding. But somehow I kept on swimming. Lucky for me, the guys on the Sea-Doo had given the boat a wide berth, and were waiting for the fire to burn out to see what was what. When they saw Russell and the rest of you approaching, they forgot about it, turned tail, and got out of there.

"I got to shore and must have passed out. I don't know how long I was out. Eventually some local kids who were smooching on the beach found me and shook me awake. Everything I had on me, the scanner, my cellphone, everything was soaked and useless. The kids insisted I go to the hospital. I guess I was bleeding pretty badly. It looked worse than it was. You know how head cuts bleed."

"Oi oi oi," my mother was almost crying.

JP leaned over and gave her lap a reassuring pat. "I'm okay now, Mrs. Quant."

"I know, I know, but eet's steel very very sad."

"When I got out of the hospital, I knew if I didn't do something fast, all our plans were going to go up in smoke. That was the day it was all supposed to go down. I knew they would be trying to get Frances to incriminate herself at Amuleto. But if that didn't work, losing all our proof meant any chance we had left to take her down was ruined."

"But didn't everything go down with the boat? Or get ruined in the water when you swam to shore?" his sister asked.

I shot JP a smile. "This, Marie-Genevieve, is where your brother proves exactly how brilliant he actually is."

"It's true," he crowed, giving his chest a Celine Dion thump.

Sereena and Jared came into the room carrying trays. Jared's held glasses and a pitcher of margaritas in honour of our successful Mexican escapade. Sereena had some eats. She held her tray in front of me, at the same time offering me a napkin and saying, "This cooking thing is really quite easy. I don't know what all the fuss is about."

I looked down at the two bowls on the tray. One was filled with salsa chips from a bag. The other with store-bought salsa.

I didn't have the heart to tell her that opening a bag and a jar did not constitute cooking. Then again, with Sereena's history in the kitchen—or rather lack of it—maybe it did.

Anthony merely rolled his eyes when he saw the "cooked" goods, and said, "Go on, JP."

"No one should ever collect electronic information without backing it up. I knew the boat wasn't a particularly safe location.

So, every piece of information I collected got downloaded to a back-up Data Traveller device. My friend Elena at the copy store in town agreed to keep it safe there for me.

"When I got out of the hospital that morning, I knew Russell and Sereena would already be on their way to their meeting with Frances. I was supposed to meet with Darren and the Mexican cops to go over everything we had before we all went to Amuleto. But I had nothing to give them. I only had a few hours to duplicate everything using the Data Traveller and put the files together again."

"I'd been keeping Kirsch abreast of what we were doing all along," I added. "So when he told Frances that he'd already begun a preliminary investigation, he wasn't lying. When they were hiding around the corner as I was trying to get Frances to slip up and admit she was a murderer for hire, he finally decided I wasn't going to get anywhere. So they burst in and arrested her for the murders we did know about. I thought all that information was lost. Darren knew better."

"And I'm willing to bet they'll find plenty more dirt on Frances, once they start digging," JP happily proclaimed.

"There's one thing I don't get," Jared said. "Didn't you begin tracking Frances through a suicide website? What does that have to do with murdering old women?"

"Soon after she killed her mother, and the inheritance money was more of a pittance than the windfall she expected," I explained, "Frances considered—for a moment or two—committing suicide. She was searching the Internet for resources, when she discovered The Ending Society. It was in that site's chatroom where Frances met a woman who truly *was* serious about killing herself. They began this rather intense cyber friendship. Eventually, Frances told her about what she'd done to her mother. She felt pretty safe doing it because the Internet is so anonymous. Her new friend began to wonder if her own life would be better—and worth living—if she got rid of *her* mother too. She was Frances's first client."

Marie-Genevieve got up and hugged her brother.

"What was that for?" he asked when she stepped back, a telltale tear in her eye.

"Jane would be so proud of you. She gave you a job as her assistant because she believed in you. She probably didn't say it out loud, but she knew you could do this. And right now, she'd be the first one to step up and say: I told you so, bub!"

Errall stood up, holding her frosty margarita high. "A toast to Jane Cross. She was one feisty broad..."

"A wonderful wife..." Marie-Genevieve added.

"A loving mother..." This from JP.

"A fine detective and a fine person," I said. And meant it. "We'll miss her. But we'll always remember her, mostly through her little Joshua."

We drank.

"There's one last piece of business we must attend to," Sereena announced. She produced a small package, beautifully gift-wrapped, and handed it to Marie-Genevieve.

"What's this?" she asked, searching our faces for an answer.

JP only shrugged. The rest of us smiled and waited.

Marie-Genevieve slowly unwrapped the parcel, revealing a small leather case. She reached inside and pulled out an impressive-looking stack of one-hundred-dollar bills, held together with a pretty ribbon. Her mouth dropped open, but nothing came out.

"It's eighty-six thousand-three-hundred dollars," Sereena told her. "Fifty-five thousand from the sale of the Korova painting..."

"Twenty-five thousand from Frances, meant as a down-payment for my bogus surgeries," Jared said. "The authorities agreed to turn a blind eye while I cashed the cheque, before they froze her accounts."

"And seex-tousand-and-tree-hundred dollar from me. Because of de odder paintings I sell to dat man's friends," my mother proudly announced. By "dat man," she meant Toraidio Garza, whose friends were still buzzing about the newest talent on the art world scene, the ever-mysterious, K, aka—Kay Quant nee Wistonchuk—aka Mom. Go figure.

"But I...why me...I don't understand this," Marie-Genevieve

got out between happy sobs.

"Come here, Sis," JP said, pulling her into a hug. "After all you've been through...having to raise Joshua alone now...you deserve this. Consider it a gift from Jane."

"I think this calls for another round of margaritas!" Anthony decreed, kissing the top of Joshua's sleepy head.

"Would anyone like me to cook up more food?" Sereena offered, taking quite nicely to her new role as Julia Child reborn.

My mother muttered something under her breath, then wobbled away toward the kitchen to begin cooking things with butter and cream.

It was a jubilant afternoon, which quickly led to early evening. Eventually, once enough of Mom's cooking had been ingested to soak up the excess salt and tequila, everyone straggled off to their own homes. Marie-Genevieve and Joshua, who were staying with us—uh, I mean staying with *me*—retired to the guest room, exhausted from all the excitement. And, I hoped, to roll around in all that money. Finally, only JP and I were left. And of course Barbra and Brutus, who'd managed to convince us to light the fire. It was a good idea. We'd left the door open a bit too long, and as the effects of the margaritas died off, the season's true intentions were evident in the still frigid night air invading the house.

"You feel like going to bed early?" JP asked, cuddling up next to me on the couch, facing the fire. "Maybe watch a movie in bed with popcorn?"

"Sure. But first, there's one more present to give out."

JP bolted upright, his sudden excitement causing Barbra to do the same. As she sat watching us with her inquiring doggie eyes, I noticed that JP was doing much the same.

I patted both their heads, then leaned forward to reach under the couch. With dramatic flare, I pulled out a long, flat package.

"Did you get me eighty-six-thousand-three-hundred dollars too?" JP asked.

I smiled at him, appreciating how the light from the fireplace's dancing flames reflected in his eyes. "Not quite," I said.

"Should I open it now?" he wondered, suddenly a little shy. He was totally not expecting this.

"First, I need something from you," I told him in all seriousness.

He responded in kind. "What is it?"

"I need you to tell me how you got into this house, tied me up, and did it all without alarming Barbra and Brutus."

JP sucked in his cheeks as he regarded me with slitted eyes. I could tell his brain was whirring away as he considered whether or not to come clean. Finally he sat back and said, "Well, I'm sorry to inform you of this, Mr. Quant, but breaking into your house, and getting by your dogs, is pitifully easy."

What? Really?

"You see, most people who have dogs get lax about home security. They either decide that having dogs is enough protection, and don't even bother buying an alarm system. Or, if they had a system before they got the dogs, they end up rebelling against having to spend lots of money to update to a more sophisticated one, once they realize their dogs, roaming free in the house, are tripping their old, no-frills alarm on a regular basis."

It was true. I'd had some issues with my security system and the dogs in the past. The dogs won, especially after one particular instance, when Barbra*, saved the day—and my life. She'd attacked a man who was bent on killing me in my own home. Who wouldn't trust a dog like that over a machine?

"The day we met..." JP continued.

I held up a hand to stop him there. "You refer to breaking into my house and hog-tying me as 'the day we met'? Really? I think in the future, when people ask how we met, we've got to come up with something a little less illicit than that. And technically, the day we met was when we tried to knock each other's blocks off in Jane's office," I pointed out. "All that aside, while we're on the topic," I rallied on, "do you mean to tell me, that you—once a man of God—think that break and enter and uncalled-for vio-

---

* *Sundowner Ubuntu*

lence towards good guys like me, is okay?"

"First of all," he calmly explained, "I was an apprentice in a monastery, not a man of God. Second of all, I think the bad-boy-cum-monk-wannabe is kind of sexy, don't you?"

I inwardly agreed, but said nothing aloud about that. "Okay, just get back to the explanation. It was the day you broke into my life...come on, go on."

"Huh," he said thoughtfully. "I kinda like that...the day I broke into your life..."

I drummed my fingers against the package on my lap. "And then what?"

"Actually, I had already *entered* your house earlier that same day. I did it all very calmly, as if I was meant to be there, so the dogs wouldn't be too freaked out. I came prepared, with plenty of kibble in my pockets." He gave Barbra an affectionate ear scratch. Brutus was still near the fire, enjoying a moment to himself. "You can't really blame them. Like all good dogs, their actions revolve around whatever smells and tastes good."

Kind of like me, I thought to myself.

"I spent a good bit of time with them, making friends. Then I checked out the food and wine situation in the fridge for my subsequent visit."

"Food and wine?"

At this juncture, JP had the good sense to act a little sheepish. "Food for the dogs—for when I came back and wanted them distracted."

"Okay, I got that. But you didn't get my dogs drunk, did you?"

"Of course not," he sounded offended by the suggestion. "I would never give alcohol to an animal. The wine was for you."

I shook my head. "I don't get it. You wanted to make sure I had wine in the fridge to drink? JP, if you're trying to tell me the reason I didn't wake up while you were breaking into my house and tying me up like a stuffed pork loin roast was because I was passed out from drinking too much wine, you're crazy. I always have wine in the fridge. But I rarely drink too much. And I certainly never pass out."

"Weeeeeeeellllllllll, not from drinking too much wine. Just from drinking some wine."

Again I shook my head, exasperated.

"When people have an open bottle of wine in the fridge, it means one of two things," he elaborated. "One, they rarely drink wine. And when they do, not very much. They put what's left in the fridge, thinking they'll finish off the bottle someday, or have it there for company. But usually, it just goes to waste and ends up down the sink a month later.

"Or, two, they like having a glass of wine on a regular basis. Probably a little each day: maybe a glass after work, or with dinner. More on the weekends. When I saw the open bottle in your fridge, I knew that you were a number two. I tasted the wine and it was fresh. It was also a mid to high-end priced bottle of something good. Not a wine you waste. I noticed you'd used one of those special corks that when attached to a pump device, sucks all the air out of the bottle after corking. You'd made an effort to keep the wine fresher longer. These are the habits of someone who usually has a glass or so every day. So, I was quite confident that you would be having a glass, if not that night, then a night very soon."

"I like your deductive thinking. Jessica Fletcher and Hercule Poirot would be very proud of you," I told him. "But I'm sorry, JP, I'm still lost. It doesn't lead to anything. So you knew I'd have a glass of wine when I got home. So what? How does that possibly make it possible for you to break in and tie me up?"

He looked away. He petted Barbra. He idly scratched at a corner of the wrapping paper that covered his present. He sipped at a glass of water. He gave me a pretty smile, which although not powerless on me, was not about to sway me from my line of questioning. He was stalling.

"Well, Russell, you have to understand one thing. I was desperate. I wasn't entirely sure of who you were, or what you were capable of. And you know I'm the kind of guy who likes to take chances. I take risks. I go out on a limb. I like to be a litt..."

"JP! Out with it!"

His answer came quickly. "I drugged your wine."

"What?"

"Just a little muscle relaxant, that's all. Something to put you in a pretty little dream state. Just long enough for me to do my business. Nobody got hurt, right?" More pleasing smiles.

I was momentarily speechless. I scrutinized him more closely than I ever had before. This guy had balls. Once again, I found myself thinking that if I hadn't been his hapless victim, I'd be more than a little impressed with his sneaky and creative ways. Sneaky and creative are very good traits in a detective. And maybe in a boyfriend too?

"Are you mad?"

"I'm not mad." I was almost seventy percent sure I was telling the truth.

Barbra whined a bit, as if in apology for her role in all this.

"It's always best to tell the truth about things like this right from the beginning," I told her. I was ignoring JP for the moment.

Barbra gave my hand a quick lick. Apparently she felt absolved of all wrong-doing and fully forgiven. She retreated to join her brother near the grate.

"Tell me what you're thinking," JP pleaded.

"I think this gift is more appropriate than ever. I think you should open it now."

"Yeah?"

"Yeah."

"But first, this." JP brought his handsome face up to mine, looked me in the eyes, smiled, then kissed me long and deeply.

When the smooching was done, JP ripped into his gift with the abandon of a ten-year-old boy expecting his first iPod.

JP's eyes widened in wonder as he revealed a long, weathered piece of wood. Attached to it were two chains. At first he didn't know what it was. He noticed writing on the wood. He turned the thing around so he could read the words. He said them quietly, almost reverentially: "Quant...& Taine, Private Investigators." He looked up at me, a big question in his gorgeous eyes.

I nodded.

"Am I....?"

Another nod.

My future never felt brighter. Over the past year of being a worldly vagabond, I'd learned a lot. I was only now suspecting that much of it, like a gift slowly unwrapping itself, I had yet to discover. But I knew this. I knew to respect my past. To be present in today. To confidently direct my future as only I knew how. I was a man in full, exuberant control of the rudder of his own boat.

Being a man who enjoys his time as a lone wolf is not a bad thing. I embrace it, but I'm also a man who welcomes new challenges, new desires, new experiences. I thrive on seeing where they take me. I love my career. It's just as much a part of who I am, as is being a son, a friend, being gay or Ukrainian, being a guy who likes baloney sandwiches and fine wine. I can be a detective and be all those things too. And more. I have been Russell Quant, PI for a long time. Now, opening this new chapter, I will be one half of Quant & Taine. Together, we would hang out our shingle for all to see. Who knows where this will lead.

Who knows.